between dog and wolf

elske rahill

THE LILLIPUT PRESS
DUBLIN

First published 2013 by
THE LILLIPUT PRESS
62–63 Sitric Road, Arbour Hill,
Dublin 7, Ireland
www.lilliputpress.ie

All characters in this publication are fictitious,
and any resemblances to real persons,
living or dead, is purely coincidental.

A CIP record for this title is available
from The British Library.

1 3 5 7 9 10 8 6 4 2

ISBN 978 1 84351 411 4

Set in 11 pt on 15 pt Caslon with
Gotham display titling by Marsha Swan
Printed by GraphyCems in Spain

One must find the history of what she could not know if one is to try and recognize her. One must find the history of what she cannot narrate, the history of her muteness, if one is to recognize her. This is not to supply the key, to fill the gap, to fill the story, but to find the relevant remnants that form the broken landscape that she is.

Judith Butler on Ettinger's *Eurydice*

prologue

IT DOESN'T CRY at all, your baby. For three days it turns in its glass box, opening and closing its fists. The fingers are pale, furling, strong as the claws of a bird. What comes from your nipples isn't milk at all. It's bright orange at first, then bright yellow. You taste it. You finger it into the small mouth, and the round tongue works vigorously. This is more important than the milk, the nurse says. It's for cleaning the stomach of you; of your blood and your insides. It's for separating the new body a little farther from your own.

You spend the third night cross-legged on the bed, rocking as the baby suckles, coaxing the milk in, touching your lips to the furred scalp. You can say it now, you think. You can tell it something true, whisper it close to the head that smells like coconuts—

—BUT THIS IS NOT for me to know: the smell of your own flesh that is also not yours; the aloneness of that. The first night in a hospital bed with sterilized sheets, the hours distilled in the night by the baby's pulse and yours; as banal and momentous as waves crashing on a beach: *katchoo, katchoo.* The head emerging from you like a battered balloon, fingers like tentacles drinking in the light, the skull-crush opening into a face knowing and stupid like an ancient fetish.

These are your things. I must try to remember that now. It was easy to forget, Helen, with someone both evasive and penetrable, like you. I couldn't help exploring you, creeping into your eyeball and crouching there, peering out at your world. I couldn't help delving into your mind, that languageless lagoon, perverting it into narrative. All that I did though – speaking for you, stealing from you, creating and undoing you, I did because I loved you.

one

HELEN HAD her back to me. She was leaning a hip against the counter, humming, waiting for the kettle to boil. I was still warm from bed and wrapped like an invalid in layers of thermal vests. Helen's feet were bare. It made me shiver just to see them naked like that: her toes purplish against the chequered floor. The floor must have looked like a chessboard once, but the white squares have yellowed since it was first put down, and the black ones are sun-bleached grey. There is a gap at one corner where the lino has curled up, and dust and stray peas and hairs and bits of tobacco gather under it. The kitchen is shared by six of us. Like the other kitchens on campus it's tiny, with the drabness, outward cleanliness and inward filth of a place unloved and tended weekly by a professional. Helen bought a fish bowl to liven the place up, but the fish keep dying. There was another dead one there this morning, floating at the top with its fins clamped to its body. Helen mustn't have noticed yet.

She was wearing a matching pyjama set of brushed cotton

with heavy, straight folds at the shoulders and up the legs. She looked clean. I was very aware, suddenly, of the pockets of stink trapped against my body. When I moved a waft of stale body heat was released up and out the neck.

'New PJs?' The sound of my own voice startled me. The words shot out like an accusation: *New PJs*? She looked down at her body as though she had forgotten what she was wearing. The pyjamas were cream. Pink moons and stars were printed on the fabric with the words 'Sleepy Girl', designed to look like a child's handwriting, floating about between them. The top buttoned up the front like a shirt, the way all pyjamas used to. It didn't look right on an adult body. It made her breasts seem heavier than usual.

'Penneys – seven euro – *such* a bargain! They're so *comfy* as well!'

I am not used to seeing Helen without make-up. All day her face is an orangey disc with shimmering lids, spider lashes, smiling mouth the colour of bubble gum. In the mornings her eyes are ringed black by the residue and a tan tidemark outlines her jaw. She must have scrubbed well last night, because this morning she had fresh, translucent skin – impossibly white. It made me think of dew. The only clues to her usual mask were the unchanging eyebrows, professionally plucked into sharp little peaks of alarm. Otherwise she looked gentle this morning, peaches-and-cream pretty. I told her she'd get a cold in her bare feet and she shrugged, sliding a big mug of tea across the Formica. She was feeling happy this morning. You can always tell how Helen is feeling at a glance. Her mind was cloudless behind her eyes.

'You slept late. Late for you, Cass.'

I shrug. Actually, I woke quite early this morning. I watched the ceiling and thought for a long time about getting up. The white paint was splattered with grey blots. It wasn't the first time I'd noticed them. If I stare at them for too long they begin to move about the ceiling like silver worms. Today it was worse; they merged and parted quickly, rolling into one another and multiplying like mercury maggots. It was so terrifying that I didn't want to see. I pulled the blankets up over my head. I wanted to shrink back to the dark like a snail. In a neighbouring room someone scrambled into their clothes and clattered away, late for something, and the sounds of the college day started up outside my window. I don't have a clock but I can count the hours from bed by the morning chats and the yelp of sneakers.

I know those noises by heart but they always shock. Their life scratches at the walls, pecking at my quietness to haul me up out of my shell.

'I have no lectures today,' Helen said, hoisting herself up onto the counter and kicking her heels against the press. A dimple curled at the edge of her mouth. Her hair is a mass of blonde wisps, barely believable, like the hair of something mythic.

'I have *ab*solutely *nothing* to do today!'

This seemed to make her proud and she hopped down again, all dimples and light. Why was she so bloody happy?

I smiled, 'What will we have for breakfast?'

'Dunno. I feel like Coco Pops. Do you have any? I'm totally addicted to Coco Pops at the moment. I ran out yesterday. I meant to buy more …'

'No.'

'Oh well. I don't know then. I'd love a fry but I'm totally broke. I spent a fortune on Saturday night …'

'There are eggs. Will I make us some pancakes?'

'Oh yeah! Cool. I haven't had pancakes in ages!'

There was no ground coffee left in the tin, which in any case belongs to Cahill down the hall. Neither of us drinks instant, so we raided Helen's penny jar, and she put on a coat and flip-flops and went to the snack stand in the computer block. While she was gone I mixed the eggs, sugar and flour into paste with a fork and then slowly, carefully, added the liquid; half milk, half water.

The first pancake was a disaster and I had to throw it out. The rest I spread with raspberry jam and sprinkled with hot chocolate powder. They were piled on the plates by the time Helen got back with coffee in cardboard cups.

So we sit on her bed, our backs against the wall and the duvet spread across us lengthways, feet sticking out the end. These rooms were decorated when paisley was either in fashion, or cheap, or both. The sixties it must have been, but I don't know. I'm no good at that sort of thing. I don't know what 'paisley' means exactly, but I know that it describes this decor: floral print curtains, brown on lighter brown, tinged orange by years of daylight. No-colour walls. Cockroach-colour carpet. The flowers join up like spreading mould. They resemble no flower and all flowers. Helen's room is bigger than the others. She has a dressing-table strewn with lipsticks and dusty make-up brushes. There are photographs stuck around the mirror in careful disarray. They're the same sort of pictures she used to put up in boarding school: party scenes of people grabbing each other in elbow hugs, clutching bottles of beer. It's her way of assuring herself that things go on outside her room, that she has fun. The room always smells like her perfume: a sweet vanilla concoction that comes in a bulbous white bottle.

She has been keeping an orphaned kitten in her room for about a week now. It mews until she lifts it onto the bed where it topples about clumsily and its tiny claws catch in the blanket, making quick, painful nicks with every move. It's a miserable little thing. It trembles constantly. When you hold it you can feel its skeleton through the loose, blubbery skin.

Helen still hasn't put on socks. We laugh about one of our lecturers – 'the woman-hating, youth-crushing cat-man', Helen calls him – who looks like a giant, bald cat, the inbred kind; pink with big ears and a pixie face. Siamese or Pekinese, Helen says they're called. He enjoys telling us that all personal morals are a social construct. He enjoys our dismay.

'... very juvenile for a middle-aged man.'

'Yes but for a *cat* ...'

We guffaw like little boys and let the hot raspberry jam trickle between our fingers and plop in sticky drops onto the plates and duvet. It is only with Helen that I get like this – giddy, laughing at things that aren't witty, nearly dribbling with stupid, clumsy laughter.

The kitten's tail sticks up straight, quivering. Its cry is sickly and hopeless. It is very young and might not live without its mother. We can hear Cahill, the Irish language student, banging the kettle and cursing me in the kitchen. He has seen the pancake in the bin. I wrapped it in newspaper and everything, but he must have spotted it somehow. He is well brought up, raised on some Irish-speaking island, and enjoys a good earnest rant about wasting food. I often think he puts on rubber gloves and trawls through the bin, searching for evidence of my wastefulness.

He marches down the hallway and bangs on my bedroom door.

'Cassandra?'

We pull Helen's duvet up to our mouths to stifle the giggles.

'He's a total nut,' Helen mouths, raising her eyebrows, curling her dimples.

'Cassandra? Cassandra? Did you make pancakes?'

'How does he know it was me?' I whisper. For some reason this makes Helen laugh more.

'Shhh. Sh. He'll hear you!'

Then he's back to the kitchen, muttering to himself as his porridge simmers.

Helen is still in hysterics, biting the duvet, tears starting in her eyes, but I don't feel like laughing any more and it annoys me that she does.

'Are you ever totally happy Helen?'

Before it's out of my mouth I am embarrassed. The question hangs there. I'm not even sure what I mean. It seemed, for a moment, as though that's what it was all about; our laughing, our eating pancakes for breakfast, that it was all about saying, 'I am *totally* happy.' I got it wrong though. I can see that now. She giggles, her head thrown back in dismissal.

'Cassy, what are you like? It's too early for all that stuff. Drink your coffee!'

She tongues the jam out from in between her fingers and wipes her hand on the duvet. I think of the smell of dried spit. Like public phones. Like blow job.

My question must have ruined her mood because she decides to go to the library for the afternoon. At least I won't miss that lecture now. I'll make it up to her. We'll go out tonight and I will be positive and fun and light-hearted. I can be like that sometimes. We'll pick up some good-looking men, laugh at tired jokes, flirt all night and leave them at the taxi rank.

OISÍN TRIED to re-button the three plastic poppers of his duvet cover where they had come undone during the night. Then he gave up because the duvet had twisted itself up inside and bundled to the bottom and the whole thing had to be redone.

The sight of her had affected him last night. She stayed with him like a sum or a crossword clue.

He had been coming home early from a party, tired, with a weight in his belly. He was a little too drunk to concentrate on his book and he tried to stare out at the wet, black road and the January darkness. When she stepped onto the bus with an air of summer and light about her he felt okay again. Suddenly he didn't mind just sitting on the bus, doing nothing. Looking at her made him feel like he was *doing* something. He watched her put on lip gloss for no one and blink at the rain. He knew her name, Helen, although he couldn't remember how he knew it. He didn't say hello. He wasn't sure whether they were supposed to recognize each other. He had nothing interesting to say anyway.

Keeping his body under the blanket, Oisín reached an arm out into the cold air and patted around the patch of floor beside his bed, feeling for his laptop. He had left it open. Grabbing the base, he heaved it up off the carpet and plonked it onto his knees. It was still on standby, hot like a hurt limb and buzzing weakly with the effort of staying alive all night. He tapped the mouse pad and it sighed, flicking the screensaver on: a picture of Kirsten Dunst wearing a pink crop top, her dimples neat as the little dent of her navel – a still from a film he hadn't seen. Then he clicked on the internet icon and waited for the page to load.

He logged in to his email account. There were no new messages, so he browsed through his old ones and found the link he was looking for in a message from his friend, Aengus: http//www.xxccklolly//grl2grl. The link turned blue when he moved the arrow over it. He clicked and waited. A picture of two identical girls flashed up: outstretched tongues touching, hands on each other's breasts, semen splattered on their faces and in the briny tangles of their hair. He liked when his mates from home emailed these links. It was easy to just click and not have to feel like a pervert searching for porn. You didn't have to pay unless you wanted a video.

At home in Tipperary he hung around with the lads. They were very different from the guys in college. They sat together in silence mostly, but they understood each other, Oisín thought. When they spoke it was without eye contact. It was loud and followed by an expletive or a guffaw. They talked about what band was 'fuckin' crackin' or who was doing the local 'fox'. Occasionally they went to gigs or to the cinema together in small groups. They were all employed, after many years of resistance, in low-ranking office jobs or serving meals-on-wheels to the elderly. They were living at home as they plodded into their thirties. One of them, Aengus, had a girlfriend.

The youngest of the lads, and the only one to go to college, Oisín had long ago vowed in a wordless part of himself not to become a snob, to never consider the lads anything less than he had when they had offered the only possibility of a social life. Whenever he was really down one of them was sure to suggest a trip away. Oisín thought of these holidays as a chance to let off steam, as though there was an uncomfortable burning in him that had to be vented abroad. He usually had fun and came back refreshed, his mind clearer. The last holiday was in Amsterdam, getting so high that they kept losing their way back to the hostel, and watching live sex shows starring mysterious-looking immigrant girls.

He was surprised to discover what 'live sex show' really meant. The first time they went Kevin had organized the tickets. He was good at that sort of thing, and often said that if it wasn't for him the lads would never do anything but sit on the couch all day and night, wanking and drinking beer.

'If it wasn't for me, fuckin' Denis would still be a fuckin' virgin! Wouldn't 'cha Denny?'

'Go 'way to fuck,' said Denis, looking into his pint, searching for something better to say. Kevin was tall with a strong jaw. He had the best score record. If the lads were picking up women he always got the pretty one. The girl's friend went to Aengus, or sometimes Oisín, and the rest of the lads had to peel off and find their own birds.

Kev was the one who had suggested the holiday in the first place, booked the hostel, collected the money. He was in charge. He bought the tickets to the sex show without asking anyone else. With half-hearted protests of 'fucking rip-off', the lads had each given him their fifty-five euro and followed him to a small brick building in the red-light district. It looked like an abandoned house. The front door was not locked. It opened inwards. Beyond the door, the building expanded like a magic wardrobe. They were in a circular lobby with a high ceiling and corridors leading off it in five directions. These corridors might lead to anywhere, thought Oisín, to more lobbies with more corridors. The building might go on and on indefinitely.

The guys waited in the lobby, kicking the carpet, trying to make jokes but too giddy to think of any. Denny, stooped and balding at the age of thirty-one, wearing a T-shirt that said 'I fucked your girlfriend', told Oisín about that time they had stolen the pint glasses from Nancy's bar.

'And Kev's face! Man i' was d' funniest thing ever!'

Oisín felt sorry for Denny. He couldn't help it. All of Denny's stories were about 'd'funniest thing ever', and he had told the story of the stolen pint glasses four times since the airport yesterday. Oisín had never allowed himself pity for any of the lads before, and it felt like treachery. He didn't know which was kinder: to slag Denny off or to laugh along. Without deciding to, he let out a deep, open-mouthed laugh that reverberated too much in the stripped room, shocking even himself. Kevin and Aengus looked at him, and then back down at their shoes. They scuffed at the worn carpet. Oisín yawned and looked at the ceiling. There was gold paint flaking off the plaster cornice.

At last a skinny usher arrived, took their tickets, told them all to follow him, and proceeded down one of the corridors. The men walked behind him in silence, falling into single file, lead by the glow of the usher's torch down a long, low passageway. Oisín felt as though they were tunnelling down under the earth. They passed closed doors. There was felt on the walls. Oisín ran his fingers along it until the tips began to burn. His throat hurt.

They arrived in a dim room with no windows. Before leaving, the usher pointed to a small built-in bar in the corner, where an Asian girl in a trim three-piece suit offered them a choice of complementary beer or vodka.

'Check out the cutie Korean!' Oisín had whispered to Kev, but Kev was busy checking her out already. A red velvet curtain, rough with dust, spanned the width of the room, dividing it almost in half. Oisín thought it would pull back and reveal a large screen. He expected a gigantic woman with heaving breasts groaning and glowing out from the wall. Then music began from somewhere. It was slow electronic music, and it made him think of how the world sounds when you dunk your head under in the bath.

The curtain screeched back, wavering gracelessly and his eyes fixed immediately on the wall behind it, thirsty for the image. There was no screen. The back wall was made of fat bricks painted a thick, glossy black. He thought briefly: 'That's varnish paint. That's not for walls.' His eyes scanned down to where the performers were positioned on the maroon carpet: a man sitting on a wooden chair, his penis almost erect, a too-young girl on her knees beside him, kneading the pink blossom of his foreskin. The scene looked shabby after Oisín's vision of monstrous breasts.

The lads walked back through the red-light district afterwards, making noise but not having conversations, hunching their shoulders, taking up space and elbowing each other when they passed a good-looking prostitute.

They were not very friendly girls. They sat on high stools, looking glum and texting on their phones. The lads mustn't have looked like potential customers. If you showed interest though, they smiled and looked down at their own bodies as though to say 'You want?' Denis was gone when they reached their hostel. He appeared two hours later, claiming to have lost his way, but smirking to show that it wasn't true. Kev slapped the back of Denny's head, 'Denny you poor bugger!'

'Bugger and more,' said Denny, 'I'm telling ye, man! You ever get a bird like the one I just had, get back to me then!' Oisín envied his balls. He wouldn't have been able to do it. He would have got too excited or something.

Later, when they were alone, he asked Denny what she had been like. He told him the girls liked Irish guys. 'They love us. Hate English lads. The English lads abuse them an' all. Hurt them. We just ask for a bit of head and a poke. And we're good looking. That's what she said. Not like them English. She liked me. She likes blue eyes. Told her she was a good girl. She was a good girl ...'

The lads went to a handful of sex shows after that, until they ran out of money and their week in Amsterdam was up. The last show was in the same place, but it was a different performance. The tickets said 'Ying and Yang'.

The girls were different colours: one brown and one very white. She could have been albino if it wasn't for the flat blue eyes. They were smiling as they licked each other, and made sounds as though they were coming. They locked eyes with each of the lads in turn as they did it, and whichever guy they were looking at said '*Whoa baby*!' or '*Oh yeah*! *Do it for Daddy*!' and things like that. Oisín hoped they wouldn't look at him; he wouldn't know what to say. He was semi-hard and he didn't want it to go away but he didn't want to get any harder either. The girls removed each other's bras. They were flimsy, transparent things with sequins sewn onto them. The pale one had pink hair and a sequined cherry on her thong, right at the top of her ass crack. She looked him in the eye and smiled. *I'm beautiful,* her eyes said, but they were lying. Her eyes were jaded. She lifted her chin and nudged her lips at him, ran her tongue over her teeth: *I want to lick you.* She wanted him to believe that, but it wasn't true either. There were thick red lines on her breasts.

He was getting harder despite this; a warm thrill tumbling down his spine, up through his testicles. His beer bottle was cool against his fingers, but it couldn't soothe him. His hands were slippery. He didn't want to look at the others to see if they were the same, and he knew they weren't looking at him. It was a matter of respect between the lads.

He stared at the black wall. It had been painted quickly. Glossy bubbles had hardened in the valleys between the bricks. He concentrated on that and the cold glass in his grip until his erection eased.

When he looked back at the girls the dark one was bending over, groaning, while the other one held the lips open, splaying the shock of pink folds, and flicked her tongue inside. He had never had sex with a black woman. His cum would look like milk on her skin.

Pink inside. That surprised him. He would have thought purple-brown. The lovely ache in his groin made him want to keel over. He felt something terrible might happen if he didn't reach down and grasp his cock: his whole pelvis might implode. That word *cock*. He wanted the one with the pink hair to say it, *cock*. She might not speak English. He would teach her that word, she would look at his lips and repeat after him. '*Cock*,' she would say, the clean tongue flashing behind clean teeth, and she would laugh. Then she slipped her littlest finger into the eye of the black girl's asshole. Usually in porn he liked that. Usually this was the moment he would go faster and faster. Something wasn't nice though, or something was too nice. Something wasn't working for him. It was to do with the way she moved her clean fingers with the glued-on nails; a child playing an instrument. Competent. The nails were pink like her hair.

'Wahayhay!' Aengus had said. 'Oh baby, yeah!'

She was looking at Oisín. He tried to say it too, '*Way – yeah, come on baby*!' but when he opened his mouth the sound didn't come – only a breath without voice. He felt nauseated. Too much dope, maybe? Too much drink? His mind was moving in all the wrong directions and he couldn't focus.

'Oisín's smitten – oooh! Hey Pinkie! Oisín lurves you – Ha ha!'

'He wants you to give him one backstage – don't you Oisín? Whatd'ya say Pinkie?'

Kevin reached out to touch her bum. Her eyes flashed. The wiry, jaundiced bodyguard stretched out an arm, restraining him gently and easily. Kevin backed away, palms up in surrender.

'Ah no – I'm only messin' baby! It's just you're a lovely looking girl you know that? Nah, you're sound-out baby, I'm only messin' with ya. You're sound-out, so you are.'

If they had known what Oisín was really thinking they would have called him a pussy, a college boy pussy! Pinkie didn't really want to say *cock*. She wanted him to think she did though, and that made it worse. That made him hate her.

Aengus and Kevin were both staring at him now. Any moment they would realize what was wrong. They would know he was a pussy college boy, too good for them, not one of the lads any more at all.

He thought '*Pussy*,' but not in a sexy way. '*Bitch*,' he thought. Then he thought the word '*Man*' – '*Man. Man. Man.*' He took a swig of beer and swished it about, wetting his cheeks and palate. He sucked a breath and the air felt cold against his teeth.

'Wooooaaah – come on Pinkie! Give it to her! Oh that's right, yeah, that's right like that. Oh yeah!'

Relief. He really meant it – she was hot, hot, HOT! He was one of the lads again. No one had even noticed him transgress. He shouted louder.

'Woooaaah baby! Good girl …'

The lads didn't speak after the performers finished. They had a drink – paying for it this time – and went back to the hostel. The barman at the hostel stayed on late into the night. When the lads were the only remaining customers, he served them something like hash, only it was black and squidgy and could be kneaded between fingers and rolled into a worm shape that lay neatly beside the tobacco. That night, his head on the damp hostel pillow, forcing his mind to wade through speech, Oisín asked Denny if he had liked the show.

'It was hot,' he said, but confessed that he preferred the private sex shows he had been to last time he was in 'Dam. They were less embarrassing. You sat in a booth in the dark, he told Oisín, not even the performers could see you, and there were clean tissues provided to wipe up your cum. He took Oisín to one the next day. He was right, they were less embarrassing.

Sitting up in bed, Oisín kept his hand pulsing on the mouse. A blonde with pigtails, a huge red lollipop entering her open mouth, gazed out from the screen. Her school shirt was torn open to reveal weighty breasts: large nipples as red as the sweet. Another girl licked the lollipop too. She was facing away from the camera. Her white knickers said 'Princess' on the bum. They weren't really schoolgirls so it was okay. They weren't really that young. Not with tits like that! Oisín reached into his jocks with one hand and kept clicking with the other.

That night after the 'Ying and Yang' show, he hadn't been able to sleep. Denny had snored heavily in the bunk below him. Every time Oisín closed his eyes he'd seen that bodyguard, the gentle, firm way he had eased Kevin back. The long neck had held up a shrunken face, a glassy-eyed expression that never changed. He looked like a meerkat, Oisín thought. His arm wasn't very thick but it was strong, and Oisín could see the ligaments and veins all twirled together and moving slightly under the yellow skin.

Sometimes at these moments – Oisín's hand moving vigorously, the delicious warmth twinging higher and higher, pounding towards release – that bodyguard would stalk into his room and run a chilly finger down his spine. That blunted his arousal. It was the girl-on-girl action that had reminded him. He clicked his way to the deep throat pictures. 'Gagging Bitches', said the link. Then there was a description of the site:

> You know what we say to foreplay? We say Fuck OFF! We take hot young cunts and fuck their little faces until they're gagging and their mascara runs. Then we fuck up all their other holes. She may weep all she likes. Stopping ain't our style …

There were twelve options: girls' names with thirty-second teasers. There was a picture of a blonde woman in a pencil skirt and a white blouse. She was wearing librarian glasses and chewing a biro: 'Joan from downstairs,' it said. 'Let's begin by smashing those specs. Watch us turn the secretary from hot whore to cumbucket. See love tunnel turn to train wreck while three men fuck her till she weeps …' Under the name 'Helen' it said 'This dumb whore thought vomiting would get her off the hook … but there's more than one way to fuck a kitty.' The picture was of a girl in red lacy underwear with a vice fixed to her jaw. She was cute as a doll. She had small, round breasts hugged proudly by the lacy red cups, cartoon-yellow hair in a high ponytail, and slutty silver eyeshadow. There was a penis in her mouth, and a man's hands holding the handles of the contraption. There was semen on her stiff, black eyelashes.

While he waited for the teaser to load, Oisín tried to think of the real Helen, the girl from last night, but she kept eluding him. The video failed to load so he scrolled down for another. The deep throat album had been updated since last time. There were more Asian girls now. Their slender necks bulged like a snake that has swallowed its prey. Oisín liked the Asian girls – they were so neat. Their red-lined lips and pink cat's tongues looked sophisticated against the slop of shaved testicles.

Aengus sent the best free porn links. His taste was the same as Oisín's: really sexy girls, definitely no airbrushing. Like Oisín, he wasn't into gross stuff. He preferred the girls with natural tits touching themselves and licking their nipples, drinking shot glasses of semen or popping beads up their bums and things like that, not the really mad shit.

As for shit – not into that at all. None of the lads were – except maybe Kevin.

Kevin had once sent him a mobile phone video of a fifteen-year-old being fucked in an alley by three different guys. It was rape. It was on the news and the boys had to go to juvenile prison. You couldn't really see much. One of the guys had recorded it and sent it to someone whose brother sent it to Kevin. That's how they got caught, by sending the video around. The girl hadn't told on them. Oisín didn't know the girl, but he recognized the uniform. She was heavy with white breasts. He had deleted the message.

Cleaning up with a piece of toilet roll, Oisín remembered about changing the sheets and decided he'd do it later. He noticed that his cum was clear this morning. It was strung together like snot. After taking a shower he made some coffee in his kitchenette, stirring the granules languidly until they were completely dissolved.

CASSANDRA IS in the shower when you leave. She hears you and roars, 'Bye Helen!'

With that simple phrase, 'Bye Helen', Cassandra makes you feel accused, as though you have betrayed her by leaving, as though you were sneaking off. This is a talent that Cassandra possesses.

You walk into the library and then out again the other side. You head up Grafton Street and down again and all the way to the quays. It's one of those dull, dank days when the cold is in your bones and your face feels too exposed. The river has risen with the rain. It has swallowed the strings of decomposing apple butts and faded crisp packets that are usually visible over the water line, dried to the cement walls of the Liffey.

You buy cat litter at the pet shop on the quays, then walk to Dunnes Stores for granary bread, hummus, and washing-up liquid for the kitchen. Then, feeling bored and careless, a tub of chocolate cornflake squares and some ready-made raspberry jelly from Marks & Spencer's that you consume in your room, stroking the kitten and reading the same page of *As You Like It* four times, each time forgetting to pay attention.

I'LL GO for a walk before that lecture. While Helen's getting dressed I take a thorough shower, exfoliating with an expensive body scrub prescribed by the make-up artist on my last modelling gig. The packet says it contains 'peach-stone extract', and 'organic walnut'. There are words like 'sensual' and 'indulgent' written across the lid, but it's unpleasant stuff really: pink, peach-smelling goo with orange grains in it. These grains represent either the peach-stone extract or the organic walnut bits. It says to use a loofah, but I only have a sponge. There are instructions on which lathering methods to use for maximum exfoliating effect. The whole project is extremely tedious and I don't think I'll have the willpower to repeat it daily, whatever the make-up artist says.

I can hear Helen's door click shut. She passes the showers without saying goodbye and starts down the stairs. I call, 'Bye Helen!' It makes me feel stupid and needy, shouting after her like that.

After making the effort to exfoliate I decide to go the whole hog and put on make-up as well; evening out my skin tone and brushing on some too-black mascara. This makes my eyes look larger and darker than they already are, which is complemented by the black of my bobbed hair. The effect I am going for is big smudges of eyes framed by a glossy black ball at the top of my neck. The bob is a bit 'two seasons ago' – Helen told me that – but if I blow-dry my hair this look works well for me. Otherwise it sticks up and out as though someone has knifed it off in clumps and I look like a crazy person. When I look like this, men don't evaluate my bum and the ladies in Brown Thomas do not offer me perfume samples. On those days I wear tracksuit bottoms. I sit in the park and no one sees me.

I change my mind about wearing jeans, and put on boots and a skirt instead.

Nothing has happened today but it's already the afternoon. The days just slip off in college; it's the sparse timetables, the hanging about. Helen's lazy, happy mood has rubbed off on me. I like the softness of the afternoon air and the pain of the cobblestones through my shoes. I even like the sound of someone playing with a guitar in his room; a vain boy's hope to be heard. What a sin to have ever been sad. I will give everything in my purse to the homeless man at the Nassau Street entrance and, having done all I can, let him drift softly out of mind. This is the best way to live. This is the only way to be happy, and sane, and good.

He is not there today. Next time, then.

Grafton Street is full of strangers. You can lose yourself in all their bustle, all their purposes, all their loves and the little pet hates, all their self-importance.

A stout refugee woman tugs at my sleeve. She is my age with proud features around her snarl. Her baby is swaddled in a filthy tiger-print shawl. It has an ancient, knowing face and its nostrils are sealed with snot. She pushes it at me so that its face is inches from mine, and we blink dumbly at one another. Its mother pulls it away again, irritated.

'Please lady.'

I am not a lady. She pouts and asks again, and there's something not right about it. Her hands are cupped with embarrassing servility. I give her a euro and feel worse than if I had ignored her. I'm saving my money for the homeless man. He might be there when I get back.

I try to recover that happiness, the feeling I had when I first set out for this walk. I should be able to do that, to carry a mood with me. I should not be so easily shaken. I try to love the crowds, the smiles of strangers and the buskers' music, the crumbling, bitter old man muttering to himself as he skulks along the wall. He growls, jabbing his elbow into me spitefully as he passes, running his other hand against my hip, his flaking grey heart desperate for the bulk and warmth of another life. The impact shocks. It makes me ashamed of my youth and my strength. I do not want to carry the weight of his loneliness. He smells of unwashed clothes, of packed dead skin.

What should I do to appease him? Too late, he's gone. He's crazy. There is nothing I can do for him. When there is nothing you can do, walk away and don't look back. Leave it in a bundle on someone's doorstep.

I sit by a window in Bewley's and stare down at the busy street, eating a chocolate doughnut made of something I can't identify. It is not chocolate on the top, that's for sure. It's chocolate flavour. I need to calm myself, slow my pulse, take stock.

Must head back for the lecture.

The homeless man still isn't there.

I wish I wasn't so early. The hall is occupied and everyone is waiting around in chatting clusters. I strike up a conversation with a few girls from my tutorial group.

'Do you know who's giving the lecture?'

'No, I hope it's Dave again, fantastic isn't he?'

'He's funny, yeah.'

Dave. I don't know which one that is.

'I had him for tutorials last term and oh my God, he is *soo* much fun ...'

CASSANDRA IS gone when you get back. She must have a lecture.

Sitting on your bed, your legs crossed, resting your fingers on a small cushion someone gave you with 'Helen' embroidered on it, you paint your nails with the 'Cherry Bomb' polish you bought yesterday. It's that new one-coat-only rapid-dry stuff that only takes a minute, but you blow on it anyway out of habit. You hold your hands out before you the way you do, fingers splayed, wrists bent back like the spine of a ballerina, head cocked like a parody of girlishness, lips puckered in concentration, while the first coat hardens. Then you apply a second layer, then a third, shrugging away your curls when they fall over your eyes.

THERE ARE a few seats in the back row of the lecture hall that aren't lit by the orangey light. Sitting here I feel hidden. It's a professor I haven't seen before. Old. Twenty minutes into the lecture and already we know that he is separated after thirty years of marriage, that we are lucky in our innocent belief in love, that we cannot understand this poetry as we have not yet experienced the disillusionment of failed love.

A strange word: love. A fool's word everyone wants to trust, even this poor, broken-hearted, obsessive old sod, dismantling his like a public autopsy. He spits his words like bile as we watch and listen and scribble notes. A caged gorilla flinging his shit at spectators. He hasn't shaved.

'Any questions?'

'Well, why is the poet so respected? What is the point in literature, if only those who have experienced the events described can empathize? Is empathy all it is? What do we learn?'

I bore myself when I start like this. It is my argument against everything: 'Isn't it just self indulgence for the middle classes/

for the upper classes/for the colonized/for the women? What is *achieved*?'

I shouldn't have started. He cares about this dead writer. He cares about this poem. God, let him have it if it matters to him. Let him be right. His wife left him, he stinks. I can smell it all the way back here. It's that rotten-love-carcass smell that makes humanity revolting. He has mustard-like gunk clotting his eyelashes, and no one will love him ever again. I bet he hates our rosy cheeks and our reverence. I bet sometimes he wakes up and wants the dark back.

The girl next to me, Alice, twists a rope of hair around her fingers, nodding.

'Good point actually.'

He glares at me. 'It used to be harder to get into this course. Before the points system. We knew the kind of minds we were to deal with. Not any more. It was about culture then. Culture. Not Leaving Certs. Not *points*.'

Helen told me it's actually worse than that – not only did his wife leave him, she left him for another man, a younger and more successful academic. '*And*,' she told me, 'this academic lectures at Cambridge. The wife and kids go and live with him. Then the guy – the guy who stole his wife and lectures at Cambridge, whose book on Chaucer was published this year – has an affair with the sixteen-year-old daughter and gets her pregnant.'

He shuffles his papers. His fingers are trembling. He's a drinker, this lecturer. If you go up close you can smell it off him. What sort of knowledge will we inherit from this elder?

He begins to explain again,

'You cannot understand. How can you possibly understand what Chaucer means, he who lost his children, who lost … who lost … everything … in a fire …'

Poor lonely old sod passing us this world like a poisoned gift: a feast of our grandmothers and our own little children, shoulder blades and eyelids and all. Our test-tube embryos served up like caviar.

I resolved to go to the library after the lecture, so I resist the temptation to go home and see if Helen's back. I wish I had removed that dead fish though. I hate to think of her noticing it alone, lifting it out with her fingers, handling the weight and the cold of that little corpse. I keep seeing his round sunken eye and the stiff curve of his body lying just below the surface of the water.

My student card does not swipe me in like it's supposed to. Instead I have to show it to the smug man at the desk, who pretends to scrutinize it. Then he faces the other way and holds two outstretched fingers towards me, the card slotted between forefinger and index. His arm is too high, and I have to reach up on my toes to snatch it back. Pushing a button under his desk, he releases the swing bar so that I can pass through. I want to say 'thanks', but only my lips move. A pain catches where the sound should be. That happens to me sometimes.

The library is simmering with synthetic light and that hostile purr computers give off. There are a lot of computers in the library. They are dotted about in pairs, stuck back-to-back and perched on metal stands that make me think of spaceships. Everybody moves about in silence, tapping at computers, turning pages, scribbling in feathery sounds with soft felt-tips, or biros that dent the paper. I walk through desks of students, computers, bookshelves, forgetting what I'm looking for. I feel loud. My shoes are making a clack-clack sound and I don't know what to do with my hands. I have no pockets, so I just hang them both on the shoulder strap of my bag, but that doesn't feel natural. I don't know why I wear heels. I am too tall as it is.

Occasionally someone at a desk lifts their head as I pass, clocks me, and returns to their work. I try to wear an expression of urgency – I need to think of a dissertation topic, and then I need to find books on it. This is not the right section of the library though. The dissertation has to be on Victorian literature, and this is the theatre section.

I hate this quiet crowding. The huge building is packed: every wide, low-ceilinged room is lined with books and periodicals and computers, and then filled with people. All these people filling the space have words, sentences, stories running in their heads. There are so many different lives racing on in here and no one speaks. Their silence is a smouldering of voices – like fire under a blanket.

My chest contracts and my eyes pulse. The people walking around the library look hazy; anything I try to focus on blurs and sways. If I am not careful I will forget how to breathe and my eyes will fog over. This is another thing that happens to me sometimes.

I make for the bathroom where it reeks of antiseptic and the kind of sewage smell you can't clean away. I dart into a vacated cubicle, bolt the door, and sit on the closed seat, shut in with that nostril-burning contradiction of bacteria and chemicals. Head between my knees, knuckles pressed into my eye sockets, I concentrate on breathing until the blood stops fizzing in my veins.

I focus on the interior of the cubicle. In front of me the door frame: white, with a black sliding lock. To my right the blue sanitary disposal unit, pregnant with knowledge of its festering contents. The scrawls on the toilet-roll holder clamour for advice:

Swallow or Spit?

I can't poo!

I'm in love with a married man, I know he loves me but he doesn't want to hurt his wife or kids – should I stay with him? Don't know what to do.

Three girls, in contrasting shades, have given her advice.

The next question is written in luminous pink felt-tip. The writing is curly, the 'i's dotted with halos.

23 and a virgin – weird?

The first reply tells her she is ugly. The second that her first advisor is a slut and that the virgin is right:

Not at all! I waited for the right person and so happy I did!

Someone else has responded to this advice:

Well so did I but it turns out he's shagged half of college and gave me two different STDs! Sex doesn't mean shit to men don't fool yourself love! Lose it to a vibrator!

There is a maxim beside it in different handwriting:

Virginity is like a balloon! One prick and it's gone!

I use my eyeliner to write on the door:

It is time to forget. The House of Atreus is better left vacant. Let the wind howl through its openings. Let worms devour the bloody carpet. It is time to forget.

I look at the words scrawled there in black charcoal and I can see they look like ravings. I use toilet paper to smear them out. At the sink I watch the water run over my hands. They're the kind of taps that you don't have to switch off, which I prefer because there seems little point in cleaning your hands if you're just going to touch the dirty tap again. They always run out too soon. I press the tap three times, using the upper side of my wrists instead of my fingers. I like when my hands become so cold it feels like they're dead.

There's a harsh, ultraviolet light in here designed to prevent you from shooting heroin on the loo. It stops you from seeing your veins. It also makes your face look like somebody else's; like you in a different world, under water, or on the moon. You in negative. It shows every pore of your skin. My reflection stares over the sink like a stranger. The nose is too big. Severe cheekbones jut in a way that gets me modelling jobs. They are unattractive. They make my face look like a man's.

I smile at the reflection, smooth some lipstick thickly onto my mouth, and step back into the library.

Between the toilets and the steps up to the Ussher Library there's an undefined area with computers and benches, no desks or books. It's supposed to be part of the library but when there are no supervisors around students talk and make phone calls here. A girl with a small, lopsided jaw is sitting on the bench talking on her mobile. From looking at her I can guess she is a Business Studies student or something like that: streaky fake tan, pastel knits, tight jeans. She scribbles on her foolscap as she speaks.

'No Mom. No, I'm not going out tonight, I *told* you. 'Kay. Ya. 'Kay. Will someone collect me from the Luas? I don't have the car. 'Kay … Oh Mom? We didn't have to go to lectures today cause – am – a girl died. Ya I know. I know – hardly bodes well for me does it? Like if some people are actually killing themselves already like – and exams haven't even started! *SUCH* a high-pressure course. I know, what a week! Yeah. Oh, she jumped out a window. I dunno, I dunno. Maybe. Ya – I know. It's so sad isn't it? Not really, like I knew her to see … I think she had problems. Ya, ya … ya, 'kay. I'll call you when I'm on the Luas. Bye! Bye. Bye-bye-bye …'

I remember what I came in for. I'm looking for a book of critical analyses of *Alice's Adventures in Wonderland*, hoping it will give me a dissertation idea. I look up the index number on the computer, write it on my hand and try to locate it on the shelves, mouthing the alphabet as I run my finger along the combinations of letters and numbers sellotaped to the book spines. I have located the space where ARTS8287 TH L5 should be, but in its place is a pale blue cloth-bound book called *The Victorians and The Cult of The Little Girl*. It's bound to have something on *Alice in Wonderland*. Bunny holes and all that … In any case it will have to do. I take it to an empty desk and sit down.

The cover feels pleasant: sack-cloth texture greased by decades of touch. I run my palm over it and then over it again before I open it. The pages are the colour of tea stains. A tiny insect, the kind that is not hatched from an egg, but born from darkness or rotting fruit, uncurls itself in the crease of the spine, and moves slowly, sleepily over the word 'truths'. The tiny life has all the magnetism of something secret, primordial, significant in a way that I will never understand. Then it unfolds its wings and pings off the page. That shocks me. I didn't imagine it having wings.

The girl beside me is left-handed. Her elbow prods mine and we both make a lethargic gesture of apology.

There's no fresh air in here, it's all been used already: inhaled and exhaled through noses and mouths; then sucked in and spewed back out by the humming air conditioner. That means the oxygen must be quite low by now, so everyone is drowsy. I am breathing someone's cough, someone's sigh, someone's silent fart, blended and filtered by the machine. In London the water is sterilized sewage. There isn't the silence here to think. Strangled words whoosh about – *Afro-American Literature and Female Identity … Swallow or Spit? … Saussure and Truth … I'm in love … Salmon Rushdie and the West … Yeats and Apocalypse … SUCH a high-pressure course … What should I do? … The Big House in Anglo-Irish Literature … What should I do? What should I do? What should I do?*

AFTER THE 'Renaissance Drama' lecture, Oisín had a few pints in the Buttery with some of his class. A slim redhead with a push-up bra laughed at his comments on the chirpy, round little lecturer, though he knew himself that his observations were not particularly funny. When she giggled her gums showed. Oisín was encouraged: 'I thought he was going to topple over, the way he kept swaying on his heels!'

Her lips shrank back like melting wax, exposing gums and teeth, and a high trill rolled out. It kept going long after it should have. Maybe he was in there. 'I rooted a ginger'; that'd be the subject title when he mailed the lads about it.

Sharon from film studies was there too, at the other side of the bar. She didn't see him. He had what might be a date with her tonight. He was suddenly a little panicked and didn't want her to see him. He would be embarrassed. She might notice his dandruff and change her mind about coming over tonight. There was a short Indian boy talking at her energetically, but Sharon gazed about the dark bar.

The skin beneath Sharon's eyes sank in brown folds like an old man's. Her hair was cropped along the jaw line, with a straight fringe that hung over her eyebrows. It was a frank, plain face, but not repulsive.

Oisín liked Sharon, he didn't know her very well but he knew he could sleep with her and that made him defensive about her ugliness. He didn't want her to be seen that way. He wanted to grant her beauty. It was something about the gape of those unbeautiful eyes, like a vacuum that sucked you warmly in.

Sharon was long-bodied with no waist and strong, wide-set shoulders. She wore dollar scarves. The Indian boy didn't notice that she wasn't listening. He looked like he was talking about maths or something. He wasn't looking at her any more. Instead his gaze was fixed on his own hands as he explained something with them, drawing lines and circles and then chopping them to pieces with a downward swoop of the hand. She put her hand on his arm, told him something gravely. The boy raised his eyebrows as though surprised or impressed. They waved at each other as she rushed out of the Buttery. She hadn't seen Oisín.

Indian men treated girls like Sharon as though they were boys. That was something Oisín had noticed. There was one in his 'Tragic Patterns in Greek Theatre' class. He spoke to plain girls as though they were not women and he didn't speak to the other girls at all. His name sounded like 'I'm Sorry', and every week he had to repeat it several times to the half-deaf lecturer, explaining that *he* was not *sorry*, his *name* was *Am-sa-ri*. He was from a different department, studying Latin and Greek, and took the course, unmatriculated, to 'contextualize' his learning. He had once explained this to Oisín walking out of class in one of his attempts to start a conversation. They were the only two men on that course so perhaps he thought they should stick together. He also told Oisín about his wife. He was married to a seventeen-year-old who was still in India and wrote him long letters in beautiful handwriting. Amsari was very proud of his wife's handwriting. He said he would show Oisín her letters if he liked.

Amsari was the first Indian man that Oisín had ever had a conversation with, apart from doctors and cashiers. Listening to him made Oisín oddly envious. Amsari fit so comfortably in his organized world. Like a wind-up toy he worked vigorously along whatever path he was pointed in, but he didn't have to navigate. He was born into a certain caste, and a certain role: a system designed to banish chaos. Amsari made it look very successful. When he was not taking notes his hands rested calmly in his lap, one folded on top of the other. His face was perfectly symmetrical, his square jaw always cleanly shaven to no more than a shadow on his golden skin. His whole being radiated a sense of peace and order. His parents had chosen his girl – a beautiful girl, Amsari told him – and lighter than her husband. To have even your sex partner chosen for you, thought Oisín – how simple, how complete. To have strong black lines marked all over the map of your life, the boundaries fixed. Beside Amsari's, Oisín's world looked like an ever-shifting sea of confusion: waves and crashes and swirls, then monotonous depths of stillness that penetrated down through the sun-warmed blue to the cold, black seabed. There was nothing but water above and dark beneath.

If he had been born in Amsari's family, thought Oisín, his life would be drawn like a bath and all he would have to do was step in. There must be some relief in that. The thought of this marriage, so different to anything he had ever encountered, so innocent, in its way, excited Oisín, but not enough to stop him from wanting to escape the man's advances towards friendship or hoping, with disproportionate terror, never to look on the young wife's letters. The other students, like Sharon, laughed and chatted with Amsari. They didn't notice that he was Indian, or else he didn't seem so exotic to them, but Oisín couldn't relax. Amsari was too polite, too earnest, his teeth too white and straight. It made Oisín uncomfortable.

No one seemed to notice how out of place Oisín really was at Trinity. He had the constant feeling of getting away with something. He was missing something, he was out of the loop. Everyone else knew things that he had never been taught. From day one that's how he had felt – like he didn't know the score, not really. The redhead kept chattering and laughing.

'I see the way you sit there staring through class,' she said, thumping his shoulder gently.

'You're not listening to a word he says are you? You hardly even take notes. I bet you ace the exams anyway though, I know guys like you!'

There were long, fine hairs resting on the powder-blue wool of her shoulders. That was probably caused by running her hands through the thick curls, which she did a lot. They criss-crossed delicately, forming a fragile mesh that shimmered like liquid in the low light.

I TRY to read the introduction but I can't concentrate with all the breathing that's going on in here. I skip to the chapter entitled 'Alice as Wonderland: Exploring the Male Gaze'. The chapter is filled with pictures of the real Alice as a girl, some photos of naked babies and postcards collected by the author. I stop reading and flick through them instead. Most of the postcards are of little girls, half naked, half understanding: their hipless waists bent to curves and a hand near the bare bumps between their legs, feigning womanly modesty. Some of them are on swings that they have well outgrown, with big bulbous seashells held to buds of breasts, eyes extinguished. This should be repulsive but I want to keep looking. I don't think I have seen a naked little girl since I was one myself. My face is following me. I catch her staring out of the evening-blacked windowpane. The eyes are big gaps in a white disc.

Two centuries ago men believed in innocence. They thought it was incorruptible. That's why these postcards were okay. Because men didn't think they were up to it – after all, who were they in the face of such a thing? They thought it was something hard and smooth that they could finger and leave down again, like a pebble. They didn't know they had the power to fracture it. They thought it would always be there, regenerating itself perpetually like a garden of paradise.

I begin to make a note of that thought, but then I realize it is irrelevant to the topic. I press the biro into the foolscap as though an idea might write itself, but it just makes a little black dent in the paper. I can't think of anything but quiet. How much I want quiet and blank inside my head.

I do not want this slow motion image that's replaying itself over and over, insensitively comical: the image of the business student with the wonky jaw floating slowly, silently, out of a window, down and down and down, her coat billowing behind her, angora scarf swirling like seaweed.

How did that happen, and when? I do not imagine her hitting the ground – I can't – so she just keeps falling indefinitely.

I will go for a walk. I only have my A4 pad and some pens to gather up, but somehow I am making a racket. I am sweating.

My eyes are stinging. Click-clock, click-clock, along the library floor. I'm getting out of here. I am leaving. I'm approaching the exit of the Lecky and soon I'll be outside breathing air – through the swing bar, the glass doors, the Arts Block, and outside. But the Arts Block is crowded and making it to the street is a battle. An earnest-looking boy hands me a flyer with a pink monotone photograph of a young Chinese man on the front. Maybe I know him, but I think I would recognize him more easily if he were in colour. The pink is a little off-putting.

'Please help to save Zeng Qiáng,' the boy implores, 'Please sign.'

Behind him is a desk where a dusty looking girl sits, leaflets, petitions, and booklets spread out before her like a lean banquet. She has a boxy haircut, a heavy fringe weighing down on deep-set, no-colour eyes.

'I think I might have signed already,' I say. My voice comes out hoarse and faint.

'Well please sign again just in case,' says the girl, her eyes widening. I envy her goodness, her earnestness, the frank ugliness of her haircut.

'Have you got our literature?'

The skin beneath her eyes is brown, puffed and covered in small blisters. Such constant desperation must be tiring. I think I recognize Zeng Qiáng – that's the same boy who's been missing since Christmas break.

'No. I'll take it. I'll sign again just in case. Is this the same boy ...?'

'He went missing on New Year's – the day before he was due to fly back here from China. He's a Falun Gong practitioner, that's why. It's a peaceful religion ... All his books are still in his room. We just found out last week that he's in a camp. He has been told his family will disappear if he tries to communicate ... so he takes a risk ...'

'That's terrible,' I say, trying not to sound cold or like I don't care. I think I do care, but the outcome is the same whether I cry over it or not.

I sign quickly, scribbling my email address and phone number as illegibly as possible. I've made the mistake before, of filling in my contact details too neatly. My email account ended up clogged with updates of various horrific and hopeless tragedies. The cutting-off of a young lesbian's breasts is the one I remember most vividly. She was forced to walk the streets with a sign saying 'I am a lesbian', while she bled to death from the two rounds of open flesh where her little breasts used to be. It was somewhere in the East. She was fourteen. Something about her age stuck with me. Hotmail kept advising me to buy more storage space but I don't have a credit card. I ended up changing my email address.

'Well good luck!' I sound sarcastic but I don't mean to.

I am grateful to be outside at last in the lamplit cold. The homeless man is folded away against the wall at the exit; he is holding a white polystyrene cup. The cup is perfectly intact. Funny, how he hasn't bitten it, or bored a hole in it, or anything. I would have. I don't give him any money.

He says 'God Bless' – a curse to make me feel bad. I stop and rustle about in my bag. There are a few coppers, which I am too embarrassed to give, receipts and what feels like breadcrumbs. I think of the word 'karma' and wonder whether Zeng believes in it, or whether Falun Gong is a different thing altogether. I can feel the man watching me as I walk away. I turn back over my shoulder and I'm right: he's staring at me. He doesn't smile when he says it, but he looks at me the same way he looked when he asked for change, imploring, 'I'd love a girl to wrap up with tonight.'

'Oh.'

I walk on. What is it like to be him? What does his mouth taste like?

Zeng Qiáng's face is pink, gazing off the cheap paper. He looks at me like he knows. Like he is better than me and I shouldn't be looking.

The crazy homeless man knew something too. The earnest and the mad see things their brains can't process, smell and taste the things that make them gag. They look in directions they're not supposed to see, at things they cannot change. They look and look and look. They look even when it does no good. They look even when the light is too bright. They keep looking while the sun frizzles their retinas. Their eyes are wounds.

Where am I going? The church, I think. I will kneel and pray. Pray away Zeng Qiáng's pale pink skin, his deeper pink pupils, his accusation. Pray away the billowy-coated girl and her high-pressure course, flying out a window with sheets and sheets of business statistics wavering slowly down around her. Pray away the homeless man's chilling horniness. Wrap these things up, tie them with a ribbon and give them away. Forget it all for now.

But the church is locked, a big chain and bolt around the gate. God's House. Is there not a rule about sanctuary or something? I suppose that must have been in the past. Things are different now. Homeless people and heroin addicts would creep in at night if it was left open, smell the place up.

It's nearly seven. I'll head back and get ready for tonight. I promised Helen we'd have fun.

ACTUALLY, Oisín was not doing very well in college. This fact embarrassed him a little. He was disappointed with the way he had turned out. In his early teens, before he had found his niche with the lads, he had read a lot for a boy his age, pursuing wisdom with fervour, preparing for something great. During this time he had a series of pleasant, undemanding relationships with the sorts of girls who understood his silences and who were always available for quiet, lights-out sex. He sat with them in their bedrooms reading books and film magazines. They exchanged novels and 'Pumpkins albums and went to the cinema together. They did not need to talk. When he grew out of this there was nothing to replace it. Literature seemed silly to him now, just a lot of confident people all voicing too many opinions to ever be heard. He was bad at his subject and that hurt him a little because English had always been his *thing*. Amongst the lads he was the clever one, the one who read books.

Oisín lived alone in a flat his father had bought him in celebration of his Leaving Cert results. The lads didn't know this, they thought he was renting. He was a little ashamed of his father's patronage, and of the quiet pride that he himself took in the decor. Oisín had picked the curtains: navy and grey tartan. He had replaced the cracked plastic toilet seat with a wooden one from Argos, and screwed it on himself. It had taken him almost forty-eight hours to settle on the positions for his five posters. For the first two days of Fresher's week he had hardly left the flat for gazing at the arrangement, shifting the posters about a little, and then reverting to the original positions. Just when he thought he had got it right, when he had settled into the couch with a beer, mentally preparing to go out to a Fresher party, he would see that the *Matrix* poster needed to be shifted a little to the right, the *Withnail and I* one needed to be less straight and he should, after all, move the picture from the A|wear autumn footwear catalogue – of the hot girl in lace-up boots gnawing at a rope twisted around her wrists – into the bedroom. The composition of the posters was now perfect. He hadn't moved them in two years.

The lads all lived at home, so they wouldn't understand the sense of competence Oisín found in doing his own laundry, hanging it to dry by the radiator, or in choosing the cheapest detergent.

Despite this pride, a waft of failure sometimes greeted Oisín when he walked into the small flat made for one. It was a dusty, carpeted place with a kitchenette-cum-living room, a bedroom, and a bathroom with a shower. The air seemed heavier inside the door of the flat. The first thing he did on arriving home was to flick on the radio and take a beer from the fridge. Sometimes he switched on the TV as well, with the volume low. Otherwise the silence and the heavy air gave him a feeling of panic and desperation, as though there was something important he was forgetting to do.

He hadn't had a girlfriend since school. There were girls he had met camping in Europe who he still kept in touch with. They lived abroad in places like Germany, Estonia, and France. When he was very lonely he sometimes called one, and said, 'So do you miss me baby?' Sometimes during these sudden torrents of loneliness, if he was drunk enough, he would invite them to stay with him for a few days. 'But where will I sleep?' Carmen had said last time. 'You can have my bed. I'll sleep on the couch …'

He didn't call them fuck buddies. Even when discussing them with the lads he usually said, 'I have a cutie Frenchy coming to stay with me,' and they knew what he meant. When it was one of the less attractive girls, or they invited themselves, he got the niggling feeling that they couldn't get a lay back in their own countries and came over for guaranteed sex. This was true, in a sense: they came over after break-ups or when their college terms finished. It didn't bother him that much. 'A ride is a ride,' as he told the lads.

The redhead wanted one badly, he thought, watching her trace a finger over painted lips and hook it to her lower teeth. Her breasts were shoved together like an offering, the small, ripe rounds nearly touching. Between them, the flesh was squashed together in three folds, making a third, miniature breast. 'So what about you?' she said, removing the finger and running it along the rim of her glass instead, 'What do you want to do after college?'

'Dunno.' He wouldn't mind giving it to her. He could imagine her going down on him in a mechanical sort of way. The red lips would be cold and thin and not moist enough.

Occasionally it occurred to him, from the 'I miss you' emails and letters, that maybe the German girl, Petra, thought there was more to their relationship than a casual friendship and the convenience and certainty of having slept together before. She had been a virgin. That probably had something to do with it. When she had come over the first time he had forwarded her money towards the flight. Maybe she misunderstood that a little. Even the lads said she was a fox – the money was a gesture of gratitude and fair exchange. Really, he had given her no reason to think that there was anything but friendliness behind these transactions.

Anyway, Oisín thought, smiling as the redhead giggled at a joke he didn't understand (she talked too fast, and through her nose), Petra may not have got the wrong idea, she may be playing and flirting with him. She sent him a tape with local birdsong on one side and her snoring on the other: 'I thought it was kinda sexy,' she wrote. That was a joke: he had once teased her about snoring and then retracted when she became embarrassed. 'No, it's sexy,' he had said, 'really! I'll miss your snoring …' and rolled on top of her again. Come to think of it Petra could be a lot of fun. Perhaps he'd send her an email.

He had cancelled work tonight for this date with Sharon. She better be on for some action 'cause it was the third time this month that he had cancelled on Martin the day before. He wanted to keep this job. The pocket money was useful, and working was good for him. It gave structure to his week. The game of earning gave order to his world.

The redhead's drink was finished. She tilted the drops of watered cream about the bottom, streaking the glass, clinking the melting ice. She probably wanted him to buy her another. Why not? He'd be able to tell the lads what colour her pubes were. That'd give them a laugh. They'd slag him for months!

The fresher behind the bar had a lot of pimples and he didn't know how to pull a Guinness; did it all in one go instead of letting it settle before topping it up. Not his fault. They should have taught him that when he started. Oisín's dad owned two pubs, so he'd been able to pull a perfect pint since he was ten.

Maybe it was because he was a barman, but going to pubs in Dublin depressed him. The whole event just depressed him. He missed the comfort, the swaddling, anonymous bosom of the lads – he could hide and relax in their gang. They stuck to the same three pubs and this drew a perimeter around a night out. He knew how to don the right laugh, the right voice, the right phrases to merge with the group – he knew them so well he didn't even have to try. Every time he went out with people from college – gelled his hair, put on aftershave, and stood around talking or just looking happy – he did it in hope of something. He wasn't sure what.

Even after a lecture he was a little disappointed that nothing had happened. He might as well not have gone. He liked when they took a roll call: it made it matter more whether he turned up or not. The lecturers always gave the impression that there was some goal to their teaching, that there was something very important about his generation and they were being prepared for something great. Something these elders didn't have the courage to do themselves would be performed by this bright, uninhibited, unafraid youth. They made passing comments like 'Oh, the naivety of youth,' and 'Read it for next week, if' (and a laugh gurgles up the gullet) 'you haven't fed the first chapter to the fire to heat your freezing little flats.' They sounded like they envied these cold flats. Oisín's actually had a very good heating system, a fact that he was a little ashamed of when these comments were made. These academics sometimes seemed a little intimidated by their students, as though they didn't think them naive at all, as though they were the clueless ones teaching the wise, brave youth of today and afraid of being found out.

He handed the redhead her drink, then changed his mind about picking her up. There was no need. He'd probably be getting some tonight. In any case, he was sure she'd begin to find him boring soon. She was very clever. He didn't remember her name either, which was bound to become embarrassing if he got anywhere with her. He'd tell the lads about rooting a ginger anyway; it was as good as true, and it'd give them a laugh. He knew that, with his bookishness, the lads considered him a little effeminate unless he kept them updated on his virility.

He went back to his flat and read a chapter of *A Very Short Introduction to Critical Theory* because someone had talked about Saussure in class that morning and he had been confused. He showered and changed for his date. Then he sat in bed and emailed Kevin about the redhead and about Sharon:

'PS. My ship's come rollin in! Got a date with a hotty with a botty tonight too! She's CUMin (ha ha) over to mine for some 'study' you'd do well here man ... college girls are HOT!'

two

IT'S THAT LOOK: directly in my face, it travels my skin. I think of flies, the lightness of their little legs, the way they fracture your image with their many-mirrored eyes. I blink him off my lashes but he's persistent. I know he wants to touch the cliff of my lip with his thumb. I have bee-stung lips, blow-job lips. I got them from my mother. Men like them. Lips and breasts are things men prefer swollen, like sores. He's trying for conversation but I have a heavy cry in my throat. Where is Helen?

'Do you want a drink?'

'Em … No. No thanks. I'm looking for a friend.'

'Well aren't we all? It can be a lonely world, little lady …'

After queuing for so long I always feel a little disappointed when I get inside. It's the name, I think, 'The Vatican'. It makes me expect some velvety secret: a forbidden interior, plush and cool as a vault. It's the doors too: thick metal like there's something to hide, something of value inside. I'm sorry I came.

I spot Helen, or someone with Helen's halo of ringlets, move away from me across the room. Someone is leading her by the hand. She isn't walking like Helen, she's not even walking like Helen when Helen's drunk. She's walking slowly, very carefully, looking at her feet and steadying herself every now and then with the bar or someone's hand. I have never seen Helen like that, but it must be her. No one else has hair that moves like that, bouncing at the small of her back like a taunt.

OISÍN TUCKED a condom into his johnny-pocket, and packed an extra few into the inside zip of his jacket for luck. Then he checked his hair.

Sharon had been friendly yesterday, asking him to come to her lunchtime show in Players. They began to chat and he'd thought happily, 'This is a conversation. This is a getting-to-know-you.' He had a passing sense of belonging. They agreed the Film Studies course was awful this term. They both hated horror movies and were dreading sitting down to *Aliens* this week. They seemed to get on. He'd heard from the director, a guy in his 'Gender and Genre' course, that she would be naked in the play, so he considered the invite might be something of a come-on.

She was kind of pretty, in a way. Her eyes were an odd shade of grey: pale and wet like an animal's.

A lot of student shows had naked girls in them but it didn't really turn him on; it was never really sexy or anything. Those plays were kind of crazy: lots of blood and nooses and screaming. And lots of talking. Not really Oisín's pint of plain. He hadn't been to a real theatre in years though. Maybe all plays were like that now.

Oisín had heard of one play last term where a girl masturbated on stage. It was something by Heiner Müller, whose collected works were on his 'Modernism' course, or his 'Post-Modernism' course, or his 'European Change' course. But the book was missing from the library. He had an idea that she had the book, the masturbating girl. He knew the girl to see. She was on his 'Nineteenth-Century Sexuality' module. She had a long face, very long hair, sharp elbows.

He'd got Sharon's number from the director guy ('Actually I've lost Sharon's number – do you have it?') and arranged the date by text message, re-writing it four times before he got it right. She'd agreed to watch *Aliens* with him. She had even suggested doing it in her room, on her laptop. That suited him. Now he didn't have to clean up or anything.

He worried how his hair looked. He had little control over his hair. Sometimes it just wouldn't sit right no matter what he did. This evening it looked sparse and flat. He checked his shoulders. At least there was no dandruff. He ran some gel through it and avoided looking at it again. That was really all he could do. Then he grabbed four beers from the fridge and stuffed them into his strapless army-surplus bag along with the DVD, making a mental note to pick up wine on the way.

Sharon opened the door with wet hair and a lot of eyeliner on, crescents of black on her lids as though to counter the brown sag beneath. She smelled of shampoo – something fruity – and the half dark of the evening made her eyes look eerie in their pits.

Oisín should have given her the wine when she opened the door. But he was still holding it when they were inside her bedroom. The air was musty and private, like someone's sleep. The cheap red wine felt like a silly gesture, presumptuous and pretentious. He didn't know shit about wine. Sharon set the bottle down on her bedside table. The edges of her mouth turned down, 'I don't have a corkscrew.' She reminded him of one of those sorrowful looking, sloppy-cheeked dogs. That old monstrous feeling of failure clenched Oisín's throat. He saw himself as she must see him: a bedraggled culchie with bad hair standing by the bed clutching his bag by the flap. The setting was too personal; her room with its cerise duvet cover and all the cushions. Some pink flyers from a humanitarian campaign she'd been canvassing for were piled on the bedside table. The light of her en-suite bathroom was on, fan whirring, cistern trickling. She must have just been to the loo.

She didn't want him here. Why had she invited him?

He kept his eyes on the wine bottle. 'I have one on my key ring.'

'Oh great. Cool. You want to open it or will I? Sit down. So … have you started your film essay? I haven't even thought of a topic …' She spoke loudly, dispersing the intimacy. She didn't allow the silence to breathe. She talked about the 'Free Zeng Qiáng' campaign, a subject Oisín avoided to disguise his ignorance and indifference. He didn't know what Falun Gong was, but it sounded freaky. Sharon didn't seem to notice his silence. She talked about her film essay, about her last essay, about that time in first year when her computer crashed.

' … so I had to type it all again from memory in like two hours! Literally! I began at two and it had to be in at four! And I got a first! Can you believe it … just shows you …'

This constant talk made Oisín relax a little. Her pupils danced and pulsed, her gaze moving everywhere. Occasionally though, they rested on his eyes in a promising way. If she kept talking like this they would be hitting it off, they would be getting on. Her chatter loaded those moments when there really was nothing to say, as though creating some connection in the space between words.

He had trouble reading her. She avoided his touch every time he tried. She kept talking more and more loudly, as though to push him away from her with the sheer volume of her voice, yet when she was quiet she looked at him as though she were horny too. After all, she had asked him to come. Every time, just as he had given up, she pulled him back with a touch of his knee. Her hands were wide and bony.

'This one play I did, the guy used to get hard every night. It was awful. I'd have to lie on my front pretending to be dead and this guy was ramming his package up my ass. Eurgh. It was horrible …'

Oisín had seen her do this before, with other boys in the class. He knew this was a conversation she often had; a self she often wheeled out for just such encounters. He had the feeling she knew the drill. Well, so did he. Next they would talk about first loves (his was made up), then about their parents. Oisín liked all this. This was a conversation. He wanted a conversation. He wanted some intimacy: some skin on skin or the gentle brush of his mind against someone else's.

The mixed message thing irritated him though. If she wanted a ride he'd give it to her, but he wasn't going to beg for it. She wasn't even hot.

They had finished the wine by the time the film ended.

They talked about college, about that feeling of non-belonging and to Oisín, who had never articulated it before, this seemed like a revelation. He could fancy her. Her sad, manly mouth, her animal eyes. *Like a wolf*, he thought, *like a fox*.

'Your eyes are amazing. They're so grey – like a fox's.' He went for it.

Once he had kissed her he knew it would happen. It was the way her lips softened open. He was glad of the sudden quiet.

He hadn't had sex in weeks. She made no sound, no groans or mutters. Just breath, faster and slower. He went down on her and listened to the breath and the silence. She didn't taste very nice.

When she came she gave a little whelp, then a quiet, throaty laugh.

'Sorry. I came.'

WHAT'S HIS NAME? Brendan? Malcolm? You can't hear him with all that music playing. You say yours, 'Helen', but he points to his ears and shakes his head. The music is too loud. You say your name again and he says 'Emma?' and you nod. He says, 'Let's get out for some air,' and you nod again. You should tell Cassandra you're leaving but where is she? He takes you by the hand before you've even finished your drink, and leads you through the bang of bodies, the knives of light, to the cold night outside. Cassandra will wonder where you are.

Outside the doors of the club there's a naked bicycle rail, black in the dark. You grasp the cool metal to steady yourself and he comes up behind you, takes your elbow, leads you somewhere and you suddenly realize how drunk you are. It's not your head – it's your body that's drunk, slow, unable to navigate itself.

This must be the side entrance of the nightclub. The wall is covered in some sort of metal or enamel; black and shiny like a beetle's back. He's leaning against it with one knee bent.

The lights in there are terrible. He's better looking than you thought, and older, with broad cheekbones and a straight, frank jaw. There is a scar flecked across one eyebrow where he must have had a piercing once.

He cups your skull in his hand with something like tenderness. Then it begins: the wetness, the breath, the textures of other people's insides.

You are away from this, as though a blister has swelled under your skin, making a big liquid bubble between you and the outside. You think *drunk. I'm drunk.* You wonder can boys tell when you're a virgin. Girls at school used to say they could tell by the way you kissed. His hands move to warm places – the small of your back, nape of your neck – searching. *What?* You want to say, *Searching for what? What?*

'You're beautiful.' The words stick, damp in your ear. The quick image of cleaning them out with a Q-tip: grey slime words on white cotton bud, wriggling like maggots. His hands move to under your skirt and you move them away again. He bites you on the neck but you only feel a pinch.

'You and me baby ain't nothin' but mammals, so let's do it like they do on the Discovery Channel ...'

That's such an old song, the music is usually quite good in there, why are they playing that song? The mammals on the Discovery Channel are powerful cats with sleek sun-lit coats, they pump hot luxurious blood through their bodies and chew shamelessly on crimson limbs.

He pushes your face down to his crotch.

In the jungle when the big cats mount each other it's with an air of leisurely boredom. None of the urgency of human lovers.

In the gap between his legs the oily armour of the nightclub reflects your face. That's you – the melting mascara – that's your face. For less than a moment you appreciate the strangeness of that; that wonder of eyes and lips and chin and how they all add up to something. The music from the nightclub seems noisier now. Maybe they upped the volume. *You and me baby.*

Fingers clumsy with the cold, you open the button on his jeans. They must be new jeans because the buttonhole is very stiff. You look up at him and wonder if he finds this sexy – this stranger with blue eyes kneeling before him in the street, unbuttoning his fly. But it doesn't seem that way. It seems like this is what you should be doing, both of you, like sexy doesn't come into it, like it's all a point of form. And the colour of your eyes, even if he could see it in this light, probably doesn't interest him. There is something that looks like a big vein bulging along the underside of his penis. You can see it through the fly of his shorts. He pushes his boxers down and the penis pongs out.

You are not sure what to do now. One of his hands is in your hair, making circular motions in your scalp. He turns, towards the wall, stretching one arm over you, balancing himself and concealing you. The penis is standing up expectantly. You'll have to do something.

You should lick it, you think, starting at the base, where it is thickest and the vein bulges hardest. You make little, flickering laps with the tip of your tongue, moving slowly up towards the tip. The taste of his skin is not disgusting. It is textured like a plucked chicken. He makes sounds of approval, moving his hand about your scalp more quickly. You're enjoying this, the way you enjoy reading strange, tragic poetry that you don't quite get.

When you reach the tip you stop. You are worried about the little oval hole. You are frightened of what it might taste like, what might come out of it.

'*You and me baby ain't nothin' but mammals …*'

Are they still playing that song? Has so little time passed? No one you can think of is like those creatures: hunting panthers and lionesses lolling in the sun.

He grabs you by the back of your head and you pull away. You didn't mean to pull away, to back out.

'Sorry. Fuck.'

You're not sure whether your words made a sound. You are too drunk, too much inside yourself. Perhaps you didn't speak at all. Your throat closes in and there's a ringing in your ears. He doesn't respond, cooler now, he tries to coax your mouth back to its task, his thumb prying your lower lip open, only you don't move. There is someone behind you. You know it. You are being watched.

'*Sorry. Fuck.*'

You did make a sound, Helen: a very little sound, but you sent the words out secretly into the deep blue nothing of the morning. You wanted an echo thrown back like an answer. But nothing gobbles these things, it is insatiable.

'Fuck,' he cries, outraged, looking behind you at the night. There is someone there.

He pumps it with his hand, ejaculates, still trying to bring your head to his crotch. You can't move. There is a lot of it. It's white, pearly white, falling over his fingers and wrist, clumping the sparse, wiry pubis.

'I came. Sorry. I'm sorry, chicken. I – I came. You're a good girl. Sorry.'

He is stuttering now, but he doesn't stop. It doesn't happen in one go but keeps coming.

Someone grabs you under the arm from behind, forces you to stand, says something.

'What?' you say. You close your lips. Your mouth has been open, gaping, this whole time. 'What?' but you don't turn.

He flumps back against the wall. You want to run but for a moment the impulse is lost in the thick of your drunkenness, *move*, you think, *move*, but it doesn't happen. Then it does. You recoil and it feels like a fall. Then you're moving.

You don't know how you got back to college, or up the stairs, but you're vomiting into the toilet bowl, grateful to be indoors. There's something in the toilet. You're vomiting on something shiny and orange, bobbing under the weight of your puke. You feel bleached. All you can do now is rest, slumped by the toilet with your open lips touching the seat, your breath coming in long, weak drags.

'Where does it hurt?' It's a voice you recognize. Cassy? Where is Cassy?

'On the TV –' you say.

Once on the TV there were pot-bellied babies begging for two pounds a month. They were black and the skin on their arms hung in folds. That must have been a long time ago because you don't use pounds any more. It must be euro now. How many euro is two pounds? How many? You try to calculate it but your brain doesn't know where to start. Suddenly this becomes important: if you can work it out you're all right, if you can't you're fucked.

How much is two pounds? You should know that but you don't 'cause you're fucked. It wasn't them who were begging anyway, the babies. They were just pictures; they were just being videoed. It was a lady's voice.

'I didn't drink much, there must have been something ...'

You don't want to move or talk. You want just to rest and not to be, but you can't breathe, your chest is snagging, the air hurts. You can't breathe. There's a scream in your stomach. You can't breathe. Vomit. You can't breathe.

'You and me baby ain't nothin' but mammals ...'

Is that song still playing?

'I need you to open your eyes for me Helen. Can you focus your eyes for me Helen? I'll have to get help if you won't look at me. What did you take?'

Everything is pain sent in from the outside through a tangle of nerves. You know that – another secret, protective knowledge – you've seen the diagram on the back of a packet of painkillers. The pain is red and the nerves are blue wires like electricity. Vomit again. This time it's just black that comes out in spatters but you can't really look at it, your eyes won't work. You know about eyes too – something about rods and cones flashes in your mind and then it's gone. Now your breath is out of control like hiccups, and coming faster and faster, pulling in. You have to spit out words between the heaves, 'I'm okay ... It'll pass ... Leave me alone, please.'

It will pass. Everything passes. You try not to wish to die because this will pass and then you will want to live again and you will be sorry if you can't. Time is folding like an accordion.

'Breathe,' the girl says.

Then someone else's voice, a boy, 'Call Front Arch! Get them to call an ambulance! I'll go. I'll go and tell them we need an ambulance ...'

'No. No, it's fine. She'll be fine. It'll pass. Don't be stupid. Just a crap pill. It'll pass.'

'Don't give her water if her drink was spiked. If it's that date rape drug water could flood her kidneys … I did a course.'

'I've got it Cahill. Go away. She'll be alright. It'll pass.'

'I did a course,' he says again, 'I'm getting help!'

'Fuck off Cahill. Go to bed. You're making it worse.'

'I'm getting help!'

You can hear him rush out the door, down the stone steps and away.

'Bloody Cahill. Fuck's sake.'

It is Cassy. She pulls back your hair. You can feel her fingers brush your face, only the feeling is far away.

It was a fish – that's what was in the toilet. The goldfish must have died. 'You'll be alright Helen. You're okay sweetheart.' She strokes your forehead, smoothing the hair back, stretching the skin on your crown.

'It will pass.'

She wipes your neck with something wet and warm. This will pass. The taste of him will pass. You are breathing now. You knew something. You are forgetting something. You have a secret but you can't remember it.

You feel the shape of your tongue pressing on the domed palate, the scummy teeth. Your breath tastes old, used up. Ashen breath and tongue and teeth all grey and dead and moving like bacteria and ions and protons and all the still but moving things this world is made of with nothing to move them but each other. Stuff of chemistry and miracles.

'You and me baby ain't nothin' but mammals …'

Sorry. I came.

three

I'M WALKING *a corridor. The ceiling gets lower as I walk and I am forced to bend my knees and squash my chin into my shoulders like a turtle. I can feel the threat of something pressing on my head. I come to steps that lead downwards to more, lower corridors and I know there are people sweeping past me, looking at me. I can feel their bodies displace the air.*

They are whispering in the space around me, these people.

There is a thread tied around my ankle, tugging, cutting into the skin. It is too dark to see, but I know that the thread is salmon pink and belongs to the sort of spool that is used with a sewing machine. There is someone on the end of the thread, wanting me to turn around and go back. They pull harder. It slices my ankle: the sting, the relief of blood.

I can't hear anything, not even my own breath, but I know there is water below, lapping in the dark. I can't smell it yet but I know it will smell cool and earthy and it will make me think of that bridge in Tuscany beneath which Brian and I once drank a bottle of cheap red wine and made love against the wall, the cold stone pressing my breasts and stomach, river swathing my ankles with clean dirt; water worms, leaves, decomposing twigs.

I reach it sooner than expected. Without seeing or smelling it first I plunge one foot in, the one with the thread. The water leaps up my foot to the ankle, as though it can smell the blood and wants it, and I am grateful for the coolness of it, the promise it makes of open places and of rain.

Then I can see in the dark, and I realize that I could see all along, and I feel stupid for ever thinking otherwise. The people in the water are angry with me for overlooking them. They have faces anonymous like rotting corpses and no tongues and their ribs are bulging with hunger. All three of them are women. They have little folds for breasts, sharp nipples. They are opening and closing their mouths, trying to speak. At first I don't mind this at all, but then the pain in my ankle begins to throb, the sting pitching higher and higher, up and up like a long, sliding vibrato on a violin string. My feet are losing their grip. It is muddy beside the river. I slip and slide flat into the water – but it's not water at all. It's solid, dry.

I lie on my back hearing myself breathe, hearing my dry eyelids open and shut. The ceiling is grey-pink like the skin of the dying.

This is the fourth-year dorm from school. I recognize it. This year every bed has a shaky woodchip partition with three drawers and a light running under the cardboard lip over the mirror. It jitters when the button is pressed before settling into a dim yellowish glow. I can't reach it without getting out of bed, stepping onto the cold cement floor.

The school is old and exclusive. Generations of girls have slept in this bed, slowly wearing a dip along the centre where the mattress has yielded to them over the years. They wore the same uniforms and spoke the same words at morning prayers.

There are too many different heartbeats here, too many different dreams clamouring about this dim space.

My lips meet and part. I try to say something but I can't. I know what's happening. I'm slipping into that dream again, the one I had all the time at school, the one that is lurking beneath every dream I have. In the dream a schoolgirl stands over me. I can't see the face, but I know it is solemn and pale, and it holds a slender hand over my mouth as though it means no harm. I can't breathe. I can't move my body. I am suffocating quickly with the hand resting gently over my mouth. I fight with my head, jerking it from side to side in the struggle. Before I pass out I see the girl's face at last; the brief, alarming flash of a pale alien-shaped head with schoolgirl's hair. It is luminous, as though a low-watt light bulb is screwed in at the neck. The eyes are smudges of dark –

I don't come out of this dream quickly, I never do. When I open my eyes I'm still half in it. I have to switch on the light to believe I'm awake, and pinch my wrist, the way I did as a child when something bad happened and I wanted to make sure it was real before grieving. I can still hear the clanking pipes, the blank drumming of time.

It was seeing Helen that way tonight – that's what brought on the dream. She was curled on her bed, snoring lightly. I wanted to kiss her on her clammy, smoke-scented forehead. I used to feel like that when she slept beside me at school. Sometimes when I woke up I'd climb into bed with her and she would cry and I never asked her why, just stroked her hair until we fell asleep. I'd never sleep for very long. I always woke from the noise of the pipes, or that nightmare, or a slap of fear that came from nowhere. I didn't kiss her then. I closed her door and got into the shower to wash the nightclub off me.

I switch on the lamp beside my bed and try to read. The book is called *Up From Slavery*, with an African man dressed like a colonist on the cover. I can't remember how I'm meant to be reading it, what it's meant to tell me. I press my back firmly against the cold wall. I can't shake the feeling that someone may creep up behind me, grab my shoulder, my face, take me somewhere. This is one of those terrible dreams that pull you down with it again and again. You can wake up in horror, have a glass of water, of whiskey, of wine, or hot chocolate, go to the loo, rub your cheeks, but as soon as you close your eyes it's there again, creeping in from the back of your brain as though you loved it.

In boarding school, one day flowed into the next, carried by the dulling current of routine. The air constantly smelled of the musty mashed potatoes that we got every day for lunch. Butter was only allowed at tea, but we each got a glass of milk at midday. Some girls poured it into the powdery white potatoes, studded with hard little eyes and grains of salt big enough to roll with your tongue.

Sister Margaret was our dorm mistress. After a nervous breakdown she was transferred from a day school where she was the principal, to the lowest position in our convent's hierarchy. She had bright, blushing skin, but her eyes were snuffed out. She kept us up until ten o'clock some nights talking about her sister's children. She had wanted to be a policewoman, she told us that a lot, but her grandmother's dying wish was that she would become a Sister. She went into the nunnery for a trial year and never left. Some girls said that she had lost both breasts to cancer. She should have been a mother, Sister Margaret. She should have been feeding babies with her breasts, not pressing it all down until her sex turned on itself. Then someone curled on her bed, maybe brushing her hair, would ask dreamily, '*Were you ever in love, Sister?*' And just as they'd hoped, the veiled old nun would stare wistfully into the past with her dulled eyes: '*I thought I was.*' Then she would pinken with the shame of her innocent sin, and for a moment we were all in a past of possibilities.

I haven't fallen asleep again. I can still feel the cold wall on my back, the soft weight of the book, but that dream bleeds into the room, that sense of other people's sleep and someone about to finger your neck. The layers of sound: clanking pipes, a dripping tap, some girl's quiet sobs, the quick slap of bare feet fading down the corridor, the dead walls and the sturdy wooden stools.

All our minds floated about in close quarters. A person could think anything in there. You didn't know if your thoughts belonged to you or the girl asleep next to you, or the ghost's head that rested over yours on the pillow.

THROUGH YOUR drunken sleep a sound beckons from another world. A tap is dripping. You are called to one of those moments that is suspended somewhere forever; sandwiched between your past and your now. You are called to where you last left a bit of yourself, Helen, where you last stepped away leaving a faint outline of you in the air.

Somewhere a tap was dripping. You didn't care. You wanted to be alone to cry. When you cried in school the nice girls climbed into bed with you, and the mean ones threw their boyfriends' rugby balls at your head. You didn't want either. You sat with your bare feet in the ancient bath, the dripping tap patiently eroding its shallow, wide valley in the enamel; a wound dealt slowly and without passion. It was a cold, frightening sort of dark, but if you turned on the light Sister Margaret would kill you. Cassandra had been talking in her sleep again. You couldn't sleep anyway. You couldn't stand it. If anyone knew they'd think you were so stupid. They'd look at you and say, 'I think every teenage girl has a crush on her English teacher, Helen,' or something like that. But that wasn't it.

You were in love with him, he was in love with you. You knew what it would feel like with your head on his solid chest, your face in his neck. You knew already the warmth of his skin and his man's smell. He'd like the scent of your hair – apple blossom and peach.

You wake too early, groggy. Take two Nurofens and lie on your side trying to get back to sleep. Your brain feels loose and heavy in your skull. There really is a tap dripping somewhere. It's not the sink in your room.

You had forgotten that night. It was uneventful. Why think of it now? Those ancient yellow baths! Sister Margaret. How archaic the whole thing was! And that crush! How often did you cry then, over that silly crush?

You got angry with him sometimes in class when he looked at you, talking about *Wuthering Heights*. 'There was more belief in true love then, but of course such love cannot exist in this world, only the less passionate love of Hareton and Cathy can survive, and only that love is purely good ...' and you drank it all in like wisdom. You had never liked English class before. He sometimes stood with the top of his thighs pushed up against your desk, touching your things, borrowing your pen, running his finger along the rim of your copybook. You got angry with him then because it was stupid of him to act like that, to think that he could. He'd call you back after class and forget what he wanted to say, he'd be all feverish and jumpy, and you were on the verge of tears for him because you wanted to touch him to still his body, and tell him, 'It's okay. Me too, me too.'

Oh – last night. You had forgotten. That man's hard penis and vomiting in the toilet. It returns in snapshots, like a film montage, and with the same muted impact. You don't mind. Let thoughts of last night go – much nicer, much warmer to think of this older, sweeter pain.

He had to supervise your table for tea on a Friday. You got a treat of chocolate spread on Fridays; you remember thinking that must be why he had chosen that day. He'd lavish it on as thick as the bread itself, but there was plenty to eat on a Friday, and there was always enough chocolate spread. Like all the other supervisors, he sat at the head of the table. Your place was right beside him.

You talked about stupid things like summer games and the exams because people were listening. He always wanted to know what you did that day, that week even, every detail, as though by picturing it he could change it so that he was there too. You lived for those evenings. You spent your days silently describing your life as you'd tell it to him, storing up anything funny, imagining how he'd laugh.

Once he kissed you right there in the refectory. Most of the other girls had left, it was your week to clear the fourth-year table and he had to supervise. The Sisters were sitting at the back of the room, discussing the roster. You were bringing the plates to wash-up and he stopped you by putting his hand out flat where your middle was. 'Go on Helen, I'll take them.'

And you didn't get butterflies, or whatever you're supposed to get. What you felt was calm, relief. It was as though you had been waiting for him to touch you like that, and tell you to leave the plates, he'd take them. You knew then that you weren't insane. It really was happening to you both, this thing that no one understands. You asked him with your eyes to tell you for sure. As he took the plates from you he leaned forward and kissed you. It was a gentle, brushing, just-touching kiss at the corner of your mouth. You said, 'Thank you, sir, goodnight,' and went upstairs.

You can't sleep. Get up and splash your face. Brush your teeth – your mouth tastes terrible. Maybe the kiss was more like a gift, a gesture of kindness, of charity even, or pity. But you cried that night from confusion, just happy-sad confusion.

You had a sports day at the end of second term. You'd been sick for a week, Helen, and weren't allowed to do games. So you sat on the slope at the side of the playing field, drinking the sweet orange cordial you only got on special days. And there he was, in shorts. You hadn't seen him for a week because you were in the infirmary. It felt like a reunion.

His thighs were muscle-packed, and hairy like his arms. And all these years later there it is: the image of his sleeves rolled up and the light playing on the hairs, changing them from black to blond and red, winking at them, camouflaging them and revealing again the delicate film of hair. That secret image you used to carry with you, that secret you would take out and handle in the dark.

The girls won the teacher-student match and then you all sat on the grass drinking the orange out of plastic cups, the sun blazing on your face and shoulders and Sister Margaret rushing out with rugs, saying you'd all go home with the flu and what would your parents say. You were wearing a powder-blue tank top, which worried her to the point of hysteria, facing the sun with your eyes lightly shut. Your hair was very long and you liked the feel of it tipping along the small of your back. The distant shrieks and splashes from the unheated pool, and then the girls clambering barefoot up the slope, freezing in their towels, cut grass sticking to their feet and calves, and you were glad you weren't allowed to do games.

You knew he was watching you. You thought he wanted you. Not sex, but *you*: your voice, your arms, your eyes. Even then you knew you would never be that beautiful to anyone again. He took some Polaroids. First one of the Sisters, and then a few of you. Click and buzz and screams from the cold water and when you opened your eyes there he was, blue whirling blobs all over him from facing the sun too long, but you could see that he looked sad and hopeless and it frightened you. He looked like he had to do something hard, like salt a slug or crush a bird with a broken wing. It had been about six weeks since the kiss and by now you knew you loved him.

There were lovely days like that – with diluted orange and cut grass, and for all their mistakes the nuns were good, resigned people – but mostly you hated school. You hated it anyway, but without him it was almost unbearable, days flowing in and out of one another with a maddening sameness no longer punctuated by his classes or your brief encounters. Then three weeks into the third term, when you had been told the substitute would be staying on for the rest of the year, you got a letter.

All it said was 'Helen', typed at the top of the page. There was no 'Dear', and no date. Lower down on the page there was a poem printed in the same font. It began, 'If I could live my life over, I would be less careful next time,' and went on about walking barefoot in the fall and eating more ice-cream and less beans. At the bottom was a phone number and an address, no name. And that was it.

You thought it was your secret but it wasn't.

You carried the poem around in the inside pocket of your school skirt for a long time. The girls used to call it your 'ST pocket', meaning sanitary towel, much like some boys in college call the small pocket at the front of their jeans their 'johnny pocket' – meaning condom. It was an all right poem. What was it about the poem that made you squirm with humiliation? He couldn't leave it at this. He wouldn't. You'd come up from study one evening and he'd be sitting there looking all out of place on the small, pink bed with its white iron frame. He would kiss you again, but on the mouth this time, and say sorry.

'I'm sorry. Sorry I left you alone with the cold and the dust and the flesh-coloured walls.'

Sorry I left you to the world. Sorry I left you to the man with the scarred eyebrow. Sorry.

It was the kitchen tap that was dripping. You fill a glass of water and take it back to bed. It must have been the tap that made you dream about boarding school. You slept to the sound of bloody taps dripping for that whole school year.

Turn over in bed and pull the duvet around you. That's the past, silly Helen. Open your eyes in the dark under the covers. Do caterpillars see through the walls of their cocoons? An unborn baby can see light and shadow through its mother's womb. Your aunt told you that when she was pregnant.

Maybe you shouldn't both have been so stupid about it, such cowards. It wasn't such a big deal. It wasn't such a scandal. It didn't have to be all stolen moments and poetry through the post.

If you'd kept the number you could ring him now and ask him about it. It wouldn't even be embarrassing. You'd act like it was so long ago, like you were a different person, that girl, that silly girl in a powder-blue tank top whose Polaroid he keeps.

'Remember me?' you'd say, 'Just found this and thought I'd find out who sent it. You taught me English in fourth year, I think I had a crush on you …'

Fall asleep Helen, fall asleep again and wake up when the past has shifted further away. Your mind is still funny after last night. Go to sleep.

IN THE MORNING he had sex with Sharon again, from behind, which is how he liked it best.

She was not very interested but let him anyway. He tried to massage her clit a bit as he did it but her breath stayed the same, quiet and even. 'It's nothing personal,' she said. 'It's just 'cause I'm on the pill. It lowers the sex drive. But keep going. I don't mind.' He cupped her breast and closed his eyes.

Pumping away, he had an image of his mother in the bath. It was something from his childhood. She was reading a book, her hands sticking up out of the water to hold it and her eyebrows focused in a frown. He tugged at lank wet strands of her hair, and poured water over her shoulders and breasts with the plastic cup she used to rinse his hair, but she kept reading. Could that be a real memory? He only ever bathed with his brothers as a child.

When would his mother have taken a bath with him?

Oisín's mam didn't catch his eye much. She rarely smiled. If she did it was a close-mouthed smile with faraway eyes. She read a lot, that's where Oisín got it from, but she never talked about the things she read. Maybe she talked to his father when Oisín wasn't about, but he doubted it. He was not very good at talking either.

It was taking him a long time to come. Weird to be thinking of his mother while he was doing this. Everything felt wrong this morning.

After he had stayed at Sharon's as long as was polite he went to the computer labs, but he didn't feel like telling the lads about Sharon. He'd tell them another time.

She had washed her hair again before he left. When he kissed her goodbye he could smell her shampoo. It was like some sort of fruit. Saliva rushed into his mouth and he thought about breakfast. She stayed by the door as he walked away. Her eyes were like an owl's now, big in their round sockets.

four

I AM NOT coming to this lecture any more. He is ranting about love again. I thought this course would be about parody, and religion, and form. I should have known better.

He hands out a sheet of suggested essay titles, and the bundle travels up from the front rows to the back, diminishing quickly. 'Chaucer and Love as Madness'; that's one of them.

'Of course you can't possibly know …' he says, focusing on a girl at the front with blonde highlights and blushing cheeks. He always directs his lecture to her, and she always blushes and then argues weakly, and blushes some more. At the end of class she often goes up and discusses something with him.

'Love, real love is so rare,' he says. 'Love: what a mad and complex and stupid and absolutely fundamental part of our thinking. Aren't we fools to believe in logic when the most basic beliefs are founded on feeling, on the blind choice of light over dark, God over Satan, pleasure over pain? When we are building our cities on the shifting sands of our healthiest madness, in a land where the rules of gravity and equations are nothing but a word game?' The girl looks down at her lap, then up at him again through her lashes. He grins like a boy.

I picture my grandmother arguing with him, dismissing his philosophizing with a swish of her hand and a wise little laugh. I wish I were like her: less concerned with the ideas of things and more with the things themselves. She has no interest in stilling reality, fixing it into a rigid logic. That's what Chaucer is to Professor Delahunt – love, the volcano victim, preserved forever in molten lava. Love, frozen like flowers in the thick glass of a paperweight. That's what he wants. Suddenly I feel as though that's what I want really, as though he has found me out. Love. I want to hold it in my hand, turn it in the sunlight and study it from every angle. I want to own it so that it cannot wriggle and shift.

THE LECTURE was called 'The Novel as Women's Literature'. The guest speaker looked like a weasel, Oisín decided. Though he didn't know what weasels looked like exactly, he thought he had a good sense of what impression they made: feral and sharp. Twitchy.

Oisín began to describe the lecturer in his head. He thought of suitable words for his features. 'Aquiline' was wrong, but he liked that word and hoped to use it someday in front of a pretty, clever girl. This man had a pointed nose, no chin and short, light brown hair that started far back on his sloping forehead. His eyes were tiny points of green light darting nervously around the auditorium. His voice, in contrast, was confident. Each word landed with a weight and certainty out of joint with the tetchy rhythm of his eyes. He left a lot of reflective pauses, as though he was just thinking up his theories on the spot. Of course he knew a lot about his subject, but his underdog Scottish accent gave him a down-to-earth quality that the girls loved. Oisín hated him.

He was talking about the novel as escapism. The popularity of the form began out of the needs of bored housewives, he said, they were erotic fantasies or romances that offered relief from the dull domesticity of their lives. There was something not right about this man scrutinizing the private lives of 'bored housewives', invading their fantasies like that. What did he know about it? Anyway, who was the lecturer's mother? What was she that was so much better than a housewife?

The first book Oisín had ever read was *Fire in the Stable*. It was one of his mother's Mills & Boon novels. She read these paperbacks at her eleven o'clock coffee break and in the evening as her reward after she had done all the housework and the boys were watching television. Sometimes, if she and Oisín were completely alone and she was bored of her book and there was no washing or ironing or vacuuming or cooking to be done, she talked to him. Sometimes she talked about places she had been when she was younger: Paris, Rome, about abortive emigration plans for Australia … or about the pony she had owned as a child. There was nothing in the present to talk about, really. She didn't feel very welcome in Clonmel and had few friends.

Neighbours occasionally called to the door, sure that this quiet, conservatively dressed young blow-in would be grateful for the company, and she made them cups of tea, offered them the best biscuits, spoke gently and responded quietly to their chatter with 'yes' and 'mmm' and 'really'. His mother just wanted to finish the housework and settle down with her book. Sometimes she hid and didn't answer the door at all, but the visitors didn't know this. As Oisín grew older he learned that locals found his mother rather strange and boring, and left her kitchen with the feeling people get after dropping change in somebody's cup.

During the occasional private conversations between them,

his mother looked at his hands or touched his hair. She listened to him. He knew she loved him, though there was a pain about his mother that made even her love a sort of accusation. As a child he followed her about the house quietly, skulking about door frames, wanting to be talked to, wanting to help and consistently failing at whatever task she gave him. He had her eyes: brown almonds.

The Mills & Boon books – and not his brothers – were Oisín's rivals. For a long time he had hidden them from her jealously – stowing them in cupboards, under beds, behind the toilet bowl. It never occurred to him to destroy them. It was only after some time that he thought of reading one.

He was nine at the time and did not find it very interesting, though he liked some of the words. He stored them in his head and whispered them to himself. They were little weapons, little empowerments – something he had belonging to his mother. Those words would not be alone with her if he couldn't be.

Some of the words he had never heard of before: 'voluptuous', 'quivering', 'unkempt'. She usually found the books when she was cleaning, and took them back without mentioning their disappearance.

His mother had wanted to be a writer. She had won the Clonmel short story competition five years ago, with a tale of a woman who one day stops speaking. The story ended with the word 'Bang' and the woman leaving, slamming the front door on her husband and two daughters. The prize was a book voucher and a fountain pen.

Oisín brought her home a copy of *A Doll's House* for Christmas after his first term of college, but she never read it. She didn't like reading plays. She said she found it hard to picture the people.

He left the lecture early, slipping out as quietly as he could, but people still looked and sighed. He didn't usually do this because it embarrassed him to be looked at, but he was in a foul mood. He was bored and he didn't like the lecturer. There was no point describing his weasel features any more because he had no one to describe them to. The lads had no interest in this kind of crap.

'LOVE IS LOVELY,' my grandmother would say, 'and terrible when it's gone. Now sit still and eat your dinner!' We used to talk about things like that over meals, or driving back to school after the holidays, a gnawing pain in my spine and between my ribs, a tickling anxiety creeping up through my whole body from the gut. I wanted to understand things. I wanted her wisdom. I understood nothing: not love, not the war she lived through, not survival. Nothing.

'But –'

'But nothing,' she would say. 'Everything is fine. Everything will be fine. Stop inventing complications. Life is complicated enough. Smile. You need to smile more. You are very pretty when you smile.'

Grandad would have loaded my cases into the boot of the car, kissed me and said to be a good girl now and be gentle to the nuns. After fifty years in Ireland he still spoke the written English he had learned from classic novels. He used a lot of clichés, but that was okay because he didn't know they were clichés.

'You need a little hypocrisy in you,' he told me more than once. 'You need to be a little tainted if you are not to be corrupted altogether.'

He loved these kind of paradoxes. He thought they were very clever. He was a great advocate of the practically impossible theory of silently questioning everything, and he was a great hypocrite: he could never keep from saying what he thought.

He would keep us too long at the front door, '… and it won't be long before you are back with us,' and my grandmother would be shivering by the car saying, 'Stop it now or she will be late,' and he'd laugh like a bold child, and draw out his speech on purpose to annoy her. Then she would laugh too and call him *sieverer*, which was a fond way of saying 'dribbling idiot' in Flemish, and they would share something no one else could ever be included in. That was love then. I remember thinking that. *That's love. What I am looking at is love. Need to get me some of that.*

We would drive along in the half-dark and every time I'd say how I loved this time of evening, though I knew I'd said it before, and she'd answer that the French called it *entre chien et loup*. I remember saying that I didn't see how canines were at all like times of day and she said that yes, it was a funny expression all right, and sighed because she had failed to tell me something.

We were silent for most of the journey and I would watch the shimmery black tarmac of the dual carriageway as it thickened and rolled on under us, taking us nearer and nearer to Wicklow. My mother and my aunt had attended the same school. I wonder if my grandmother thought about that while we drove through the early dark, whether the journey reminded her of my mother as a girl, and whether I was anything like she had been.

I comforted myself with the knowledge that my tuck box was filled with surprises: cold pancakes and sandwiches for that evening, seedless grapes and a two-week supply of apples and oranges. After that I'd live on tortilla chips and Kinder bars. There'd be a few clean hankies in there, which I never used, and that made me cry because they smelled of my grandmother and our utility room: a smell of brown soap, and care, and fabric softener, and not the itchy industrial stuff they used at school. I used to think that if I willed it enough she'd miss the turn, but even when that happened we were only delayed a little. Eventually we'd crunch up the gravel drive. I wouldn't let her come in with me. I'd kiss her outside the car and then trundle in with too many bags. The candlelight and the familiar stench of floor polish said that really, it wasn't so bad.

'Love … so mysterious, so intangible … so … unrealistic, if you will.' The lecturer addresses the girl in the front row. Her hand shoots up. He pauses, looking at her, waiting.

'Why?'

He raises an eyebrow.

'Excuse me?'

She swallows, 'Professor, why "unrealistic"? Why do you say "unrealistic"?'

'U HOME?'

She didn't use his name. Maybe the text message was meant for someone else? He knew he shouldn't reply but he had nothing better to do. 'Just left a lecture 2 boring wot u up 2?' The reply startled him: 'NOTHN CAN I CALL IN?' Did she think she was his girlfriend? He hadn't had Sharon down as that type at all. He thought she slept with lots of guys. He put the phone back in his pocket and continued home. The flat was a mess, mugs piled in the sink, last night's pasta dried into the bowl. He pulled the mugs out of the cold, slimy water, stacking them in twos on the draining board, and rinsed his fingers. Then he scraped the shrunken swirls into the plastic bag he'd been using as a bin, and filled the bowl with water to re-hydrate those bits he couldn't get off. He boiled the kettle, switched on the TV, and re-read the message, 'NOTHN CAN I CALL IN?' Had he ever told her where he lived? It looked like the message of a stalker – all those capitals – but he was bored. 'Sure. Jst havin cup t.'

She arrived minutes later, her eyes and lips puffy, her voice small.

'Hey Oisín.'

'Hi.'

He couldn't believe he had slept with her. He couldn't picture her breasts now and he thought her skin smell would turn him off. She didn't seem like the kind of girl he could get physically close to at all. She had a bottle of red wine in her hand. He took it, and put it in the kitchen without thinking to open it for them. Unzipping herself from a tight suede jacket, she sat down on his couch. Underneath she was wearing a sweater like a giant child's with an eighties colour scheme; it was brown with orange and yellow cuffs and two small, useless pockets. Her attitude made him uncomfortable. She had a sense of knowing the space, of having a right to be in it.

'I hope I'm not disturbing you?'

'No.'

She sniffed, tucking her hands up under her sleeves, kicking off her pumps and folding her knees under herself. She rubbed her face. 'Oh dear,' she said, and sighed. 'Could I have a cup of tea?'

Her eyes frightened him. They were too big and watery. The grey was pinkish like the white part. It reminded him of when they had dissected a sheep's eyeball in school.

He boiled the kettle and there was no conversation. Every sound he made – the clack of the kettle, the soft thud of the presses – seemed too loud, embarrassing.

'Sorry to burst in on you like this Oisín.'

'No it's cool, it's cool. Lecture was really boring. Did you take "The Novel" last term? The lecturer is a wanker.'

'I just ... Oh God, I mean. I don't know why I'm even here. I ... my sister's going into hospital. She has anorexia. I just ...'

Oisín knew he was supposed to interrupt here with some expression of shock or sympathy, a hand on her shoulder even, her face, her neck ... but he didn't. He pretended to wash a mug, rubbing his fingers around the bottom over and over. She continued to talk. From what he gathered her sister was starving herself to death, and her family was broke, and she had got a 2.2 in her last essay. He made the tea slowly, handed it to her, and sat next to her on the couch, examining her shoulders and mouth and the broad chin as she spoke. He avoided the eyes. In his mind he sectioned the sheep's eyeball again. It had been neater than expected, the whole affair. Usually real things looked nothing like the diagrams. Vegetable cells, for example, didn't relate very well to the neat bricks in the science book, but the eyeball had made sense. They could easily label the parts: retina, iris, and what was the name of that hard bit? The bit that looked like a glass pebble? It acted like a mirror, un-jumbled the image before sending it to the brain. Reflected it backwards and upside down and then right way up again, so that the image that reached the brain wasn't the raw reality at all.

'Thanks Oisín, for listening. I just need a friend, you know? My friend Lucy is away. And John. John is a good friend, my best friend. He's away too. On Erasmus. I have a lot of friends you know. Don't think it's that I don't have friends, it's just, there's something about you Oisín. I think we get each other.'

HE STUTTERS, this lecturer, mirroring the blushing student, 'Because … well. You will see. You are too young, all of you. You are too young.' As a child I felt too old, always.

When I got to school I'd unpack and sit on my bed listening to various lies about the other girls' holidays, about what they were wearing to the races and who would be there, discussions on who would make head girl and why and whether this was fair. I tried to join in sometimes and they tried to include me but I felt foolish. My interest was unconvincing. They knew I didn't get it – the races, the boys, how to wear the kind of dress that is respectable and sexy both at the same time. Until fifth year, when I met

Brian, I stayed at home with my grandparents during the holidays, wearing jeans and baggy T-shirts and my grandad's cardigans. The worst thing of all, my dark secret, was that I liked it. That was where I was happiest. I didn't care at all who would be head girl.

When I was homesick I'd think of my dead mother and blame her for my loneliness. The poor ghost-girl whom I have pieced together from stories and hazy, ever-changing fragments of memory. My father was never very real to me. I didn't suffer from his absence. I occasionally wondered what he looked like but never blamed him or cared much where he was, or whether he loved me. I blamed my mother. I hated her as you can only hate those the heart chooses too soon.

I had some memories that still felt real. I knew that sometimes she would leave me on my grandparents' doorstep when I was bold, saying she wanted nothing to do with me, I had ruined it all. For some reason I can't remember, I would never ring the bell, but would sit in the darkening air and let my blood stagnate. I used to enjoy that feeling, thinking about mongooses from the Discovery Channel, or trying to figure out how they made balloons. I had a useful way of shrinking into my head, away from my body with its cold fingers and all those unnamed feelings that burrowed away in the pit of my stomach. Or maybe that was just once. Memory is funny like that. I don't know.

When my grandmother opened the door she would lift me up into the powdery, floral heat of her body and carry me silently into the pine glow of the kitchen. I was wrapped in my grandad's cardigan and placed on his lap to watch my grandmother move about the kitchen. Her methods of comfort were hot chocolate with a gloopy skin, camomile tea, brown sugar biscuits, and carrot cake. The carrot cake had white icing that was soft like cream.

My grandfather knew everything. He spoke eight different languages and could explain the merits and flaws of every religion and every prophet. His library was the very cold basement that smelled of disinfectant more than of books. The walls were lined with full shelves and fat, titleless volumes were stacked up from the floor. A large freezer hummed in the farthest corner of the room. We used it to store raspberries and peas from the glasshouse when we couldn't eat them all.

To show me a book he'd take it into the sitting room and open it on his lap for me to follow the words as he read. The sitting room smelled of clean. It had a big mustard-coloured velvet couch with swallowing cushions. We read a lot of books. There was one with pictures. It was called *The Silly Duck*. It was a 'My First Reader' book, but we kept reading it long after I had mastered the skill. It was about a little duckling that hatches from an egg in the reeds. The first thing it lays its eyes on is a fox. Ducklings think the first thing they see is their mother and fall in love with it. The fox would normally eat the duckling, but he is so touched by the naivety of the fluffy little thing that he cannot. The fox raises the duckling until it is time for the duckling to join a flock of ducks. My grandfather thought it was hilarious – I remember him chuckling on and on, and I would become embarrassed waiting for his laughter to finish. 'Such a simple idea,' he would say, 'but brilliant!'

I remember *The Little Prince* as well, and *Marcus Aurelius*, but the rest has sunk into the past. It was important to him that I read these books. After each chapter he would ask me what I thought and we would argue together. We both knew we had to reach a conclusion before my grandmother poked her head into the room and called us for dinner, '*A table*!' I thought we were important, the pair of us. We were on a quest together, and together we would eventually find that solid thing – the right knowledge. I would hold it in my fist and hand it to him and we would right forever's wrongs.

My grandfather would always make everything clear. The night of my mother's funeral he sat on the bed with a box of Laughing

Cow cheese in one hand, and a mug steaming with hot malt in the other. The cow on the box was smiling and she had two round boxes of Laughing Cow cheese for earrings. 'And the same pictures must be on this cow's earrings, and the same on those. Imagine, forever, never ending.' I could not imagine it, and it terrified me to try. Forever was inconceivable. The thought was unbearable. I understood why people had to die.

I wish I could recover the glimpse I had then, because it was a glimpse of something. I understood something. It was okay that life was not perfect, that people were unhappy, and that people died. The whole mess had value regardless. I wish I could remember that.

At night we would sit together drinking from rose-patterned teacups and I was safe and content in the knowledge that there was nothing Grandad didn't know that we couldn't find together. But he shook his head slowly: 'What happened, you would never have foreseen it, she was never like this as a child.'

That was true. My mother used to be young and happy and beautiful. She used to have soft black hair that moved like waves. She used to sit on the grass in fields of tiny blurred flowers, decorated with pastel pinks and blues, squinting in the white sunlight of fading photographs.

Even before my mother died, I had a little pine bed in my grandparents' house. The sheets were clean and cool. After sliding my bathed body flat between the stiff cotton, investing my heat in the brittle white, I would lie still, listening – though I didn't want to hear – to the sound of my grandmother downstairs, dialling. I knew they liked to have me there, to teach me, feed me, watch me paint with big flat brushes and bottles of squeezy colour. So why would she ring my mother's flat? Every time: 'She's your child, darling.' Then she would hang up and cry and I knew that my grandfather was shaking his head impotently and sighing because she was never like this as a child, while my grandmother sobbed angrily into the soft crêpe of her palms. I understood that for my mother our life was a dark thing now, something that existed too long, after everything had stopped mattering. Even when she loved me it was a copy, a flailing effort.

My mother. Mummy; woman with the prosthetic heart.

I enjoyed it when she let me watch as she put on her face. It was a lovely face with rosy cheeks and a smile painted over her big, sad lips. When she was not angry she would wear a black, wide-rimmed hat with a thick pink bow around it and smoke through a long black-and-gold holder. The smoke twirled like a dreaming ballerina, like choking seaweed. We would sit at the kitchen table, mother and child, me with a mug of water or Coke and Mummy with a glass of yellowish liquid that she would down with a knock of the head. It smelled like her nail polish while it was still in the bottle. She would roll her 'r's and hiss her 's's and lean across the table to give the moist whisper: 'Remember my beautiful darling, there are no parts for women – it's a man's world, baby, it's a man's world, my beautiful little baby! There are no parts for us worth playing.' Then Mum would laugh, and then she would cry. Sometimes she would start to take photographs of me. 'Beautiful. Beautiful. Look at that face …' It didn't seem to bother her if I didn't smile for these photos. I think a lot of them have been thrown out because they made my grandmother sad afterwards.

On these evenings Mum often told me stories: 'And I told them, princess, you stupid little man, I said. I mean to say. Stupid little man!' Her voice would sway in and out. I knew all the characters of our tragic fairy tale. The short, moustached agent would shake his bald head and say, in the stout voice for which Mum buried her chin in her neck: 'It just isn't working Marie, it simply isn't worth our while …' and the conversation would circle.

The lecturer looks like a politician. He puts so much feeling into every word that his whole frame shakes.

'And what Chaucer under*stood*, about love, was that *afterwards* … afterwards *nothing is the same*. Something is lost. But not just something, the very essence of a person, the very *thing*, the *thing* …'

He is still talking to the girl with the highlights. I wonder what she thinks of all this. I draw a droplet on my foolscap, and a smaller one under it. Then I draw the splash when the drops hit the end of the page; an upside-down tear and lots of little ones all around it. I used to be good at art.

At twenty-three my mother's life was over. For her the present did not exist, it was a dream beyond the day and she killed it with a tiny shot glass of liquid gold. Or many glasses. In my memory it is always the same one. Mum loved me and hated me because I had my father's eyes, because I frightened him away, because I was very young.

I was only very young, and I loved her. I would have been whatever she wanted me to be. Love: the thing that makes the blood fizz. The cruel thing that blurs the mind with gentle bubbles. Hubble Bubble.

I am always hoping to close the book on the story of my mother, to think her out. But my thoughts work in circles, panting persistently like a choo-choo train.

She didn't always hate me, and if I was her demon I was also the light of her world. If she didn't love me why would she keep me locked in our flat while Grandad banged on the door? And if he did drag me to school, why would she pine for me? She'd open the door, hugging herself in too-big pyjamas that made her so tiny it hurt to look.

'I'm glad you're home my angel, I've been so lonely all day without you.' We'd climb into her bed and she would kiss my head, my eyelids, my ears, my face and neck and arms, then each little finger and each little toe: 'One, two, three, four, five – all there!' and she said she loved me, she loved me so much. She loved me. I could never know how much. I could never understand how much. Her bed was warm and comfortable and smelled of her sleep and her farts and her drink.

She folded me as small as I could go and tucked me between her breasts; I was beloved. She traced my profile with her ring finger; I was beautiful. She followed the blue path of my pulse where it showed at the wrists; I was strong.

Unlike me, my mother was small with a neat nose, swollen, geisha lips and Bambi eyes. She was made differently to me. These big, jutting cheekbones must be my father's doing, because she had limbs that thrilled men with their fragility. In the street or the pub or the post office, I saw the way men watched her wrists, her hips, her calves, and I clung tighter to her. They wanted the feeling you get when you hold something tiny and trembling and beautiful at your mercy, a small bird on your palm. That must have been what my father liked. It must have been why he had stayed so long before I came along, while his wife, who was more successful, but not as good an actress as Mum, hated us and bawled until he went back to her and put her in another play.

I gave Mum stretch marks. Some evenings she would lie on her back and cry over them, and I would trace each silvery snail-trail with my fingers as though I could heal what I had done. She had a pink ridge that curved under her pelvis. That's where they cut me out. 'You wouldn't get out of me, would you, baby? You were tight as a shrimp, stuck. You wanted to stay there until your daddy came back for us. They had to pry you out. You were a ball clamped shut like an oyster, with tiny red fists, screaming at the world. The midwife uncurled you and made me hold you but you didn't want me. My milk made you sick. We waited in the hospital for three days. He never came.'

I understood this story very well. He didn't love Mum, or want to put her in his plays now because she was no longer that girl, that woman who could play fourteen and no one would suspect. He might come back though. I was put on lookout while she drank in her bed. I would know him by his red hair. We had very few rules in our home, but those she made, I obeyed. My feet made imprints in our carpet where I stood for hours, forbidden to move from that spot by the window in case Eoin, that was my dad, came back. On the last evening I was put on lookout again while she wrote me a note and put herself to sleep. I gazed out the window until my vision blurred.

She did her best. Well, we all do our best. In our own ways we all do our best all the time, don't we? We do what we do. We are no better than that. No better, and no worse.

I need to remember my mother. I need to shake off her kiss, tug out the fragile, intricate weave of memories and spread her like a ribbon before me, outside my head, so she cannot watch me while I sleep. Someday I will light the ribbon and watch it taper into ash.

Until then I must stop thinking the same things over and over. I must stop.

I stuff my foolscap and the list of essay titles into my bag and stand up. The lecturer spots me. He looks stricken and stops speaking. A few students turn to look at me, straining their necks because I'm at the very back. I pretend not to notice and leave urgently.

I slouch back to my room, hunched against the drizzle and cold. My mind is full of noise. I can't unknot the shapeless, nameless thoughts filling it. When there is nothing left to do, walk away and don't look back. Leave the problem in a bundle on someone's doorstep. Forget.

I lie on the bed and gaze at a smudge of lamplight reflected on the wall. I try to cry about love and the things it does to people, but that feels too stupid and I give up. I watch the light blankly and wait for sleep.

IT WASN'T PLANNED. Not at all. He didn't even fancy Sharon, but suddenly his tongue was in her mouth, his hands under her sweater. She wasn't wearing a bra. Now he remembered; she had flopping breasts, long and shapeless, with flat nipples. She opened his fly and it all happened very quickly. No foreplay. He bent her over the couch and grabbed her ass on either side, spreading the cheeks as much as he thought she'd allow. She was so dry it hurt to enter her. Afterwards they sat on the couch. She rested her head on his bare chest. She wasn't crying any more.

'Oisín? Thanks for listening. I just want to know, cause I've been sleeping with this guy lately and I should stop if we're ... I just want to be clear about everything. Are we ...?'

'I thought we were just mates.'

'Yeah, yeah, I just wanted to be clear. Okay. No. That's cool. Okay.'

She cried a little, her nose and eyes wetting his skin. He straightened his back. 'Beer?'

'No. I should be going. I'm glad we're friends Oisín. I think you're cool.'

'Cool. Me too. Stay as long as you like. I'm going to take a shower.'

In the shower he thought about the sheep's eye in school. The smell of it; not like meat but clean and sour the way poison might smell. He turned the temperature up as hot as he could bear and worked up a lather in the long hair under his arms. He scrubbed the back of his neck and stood with his face to the faucet, letting it all rinse off. Then he switched off the water and dried himself vigorously inside the shower. That was something he always did, to avoid wetting the floor. He hoped she wouldn't make a habit of this. Those deep round eyes. They had a draining effect.

Towel around his waist he put his head around the door of the kitchen-dining area. She was gone. The bedroom was warmer than the bathroom had been, and he dropped his towel while he searched for his boxers. He couldn't find them. That shower hadn't satisfied him. He didn't feel refreshed. He opened the wardrobe door and rooted about in a pile of clean laundry.

On the inside of the wardrobe door there was a full-length mirror that he had always hated. It belonged to a girl's room, he thought. His body looked silly and wrong in it. There was something unbalanced about his naked body. He always thought that. It looked as though there was something missing at the waist, like the two halves of a man sandwiched together. He straightened up and looked at himself, trying to decide once and for all what it was that was wrong with him. It was the connection for sure, the connection between the top half and the bottom half of him.

Oisín was tall, widely built. He was rugged looking, he knew that was his charm. He looked best with a little stubble. His chin hair was black, but certain light showed up red bits. He hated seeing his penis lax like this. It looked stupid and useless. He felt like laughing at it. He jumped up and down and it wiggled flabbily. It was nauseating.

Then he did something he hadn't done since he was a boy. He tucked it back between his legs and looked at himself. He smoothed his hand down over his stomach and the triangular slope that was left. Then he looked from the side. You couldn't see a thing. Another thing he had learned in science class was that all embryos started as girls. Then some of them turned into boys. That's why men had nipples.

five

IT MIGHT HAVE happened easily with your English teacher, Helen. Like tripping on your shoelace, like dreaming, like going with the flow, like swimming. With the schoolboys though, everything was effort. Talk was awkward and always felt a little embarrassing. It didn't seem like a possibility, that passing from the outside of them – the skin, the ironed shirts, the lips – to inside their mouths. So it never happened. The girls called you a 'kiss-virgin' and 'lip-tight'.

At one of the inter-school socials, when you had spent the whole evening standing with Cassandra beside a bowl of tortilla chips, passing them one by one into your mouth for want of something to do, Cassandra raising her eyes to heaven every time anyone approached, Antonia from your dorm tapped you on the shoulder.

'Will you be with that guy?' she gestured to a boy a few feet behind her. He was holding a mobile phone – that was before everyone had them – pushing the buttons and frowning at the screen. There was mouse-coloured fluff on his chin and upper lip. He looked very clean, as though he had been vigorously towel-dried after a long bath. Even his pimples were scrubbed raw.

They were Clongowes Wood College boys, from good families. Getting kissed at one of these socials was almost encouraged by the Sisters.

You thought you must have been pretty. You had no spots and a good figure and you dressed just right. It embarrassed your uncles to see your naked legs or shoulders. You had come to expect a double-take from men in the street. There were boys who would kiss you if you let them, but you never really knew how to let them. How did it go from them liking you, chatting to you, smiling at you, to kissing up against a wall? How did that happen? It seemed miraculous, the way the others did it. One minute they were grinning, talking, touching the boy's biceps, the next they were gone. The things that could happen during the disappearance: deep, wet kissing, love bites like berry stains on necks and chests, even fingering, even blow jobs, sometimes, if you believed the girls.

You never did it though. Cassandra didn't either, but it was different for her. She had no fear of inexperience. By fifth year she had started modelling, and she had an older boyfriend. She went to arty, adult parties where people rolled joints. She was way ahead.

'His name is Henry,' said Antonia, 'My parents know his parents. His dad practically *owns* RTÉ.' You shook your head. She scrunched her nose, shrugged, and as she spun around, muttered the word 'lezos'. Antonia kissed him herself about an hour later though, and he became her boyfriend, so it all worked out.

Your virginity, and your secret one-and-only-kiss took on a sacred quality. If the nuns dedicated their virginity to God, you dedicated yours to Mr O'Hara.

By the time you got to college you were far too old never to have kissed a boy. It became a shameful secret. You hoped to fall in love again, and to be loved. That would solve the whole thing, but that seemed less and less likely as you dampened out from a lithe seventeen-year-old to a muffin-topped twenty-one.

You started kissing in second year of college, getting drunk and letting it happen so you would know there was no mystery. You worked it out one night. It's about letting them know you'll let them. It's about vibes. The blow job was a first. At least now you know. At least you know what a man's erection is like – not like a dog's. That's what you had imagined: something pink and slithery drawing out from a wrinkled sheath, flailing about. That's what your dog's looked like.

I MUST HAVE been lying like this for a long time, though I didn't fall asleep. It's that numb thing I can do with my brain sometimes. The evening has closed in around me, wrapping the room like a blanket. I am still looking at the lamplight, and it glows orange and more distinct in the dark.

It takes effort to lift my head off the bed, like pulling a plant up out of heavy earth. I can almost feel the little rips as the thread roots snap. How late is it? Helen and I were meant to do something tonight – go to some gig. I should put on mascara, brush my hair. I open the wardrobe. There is a mirror on the inner door that someone has stuck on with thick grey glue. My room is full of things like that – evidence of previous occupancy – it does not feel like mine, and I have no desire to mark it with pictures, or silk scarves draped from the coat hook or curtain rail.

All that is here of me is a red duvet cover on the bed with the clashing pastel quilt my grandmother made for me when I was born, and some piles of books. The rest is bare but for half-removed stickers on the door; initials carved into the wall, flaking sequins glued to the light-switch. The mirror has a gilt frame around it. It is probably designed to hang from a hook, not to be stuck onto a wardrobe door with glue.

I look at myself reflected there. I am taller than I feel, better looking than I feel, with much kinder eyes than I should have: large, brown, welcoming eyes like a gentle animal's. Maybe that's the way I was meant to be, kind like my eyes. Maybe this isn't me at all. It's just a chemical imbalance. The cheekbones and shoulders are broad, manly. That's what gets me modelling jobs; high street fashion catalogues, nothing too glamorous. Some of the other models are so beautiful, so aesthetically balanced, so healthy, that it is hard to stop looking at them. But most of them are like me. Not pretty, exactly, but properly made: tall and thin, with something alarming about them – cat eyes, or children's noses. I squirt a little glob of foundation into the space between the thumb and forefinger of my left hand and begin applying it with my right. That's one good thing about modelling: the make-up tips.

My phone rings. It's this ascending electronic version of an old-fashioned phone ring. I haven't figured out how to change it. I used to ignore my phone a lot, but since my grandfather became ill I always answer it. Even if his body means nothing to me now – its last sighs just any corpse's jaded old lungs filling up and emptying out again – I should be there for my grandmother when he goes, because to her it means a lot, that pulsing of the veins, that breath. To her that's still him. 'Became ill', that's my grandmother's phrase, it's what she calls it. Actually, he took an entire bottle of sleeping pills. He didn't become ill at all, he became comatose. Just that inch too far from death.

He always told us he would do it. 'Shoot me before I become a burden like that,' he'd say, on passing some grumpy old hunchback who was poking children away with his stick, 'or if you won't I'll take some pills. As soon as I start going toodle-loot,' he'd say, whirring his finger around near his temple, 'I'm off.' Then he'd do the finger-whoosh towards heaven. We never believed him. It made me angry. I thought he was threatening us. As it turns out it was just a warning.

It's a number I don't recognize. I don't have anything to clean my hands on so I end up getting flesh-coloured fingerprints all over the phone.

'Cassandra? Hi. It's Brian.'

For the year since we broke up he has called almost monthly, a sort of booty call, I think, but so far I've never given in.

'Oh. Brian. Hi.' I sound as though I love him.

'How are you, Cassy?' He always did that. Talked to me like I was senile or imbecilic.

'Fine. Grand. Just rushing out though. I'll call you back.'

I hate talking on mobile phones. I never feel secure about it. The words are not safely contained in wires the way they are on a landline. Instead they're floating about, blipping up to space and down to some soundboard on some island and then back into the person's ear. It makes me panic if I think about it. So I try not to think about it.

'My number has changed. Can I give it to you?'

'It'll be logged on my phone, Brian. I'll save it.'

'Not this number.'

'Okay.'

'You have a pen?'

I don't answer. I want him to know I'm not really writing it down.

'You have a pen – yeah? Oh-one … Six, seven, seven …'

I don't repeat the number. There is a silence. Then I hear him breathe in slowly. 'You taking it down, Cassandra?'

'Mmm.'

'I saw you in the Morgan catalogue, you're doing fashion now?'

'A bit. Have to go Brian. Talk to you later, bye.'

I hang up, exhale slowly. He's made my face hot, and something in me crackles and melts like tinfoil in fire. I begin to write the number on the mirror with eyeliner while I still remember it, but smudge it away again. I'm not going to cry over it. I am very ugly when I cry. He told me that once.

I make a special effort with my make-up, put on under-eye concealer and everything, and dress in an outfit I bought recently. Not one he has seen. Not one he likes my bum in. Not one he has taken off.

Helen breezes in, wearing that awful sparkly pink top that she thinks is sexy. She has the kitten with her, and is holding it over her shoulder like a baby, stroking its head with one finger. It's still mewing pitifully and evenly. Helen picks the little claws out of her hair and puts the kitten on my bed, where it continues to mew. It smells like dust and dried poo. She plonks herself down and grins. The top has only one sleeve and it shows a sloped shoulder to her disadvantage, but I don't tell her this.

'I'm going to wear that mad glittery eye shadow tonight,' she says, excited, wanting my approval. There is a pinch of fat between her underarm and the fabric. I want to tell her to change, but I don't know how.

'What time is it?' I say.

'Seven.'

'I thought it was later.'

We walk to Whelan's. It's cold and the streets are dangerous at this time, full of addicts asking for change. My shoes slice into the back of my heel. Tall girls shouldn't wear heels anyway. My grandmother is always telling me that. I haven't called my grandmother all week. I will phone in the morning. I will ask that ridiculous question, 'How is my Bompa?' and she will answer at length.

What horrifies my aunt is the word 'suicide': the thought of it, and the embarrassment. She prefers to think it was a mistake, though my grandmother insists it wasn't – 'What do you think he is? Some idiot is it? A mistake ... he is no idiot.' To me what is sad is not the unpopular attitude he held, but the failure. He got exactly what he didn't want, a dragged-out end. He's become exactly what he didn't want to be: a family burden with a nappy and a feed-bag, and totally 'toodle-loot'.

We arrive early. The gig won't start for ages but there's already a smothering crowd. I hate this. It's a waste of time, standing in a crowd like this. It's too loud to talk, and there's nowhere to sit down. We have to force our way through to get anywhere, loll against walls, sip drinks because there's nothing else to do with our mouths or our hands.

In this light Helen looks beautiful again: cherubic, all dimples and curls. The whites of her eyes and the pink hearts glint in the light. How is that? That Helen's beauty comes and goes like a mood?

She wants to get a drink so we push through the crowd to the bar and as we squash between two groups of men she grabs my hand so that we don't lose each other. That's why she takes my hand, so that we don't lose each other. She doesn't want to spend all night searching for me. She's no pockets. She's checked in her bag and I'm carrying her phone and purse for her. I know this is why she took my hand, or rather, gave me hers, but even so it feels like a gift. I haven't held someone's hand like that in a long time: firmly and like it is my right. Her fingers are cool, slender. The bones feel breakable. I grip her hand tighter, and we squeeze through backs and bums and elbows.

YOU HAVE DECIDED on the glittery pink eye shadow tonight, and that top with only one sleeve and pink hearts on it. Whelan's is crowded, and you have to concentrate on weaving your way through all the bodies. Cassandra is pressing on towards the bar, gripping your hand in the emergency. You like this sort of thing, this sort of panic, this fizz in the air: it excites you, unable to move without pushing through bodies, all vibrating with expectation, banging elbows, foamy beer that slops and slides down the sides of glasses, onto the floor, onto someone's good top. This makes you feel like you are enjoying life, making use of it.

You have your glow on tonight. You never know whether you have your glow on or not until you walk into a room like this. People look at you, men and women. They feel you behind them and they turn around. Your glow is a feathery joy that brushes your cheek and fills you up from the inside like light, surrounds you. The noise barely touches you, it passes over you like waves of heat.

Cassandra orders the drinks briskly and leans back on the bar. Her top inches over the horizon of her low-cut jeans showing her tummy, jutting pelvic bones, concave stomach and the faint shadow trail that leads down to her pubes. Cassandra's problem, you think, is that she doesn't know she's pretty. If she did she would smile more.

She's smiling now, lifting the drink to her lips, sipping, then smiling again, but it's a forced smile, serious with the business of having fun.

So when do you notice him? And what does it feel like when you do?

Your face drops.

He is with a group of friends, all very grown-up and cool. The three women have trendy hairstyles and subtle make-up. There is another man with them. He is slim-hipped, wearing a concert T-shirt, an arm slung about your teacher's neck, and your teacher's hand – the wide, bristled hand that used to touch your pencil case like it was your body – is around the man's waist.

Maybe it all clicks into place in one go. Maybe the sight of him is like the time you noticed that the woman plucking your eyebrows had a foetal-sized extra thumb; there's a brief black-out, a moment of dizziness, a double take. For a beat you forget to swallow. Cassandra twists her head around to see what you are looking at.

'It's Mr O'Hara from Our Lady's!' She says, 'He's with Paul – I know that guy he's with. That's Paul. He's an artist.'

The teacher hasn't changed, not at all. Not even the hair, the dark arms, the stubble. You remember his smile. You remember how his mouth moves when he talks. You have changed though, and you feel that suddenly – how unnatural the peroxide hair is, your shoulders and hips rounded with chub, heavy like a farm animal. Not that it matters now after all.

One of the women touches his elbow and whispers something. He doesn't hear her, stoops closer. She is looking your way. In a moment he will see you.

'I didn't know Mr O'Hara was gay, Helen, did you?'

'No.'

'Maybe he's bi. He must be bi because he definitely … you definitely …'

He sees you. A nod and a fingery half-wave. The man he is with looks horrified, whispers something to him, his fingers at the back of your teacher's neck.

Cassandra grabs your hand again and it irritates you, this grabbing of your hands as though you were her child, and you pull away.

He and the other man are gone by the time she drags you over to the gathering of friends. They eye you with humour and vague curiosity. Some kid he taught. Or maybe he has told them, 'This kid who had a crush on me,' and maybe they laughed and thought 'how cute', or maybe they made that sound from *Psycho*, raised their arms with mimed knives – *nee nee nee nee* – as though you were a stalker.

So that's that then. Cassandra is embarrassed.

'That's a bit rude, isn't it?'

'Mmm. who's playing tonight, Cassy?'

'Dunno.'

'Want to go somewhere else?'

'We've paid in Helen!'

Bash your way back to the bar. Cassandra orders more drinks and you wait for the gig to start.

BRIAN TOLD ME once, 'You know, Cassandra, you are ugly when you cry.' I said 'Oh.' Just 'Oh.' Not 'Thanks Brian,' or 'That's a bit insensitive Brian,' just 'Oh,' as though I would note it for future, which I suppose I did. He grafted a huge fake tear onto my cheek once, and carefully painted crow's feet and a smile onto the other half of my face. On that side of my face he blanked out my pout with clown white so that he could draw the smile. I was immersed in water to my shoulders. He used a very slow shutter speed and a tripod so I had to stay utterly still. The pictures were taken in the bath, and at first the water was warm, but by the time he was finished I had to clench my jaw to keep from shivering. He had to wrap me in a towel and carry me into the bedroom.

The photos were beautiful.

At the opening night of the exhibition I wore a long dress the colour of a tropical sea that draped in folds about my breasts, skimmed my waist and had a deep, brutal cut all the way up the leg to the hip. My shoes had strings that coiled around my calves like seaweed. They thought I was beautiful, all his friends. They thought that the 'piece' was exquisite. I was quite a hit. I was better at that scene than he was, in fact. I sipped wine with poise, and without staining my teeth. I talked intelligently. The other men were jealous of him, taking along this young thing half his age. I loved that.

There was a young artist there, nearly as young as me, gay. Brian introduced me to him and then disappeared to mingle. We spent the evening out the back of the exhibition hall, under a glowing patio heater. Paul, that was the young artist's name, wore a black T-shirt and a grey silk scarf and smoked. His boyfriend was an art critic who had been invited to the opening, but he too had disappeared. Paul was an installation artist. He told me all about the piece he would be doing for The Edge Arts Centre soon: naked women with clipped pussies and dildos and whips, necklaces of little embryos strung around their necks, possibly murdering their aproned mothers, he hadn't decided yet. 'Misogynist Feminism,' he explained, and I thought I understood. 'Exactly,' I said. He knew someone in London who was sleeping with someone who might be able to get him real human embryos from an abortion clinic. He would display them in little glass pods for the exhibition. 'Wouldn't that be fan*tast*ic?' he said.

We talked about feminism, pornography, art and agreed with each other and agreed and agreed. 'Exactly!' we said, nodding at each other, 'Ex*actly*!' We got drunk gracefully and laughed and thought we were both such bright young things, such keen intellects. We didn't know what we thought until it came out of our mouths but we agreed with each other so much and the concepts were so convoluted, the terms so esoteric, that we knew we were right. Misogynist feminism – *exactly*! We were more educated than our boyfriends, we knew that. A generation of third-levellers, we knew we were pedalling faster than they could. I was in first year of college. Paul was about to graduate.

Brian came to get me around closing time. Those of us with contacts or prestige headed to a little bar nearby. It was a tiny, narrow place, shaped like a corridor, with nowhere to mingle but the doorway and a nook at the back. There were stills from obscure movies on the walls. By the bar a tall drag queen, draped and sequinned, wearing a flapper's headband, shrieked like a mad bird. I thought something awful had happened and jumped, but Paul said she was doing poppers, that was all. Then she keeled over, the drag queen, cackling unnaturally the way a person might when confronted with some tragedy they can't process. Everyone around her laughed too, but lightly, prettily, and looked away, then sipped their drinks.

Paul and I stood near the exit, holding the delicate stems of champagne glasses between two fingers, sipping some blue sparkling concoction that our boyfriends had passed to us. He smoked. We tried to remember what we had been talking about, agreeing about. Our boyfriends had disappeared again. We talked frantically about Kant, to no real purpose, like children remembering their times tables. We used big words. At last, at 4 AM, we were shooed out of there too, and we all took over the desolate streets, sure of our importance, sure we were all artists, sure that that meant something, gesticulating wildly, gradually dispersing, disappearing into taxis and city apartments.

Paul and his boyfriend lived in Temple Bar. He hugged me. 'The old man's getting edgy! Needs a servicing! Yours too by the looks of it!'

He was looking at Brian, who was stroking my bare shoulder with the back of a finger. Paul's man was holding him by the hips. Paul looked like a boy suddenly. He clutched my hands.

'Cassandra I'm so glad we've met. We're really … you know. I've loved talking to you.'

'Me too.'

Paul nodded and kissed my cheek, 'I think we get each other don't we?' His boyfriend rolled his eyes to heaven, 'Come on babes!'

As he was lead off, Paul called, 'Listen, come to the exhibition!'

It was only me and Brian, and three artists still carousing down the street with a bottle of absinthe that someone had stolen from some illegal stash behind the bar. There was a stiff pickled snake coiled at the bottom of the bottle, eyes jellied by the green liquid. Someone said that in Asia they used it as an aphrodisiac. There was a name for it, but I don't remember. I wanted to go home, but

Brian wanted to go back to someone's studio. It would be fun, he said, you never knew what would happen at Rajim's studio, but it was always wild. We were arguing about this when a tall woman with cropped, pink hair, who had been talking to Brian all night, scooped me around the waist. 'She's a little nymph, Brian,' she said, and she kissed me hard on the mouth. Brian laughed and kissed my neck, while she still held my waist, moved her tongue inside my mouth, and ran long nails through my hair.

I won the argument. When we got home he gave me a small pill. I hid it under my tongue. He swallowed one and made love to me for hours, pressing me into the bed from behind, his hands clenched over mine. I pushed the pill quietly into the pillow with my tongue.

'I loved that,' he whispered; wet lips, fists crushing my hands, 'the way you let Eileen kiss you. You're my little Lolita aren't you baby? My little bitch. They all wish you were theirs. Tell me you love me, Lol.'

'I love you.'

I love you.

THE WOMAN in front of you in the bathroom queue drags her gaze up and down the length of your body, glaring. You must still have your glow on then, Helen, despite yourself. The woman is a little drunk, a little too old for her outfit, with dead, too-black hair. You are her rival – that much is clear, but rival for what?

One of the toilets has been locked for a long time. It's silent in there. The woman raps her knuckles on the door and there is a faint sound of giggling, sliding heels, and then the quiet, quick, no-nonsense snort of coke sweeping up nostrils. The lock slides open and two models walk out with bright eyes. They must be models. In fact, you recognize one of them from the window of Oasis. They are impossibly tall and narrow, but without the stoop that lanky girls have. They are beautiful. They love their own faces, their own bodies. They are happy, you think, not having to wonder whether they are pretty or not, they *know*. That must feel wonderful. You said that to Cassandra once – that it must be wonderful not to have to wonder, but she didn't get what you meant.

The woman darts past the models. 'Well you took your time girls!' They look at each other and laugh and you hear the woman's piss hit the toilet bowl.

When it is your turn you bolt yourself in and sit on the closed seat. After staring at two Health Board ads for some time, you leave and wash your hands.

One of the ads told you to carry a condom, the other said not to forget to wash your hands. They had the same Health Board symbol in the lower right-hand corner, but they were very different posters. The wash-your-hands one was a hand-drawn, two-tone poster that looked like it was made in the sixties: a picture of hands being washed. It's the same one they had in your school toilets and on the walls of the infirmary. The sexual health one was trendier, cooler, designed especially for the youth of today, a grainy close-up of flesh on flesh.

You massage the frothy soap slowly and with care, watching it as though it means something. Now look at your face, Helen. You are beautiful tonight. What for? You return to Cassandra, resolved to tell her that you're not well and will head home. It's a waste of time this, all of this.

She's bumped into a group from college, and it will be easier now, you won't be leaving her alone. You don't really recognize any of them, but she seems to know them well. She is smiling her superior smile while one of them, a boy with dreadlocks wearing a T-shirt that says '21 cotton farmers killed themselves last week and all I got was this lousy T-shirt', talks to her. She doesn't introduce you, she barely acknowledges you at all. One of these students, a boy you've never met before, walks right up to you, stands too close, puts out his hand. 'I'm Oisín.'

It is not the way people usually introduce themselves. There's something barefaced about it. He seems to be missing something, a sort of self-awareness, a self-consciousness, the social grace that would make such bluntness impossible. He has a country accent. You let him shake your hand, 'Helen.'

He has dodgy hair, fluffy and sparse like a newly hatched chick, wetted with gel or something. You don't know what to say now. Why did he shake your hand? You turn to Cassandra, stroke the crook of her elbow. 'I'm going to head, Cassy. I'm not feeling well.'

Oisín insists that he was just going and will walk with you. He is hyper, babbling about books and films. He tells you that *The Matrix* is the best film ever made, that it actually *says* things about society, that it's actually *really* important. That even the lads at home – who wouldn't usually be into films and shit – thought it was good, that that just shows how good it is. You don't tell him that you hated *The Matrix*, that yourself and Cassandra went for chips after seeing it and slagged it all evening, not only the film, but the sort of people who would like it. 'The kind of guy,' Cassandra said, 'who thinks he's a genius 'cause he can see the *meaning* in it …'

'I must watch it,' you say.

Your mind is tender at the moment and even the effort of talking hurts a little. You do not want to be asked out or kissed right now. You are sad. Your own silly obsession with Mr O'Hara becomes clear now. Love. God, you had actually thought love.

'Have a hot whiskey in the Buttery before you go home.'

'I'm really tired.'

You think of something Cassandra once said to you, a quote from her grandad, that you need a little corruption if you're not to be ruined altogether, that you need to harden the heart so it doesn't break. Stupid to be broken-hearted over something like this.

He nods. 'Maybe tomorrow?'

He asks for your number. He gives you the feeling of being looked at straight on, and that sense that he is not aware that he is breaking a sort of rule; he is oddly, disarmingly direct. He has a pen and you write your number on his arm, touching his fingers with your other hand accidentally-on-purpose.

The heart is very adaptable. It lives off love; it will love anything if you let it. Be careful, Duckling. The heart is not as hardy as you think and your mind will not protect it. The heart is very naive, very gullible. It is apt to believe its own lies.

You raise yourself up on your toes and kiss his cheek like a child, but he holds you to him and he doesn't move his cheek away after the peck. He moves his lips over yours, brushes them very gently. You open your mouth to the kiss. It feels like surrender.

six

I TRY to finish the dream, even now that I am awake. I try to see the girl's face and tell her to take her hand away, 'I don't need you or want you. Go away – ' but I can't picture her. Even now that I am awake that face eludes me. I can't shake the feeling of being smothered by someone's dead hand. She means no harm by it, the girl in the dream. She thinks she's doing me a favour.

I pull the duvet over my head and try to sleep, but I can't stand the warmth of my breath, the sound of my own pulse. I want to stop having these dreams. I want to go forward now, into something else. There are tablets you can take. Brian took them. He didn't dream at all. I resolve to get myself some. He thought they affected his art and his libido, but I don't have any sort of art that would be cheapened by a lack of dreams.

That night at the gig Helen left early. I talked to a boy from my class who was wearing an ethical T-shirt and had tried to kiss me in Fresher's Week. Later, at the bar, I saw Paul and he ignored me again, and I thought of him holding my hand that night and saying, 'I think we get each other.' I went alone to his exhibition six months later. It was nothing like he'd described. There were dummies with whips and Brazilians and plastic embryos, but it said none of the things he had meant it to. All of the other visitors were tourists. They took photos of themselves with their arms slung over the dummies' shoulders and their thumbs up.

I get up and make a coffee. Sometimes when I wake at night Helen hears me in the kitchen and comes in, but she is busy with that boy tonight. He's probably boning away at her now, grinding her into the mattress. The kitten has been banished to the kitchen at night for bothering Helen, sitting on her face when she's asleep. Its litter tray is beside the bin. The cleaning lady said she wouldn't tell on us. She has two cats herself, she said. I pick it up and it rubs its wet nose against mine, then its ears. Miserable thing. It still has no name. It perches on my shoulder like a parrot while I make the coffee. Oddly it shows no interest in the fish bowl, which is on top of the fridge now in case the cat gets any ideas, and contains two new fish, both mottled black and white and orange.

Oisín has been around for six weeks, and Helen has gradually lost that glow, as though something in her is stepping lower and lower out of sight. She has become quiet with me, as though she has let me down. When I asked her if she was still a virgin she told me to fuck off.

I cover the bottom of a mug with milk and bring it, and the plunger, back to bed. I wait for ten minutes, while the kitten claws the duvet. When the coffee is very strong I push down the sieve and pour. It is not as hot as I would like. That's from putting the milk in first and not scalding the mug. I read in bed with the covers pulled over my head, nothing but my eyes and the tips of my fingers uncovered. This is my favorite thing to do. I feel a little better now, and I know I will go to all my lectures today.

THEIR BODIES were tangled when Oisín woke up, their fingers entwined, her round bum in his lap, skin on clammy skin, his face in her neck, mouth in her hair, breathing her sleep. He wanted to make love to her while she slept. He unknotted his hand from hers as gently as he could and rested the pads of two fingertips on her skin. He moved his touch slowly over the curve of her shoulder, under the duvet, down the slope of her waist, over the round of her buttocks and ran a finger along the lips of her furred pussy. He wanted to move it inside, find her clit, make her wet at a time when she couldn't fake it, wake her with pleasure ... then he changed his mind. Something about it made him shudder. They touched so gently, the lips, like a mouth about to kiss.

He dislodged himself from her limbs, but not too carefully. He wanted her to wake up. He was lonely without her. He rolled onto his back, put his hands behind his head, turned his face to the window.

The bed was too narrow for them both. The curtains were crap. They were slug-orange with a brown pattern like leaves, or like whales if you looked at it differently. Not only were they thin enough to let the light in, they didn't quite cover the window. There were gaps, through which he could see the wet leaves of a tree and the pink morning light. Helen's floor was low enough that the tops of heads passed her window. He was glad. At night it gave him a thrill to hear people pass, see their shadows crossing the walls as he did Helen, his fingers in her mouth to stop her from screaming; their sex talk low and breathy against the talk passing beyond the window. When he was having sex with Helen everything else seemed like bullshit. It turned out she was a screamer. He wouldn't have known that.

There were students rushing past the window now to early lectures, chatting, or listening to too-loud iPods. They made silhouettes on the curtains, head shapes cut out of the morning sunlight. All a passer-by would have to do was peer through the window and they would see her sleeping, and they would see him beside her, and they would know they were missing something. They would know he was a lucky guy.

The lads couldn't even imagine this. He was still sending them emails about the other girls. He didn't know what to say about her. What he couldn't explain to them was that she *got* him.

The kitten was scratching at the door now, mewing desperately. Helen gave a little snorty, purry, inward-breathing snore, and turned in her sleep to face him. He wanted her to open her eyes. He had noticed yesterday that when Helen opened her eyes they were navy for a moment before the pupils shrank and the irises lightened to the shade of a thrush's egg ringed with midnight blue. He relished the new discovery, and now he watched for it every time she opened her eyes.

Things were slotting into place at last, coming together, making sense. Everything that happened now had a déjà-vu feel to it that made Oisín believe it was always meant to happen. He was different since he'd started seeing Helen. He followed happiness, now. Now it didn't bother him that there was no point to his lectures, no point to his days: he could be happy just like this. Simple as.

Going back to his flat no longer gave him that sense of despair. If he was alone in the flat, something that happened only rarely now, he walked around the two rooms, checking everything. He checked that the fridge was stocked so that he didn't have to go and get milk in the middle of the night when she felt like a Bailey's hot chocolate. He found himself wandering into the bathroom just to look at her toothbrush lying at the side of the sink. He liked to have her clothes there too, hanging in the wardrobe or bundled at the end of the bed.

It occurred to him that this might end, but he only had to remember that he had the surety of history now. If it all stopped tomorrow nothing could change that he had watched her sleep, warmed her small hands in his, been surprised by her sudden kiss. He had made her laugh until her back arched and her neck opened to the sky. He had pumped his cum into her as deep as he could and she had liked it. He wanted to get some photos of her. He had no photos.

The kitten groaned, mewed one more time, a long, final wail, and scampered off. Let it annoy that other girl, Helen's friend, Cassandra. It was her kitten too.

The best thing of all was that when they made love they both came at the same time, Helen's eyebrows lifting as though shocked by the pleasure, pussy tightening to pull him even more inside her, as though his cum were precious and she wanted every drop. He could fall asleep afterwards without feeling the need for a shower, and he could make love to her again soon after, even if the cum from earlier was still on her tummy or breasts or back in crusty white streaks.

One night he came five times, and twice the morning after. He would tell the lads that. That's how he'd explain what he meant about Helen.

He had told her he loved her. It was at the beginning, one of the first days. She was straddling him, her jean-clad legs either side of his, her arms over his shoulders, her breasts near his face. A tight pink T-shirt. He hadn't even seen her tits yet. They had been laughing, giddy. Then they had stopped laughing and they had stopped talking and they were looking at each other. She had raised her eyebrows in a question, and he said it, 'I think I love you.' She kissed him and fingered the buttons on his jeans and he cupped her breasts and she laughed as though his desire were silly. She didn't say it back for three weeks. That's another thing that amazed him about her.

'You're amazing; cool and vulnerable at once. It makes me want to fuck you all the time.' She laughed. It was a dismissive laugh that made him laugh at himself and forgive himself because it said that it didn't really matter how corny he was, or how crude, because he was only a tiny person in a very big world that plodded on with or without him. It didn't really matter who he was. She liked him anyway.

The first time they went out he took her to the cinema. He bought the tickets but she insisted on buying popcorn and ice-cream and a big bag of Pick 'n Mix. They only had Virgin Cola, which she didn't like, so she left him holding it all in the cinema lobby while she ran next door to the newsagents to get cans of Coke.

They saw *Eight Women*, a mad French film he didn't really watch. He watched her watching the film. He watched her suck her upper lip, a habit he thought made her look mildly retarded. He watched her lopsided, curly grin become a girly giggle that surrendered the underbelly of her throat. His mind contained an ever-growing Helen file: Helen concentrating; Helen in pain; Helen eating; Helen thinking distant thoughts, unaware she's being watched.

Lit by the colourful, flickering light of the film, her beauty petrified him. He could not touch her for the first four hours of their outing. Her whole attitude confused him. She was so willing to be with him but she didn't seem to care what he thought of her. Nothing surprised her: anything he told her about himself, or his family, or the lads. She didn't really care about the details. If he made a crap joke she would raise her eyes to heaven as though she knew already what he was like. She just liked him for no reason at all. She expected nothing from him.

It was only after the film, walking back to college, that a drunken homeless man gave him the opportunity to touch her, to mind her. The drunk was meandering along the path towards them, his face streaming with tears. He had the croaky, swollen-gummed speech of the truly desperate and was holding a bleeding hand before him in the air like a trophy, screaming at real or imaginary passers-by:

'You wanna suck this? Wanna suck my blood? Hey, hey – you want … yousuckmine an' – I'll-suck-yurrrs. You. Want. Does

AN-Y-ONE wannasharemyblood? Do I have any takers? You. Anyone wanna SHARE ...'

Oisín had put his arm around her, curling his fingers daringly at the waist and steering her across to the other side of the road. That look on her face – wide blue eyes, the whites glowing in the lamplight, her sad, sad mouth – not frightened, but sad.

He looked forward to winding his comprehension all the way around hers and holding her like a right answer in his mind. They kissed deeper and longer than he had expected that night. When he kissed her she arched her back and let her hands drop to her sides.

There were boys outside her window now, leaning on the wall, talking shit he couldn't make out. He wanted to pull back the curtain, show them what he had here: Helen's wet, puffed-out, sleepy lips that had taken his balls only a few hours ago, the wide pink nipples.

She wasn't perfect. There were things he wouldn't tell the lads about. She sometimes bitched about her mother. She was sometimes so moody that he felt he had done something wrong but it turned out he hadn't. She sometimes cried for no reason. There were lots of things he could have complained to the lads about, but even the thought of that – of a time when he might complain to the lads about her, a time when she might securely be his 'girlfriend' even – gave him a thrill.

He hadn't known she was a virgin until she began to wince and cry. The German girl hadn't done that. There had just been blood afterwards and then she had told him. Helen was so tight that it was like cracking something open. It had made him feel sorry and heavy. He felt he was seeing her for real then, her face ugly with pain, accusing, round-eyed, and for a moment he didn't like her at all. Then there was a pop when he broke the hymen, a seal being snapped. She put her face into his neck, took a sharp gasp and breathed out slowly. 'Ow.' Her hot tears ran into his ear and he felt nauseous. He was surprised that he was still hard. That was when she had said she loved him, with him inside her, with tears over her cheeks, with a wavery voice, as though it were a resolution she was making right there; *I love you.*

Heaving, frowning, trying to come without hurting her, he returned the compliment.

For the next while Oisín had the feeling of triumph. He was a little closer to possessing Helen with the whole of his understanding. And he definitely had history on his side.

Still asleep, she turned onto her back, a breast showing over the duvet. He put his hand over it, squeezed it, massaged the nipple. Her back arched. Then he pulled the duvet over it, to protect her from the voices of the men outside the window. Talking shit. They had no idea what he had here.

When she woke up he would take her for a banquet breakfast. She was always hungry when she woke up. There was a place in Temple Bar that did steak and ginger ale for breakfast. That's where the lads went the morning after a Dublin piss-up. He'd sit by the window with her and eat a bloody breakfast steak and fried eggs and everyone that walked by the window would know just why they were both so hungry. He'd get up in a minute and shower. Maybe then if she was still asleep he'd go there on his own and bring her back a take-away fry, though that might not be the same.

The small bed was uncomfortable but he found it hard to leave, to un-stick his skin from hers and wash their love-making off. He wanted her suddenly. He wanted to go under the duvet and kiss her. She would wake as she came, wetness flushing his mouth.

He loved being in her little college room. It gave him the feeling of being inside her mind. He loved the laundry drying on a bit of rope strung between the curtain rail and a picture hook, and her walls plastered with pictures of her unnumbered sisters and images of faraway places: a sky, a fairy grove, Venice, the high-rise skyline of New York. The pictures opened out the room like windows, as though she was expanding her world from inside her space, as though life was not big enough for her. Any white spaces on the wall were graffitied with telephone numbers, Shakespearean sonnets, bits of songs.

'Are you sure it's language that's broken,' he had asked, 'not light?'

She had kissed his neck, put her hands under his T-shirt and stroked his chest, 'Dunno …'

YOUR FIRST TIME was a prayer to a man who could have loved you. It hurt. You offered up the pain to him, knowing in your sanity that he had cringed and forgotten you long ago, and that this pain could never reach him. Out there is only space, you know, and space is insatiable. It gobbles all it can.

You bled a bit afterwards, but not as much as you would have thought. You imagined another, who might have been kind, and not fallen into a doze with a satisfied Cheshire-cat grin while you swallowed into the pillow, who might have attached some archaic value to your virginity.

Oisín rolls out of his half-sleep and reaches for your breast. You decide that this will be the last time you'll think of him: his hands and his warmth and his man's smell. The gentle, brushing, just-touching kiss.

seven

ONE WALL of the waiting room is covered by a rack full of leaflets on eating disorders, suicide, sexual health, sexual abuse, testicular cancer, family problems, money problems … all in varying pastel shades. The boy opposite avoids my gaze, staring instead at a leaflet on financial loans. He thinks I am interested in the fact that he is here and that I care why. He thinks this is a secret, safe place. He thinks his pain is special, his story is special and someone here cares.

I have my own delusions too, my own hopes. I hope this person I am going to see is not some psychology student who just passed their finals, but one who will see into me, assess the cogs and bolts of my faulty mind, see what's missing and maybe fix me. Better still, maybe they will tell me there is nothing wrong with me at all, that someone else is to blame, someone else made me unfit for this world. Maybe they could break it all down, disassemble all the machinery of my mind, and let me start again.

A woman emerges from the open doorway. 'Gavin?' He looks up and smiles and she smiles. This is all conducted in a whispery way, as though he is an invalid and sound might hurt him. 'I'm ready for you now if you want to come on through?' They both pad softly along the green carpet to her room.

After flicking through all the brochures I stare at my fingernails and pull off one of the cuticles. At last a girl appears with the same soft voice, the same long, insipid face, the same gentle manner as the first woman, but with darker hair.

'Cassandra? Hi. I'm Amelia.'

When we are seated in her office, her back to the door and my back to the window, we begin.

'So. Cassandra, is it?'

'Cassandra, yes.'

'Unusual name.'

'Yes.'

'I'm Amelia.'

'Hi. Nice to meet you.'

'So.'

'Yes.'

'So, what can I do for you Cassandra?'

'I don't know.'

'What prompted you to make the appointment? What do you need to talk about?'

'I have a new boyfriend.'

I had no intention – absolutely no intention, when I came in here – of lying.

'I see.'

Her fingers are slender and clean with pink, oval nails. I wonder whether she does that herself or if she has just treated herself to a professional manicure. I tell her he is my first and I feel jealous of his past – I feel so insecure. I feel, I say, like I am sinking away from myself, like I don't know who I am and like I don't know why he'd love me, why I would be any better than any of the women before.

'I have no reason to believe he will be unfaithful to me but I can't stop thinking about all the girls he's slept with.' She sighs. 'That's very difficult.' Then, after a silence, she says, 'It reminds me of a song … what's the name of the singer? It's on the tip of my tongue …' She frowns and there is a long pause during which I tear off another cuticle.

'I don't know,' I say.

'It'll come to me,' she says, 'the brain is like a filing cabinet.'

'Yes,' I say, 'I've heard that. You just have to press "search", and wait.'

I resist the temptation to pick at my damaged finger while we wait. Then it comes to her, and without warning she recites a song to me about a man who is in love with a woman but has had a lot of women before her.

> *You are the only one that has my heart*
> *But all the loves that have gone before*
> *You can never be sure. No you can never be sure.*

I don't know what to say now and nor does she. She looks at her notepad, and then back at me.

'Have you any idea where this insecurity is coming from? I mean, apart from the fact that he has had a lot of partners?'

'No.'

'Well, how was your childhood? What was your relationship like with your parents?'

This is too boring. I know my own story too well. I explain myself over and over and over in my mind, and that doesn't help, I know why I'm depressed but I'm still depressed. My worth is not the same as that of someone whose mummy wanted them, or someone who saved their mummy from the place that mine wandered to. That's just life and it would be a lie to pretend otherwise. Even if it were possible there would be no point in reliving my short and uneventful past to Amelia.

'I don't want to do this,' I say, 'I don't want to have to go to counselling. There isn't time. It seems such a waste – no offence – but it seems such a waste. When there is so much life I should be having. It just seems a waste to do this.'

Amelia frowns: 'I'm not sure I understand. But I do think it is worth taking the time to work through things.'

'God.' I say, 'God. But life is so slow – isn't it? It is so slow and short.'

'I really – Cassandra I am having trouble understanding what it is you are saying. I think it might be useful to talk about your childhood … your parents … how are things at home?'

'Fine.'

Then, without planning to, I add, 'My mother's dead though.'

'I see,' she says, 'When did she pass away – on. When did she pass on?'

I didn't mean to tell her that. I don't want to talk about my mother, give rein to that cry. If I talk about her I feel as though she is at my shoulder, my mother, touching my neck, touching my hands, touching my face as though she means no harm. I feel the drunken spittle whispers in my ears. I do not want to talk about the dead, just as my grandmother does not want to talk about the war. The dead have nothing to teach us. The dead are just dead. That doesn't make them wise, or worthy. That doesn't make them anything.

'Two months ago. She walked into an electricity box. The ones with the signs on them, saying "Danger" with a picture of a man being electrocuted …'

I don't mean to say that either. I didn't plan on lying. I am aiming for profanity, I think, but I am behaving ludicrously. The joke is on me.

'I didn't know they still had those,' says Amelia, 'Did you get on to the council?'

I'm about to laugh but instead I start to cry. Do I hate my mother so much that I would have her walk into an electricity box? And how is it possible, anyway, to hate the dead, or love the dead? How can the past hope for a resolution? What can it hope to achieve by haunting the present like this? What can the living offer the dead? And there is nothing at all that my mother can do for me now – nothing I can do to extract what I need from her – not talking about her, not thinking about her, not hating her – nothing.

'Take your time.' Amelia tells me, 'You are in a lot of pain.'

'Yes I am. I am having bad dreams. Is there something I could take?'

'What kind of dreams?'

'Bad dreams,' I say, 'terrible dreams. Dead people in them. The women always dead. I don't want to re-live them, please.'

'What kind of dreams?'

She's very interested in the dreams thing. I thought other people's dreams were famously boring, but maybe not. Not for Amelia. It occurs to me then that maybe she is a writer gathering material, not a counsellor at all, but that's just paranoia. I am a little ashamed of my dreams.

They are all about me, just me. They have no social conscience at all. The night the twin towers were hit, the night war was launched on Iraq, the night children were being shot in some shanty school, I dreamed about me, my mummy, my ex-boyfriend. I tell Amelia that I dream about the Holocaust. I am the victim and sometimes a Nazi. My grandparents were involved, I say, in anti-communism.

'That was before the Nazi camps, before Hitler was even up and running; that was when Stalin had already killed more people in the Gulag than were to die from Nazi persecution ...' I must be careful she doesn't think I'm a Nazi for saying this. Her degree is not in history. Mine neither. I wasn't there either anyway was I? So how would I know? It is my grandfather's cant I'm using, and some facts from a book I read last week. I try to be honest, I try to be myself.

'I don't think they really believe the Holocaust happened – is it illegal to say that? I don't think they can get their heads around it, are surprised by it still ...'

'You have inherited that guilt?' says Amelia, writing it down on her notepad as though she has cracked a code. She is proud of that phrase, so neat, so articulate, *inherited guilt*, she writes.

'That's what I'm saying, Amelia. Yes, exactly, Amelia.' I tell her I dream about the war.

'Which war?' she asks. 'The war,' I say, 'the one in Iraq. Isn't it a war?'

I go on and on with these made-up dreams, and she seems pleased with them. Maybe they are sort of true anyway, seeing as I made them up. Maybe it's her job to figure it out. I tell her I see children's faces covered in that curiously clean-looking blood, guns in their dead fingers. I tell her about Zeng Qiáng's face haunting me, the email about the breastless lesbian, the way I don't know what to do with that sort of information.

'He's been released,' says Amelia, 'Zeng Qiáng has been released. I think he's coming back to college. They've held his place for him.'

'Oh.'

'So you don't need to worry about that any more anyway.'

'I suppose not.'

'Okay,' she says, 'I want you to keep a dream diary for me, okay? You don't have to show me, but I want you to write them down. I'm also going to refer you to student health. They might prescribe you some Prozac or something. Just for the moment. To get you through the grief.'

'Prozac? Do people still take Prozac? Is there anything just for the dreams?'

'Yes, they'll give you something for the dreams I'd say. I don't know actually. It's not my field. That's more psychiatry, as opposed to counselling. I'm a counsellor. But I'm hoping to train as a psychiatrist as well ...'

‘That’s good.’

‘We’re going to have to finish up now,’ says Amelia, ‘I have another client coming in at twelve, but if you want to make another appointment I’m here on Tuesdays and Thursdays. Look after yourself. You look like you should be eating more.’

‘I’m a model,’ I say, making it sound very glamorous. Coke and bulimia and a lot of money glitter under my voice. ‘I’m supposed to look like this.’

eight

IT WAS the first sunny day of the year. They skipped lectures and went to Howth on a day trip. It was supposed to be a surprise but he couldn't blindfold her the whole way to the Dart station. He bought two return tickets to Howth, led her to platform one and gave her three guesses as to where they were going, and she pretended to think they were going to all kinds of unlikely boring and exotic places.

'Prague?'

'Funderland?'

'The National Library?'

She was wearing a sleeveless yellow top with silly pink buttons for straps and he kissed her bare shoulder as she gazed out at the sea whooshing by. An old woman on the Dart smiled at them, her head bopping along with the train as though her skull were weightless under the frill of blue curls.

In Howth they walked around the second-hand bookshops and he bought an illustrated pocket-book of terriers for seventy-five cent because the dog on the third page looked like the dog he had as a child. He told her about Koogo and she listened even though she had heard it before.

Then they got fish and chips from Beshoff's and sat on the grass in the sun, using their hands to eat the chips and battered cod drenched in vinegar and ketchup, and afterwards they both smelled of chipper. They licked their fingers and wiped them on their jeans but they still stank.

He lay on his back and she crawled up to him from behind and kissed him upside down and he grabbed her and flipped her over and kissed her the right way up.

Then they bought whipped ice-cream cones and went down by the shore and sat on the cold rocks and shivered because the sun was sinking now. He gave out to her for not bringing a jacket and took off his jumper, which she didn't want him to do. She refused to put it on so he stretched the neck and popped it over both their heads and held her under the wool. The sky was luminous blue with an early moon seeping through, faint as a watermark. He said he had always thought it was impossible for the sun and the moon to be up at the same time and she said they were both only half up and they finished their ice-creams in silence.

Her lips were very red from the cold. They were alone and he thought briefly about making love to her there on the rocks but decided it wasn't the right moment and she might get scratched. She talked about college, and about a board game called 'Guess Who?' which he had never played. He talked about hating his dad, and about a girl he had sex with when he was seventeen. He didn't know that the girl thought it meant something and she became very angry and clingy. He ignored her letters and calls and never said sorry, but he has always felt bad about it. He told Helen this like a confession and he could see she was trying to say the right thing to absolve him.

Then they moved down closer to the sea and picked up stones that they thought looked like things: horses and hearts and Coke bottles, and one that looked like a dog. Oisín put the heart-shaped one in his pocket. He wanted something to keep.

By accident she stepped in a little pool between the rocks and screamed when she felt the cold water seep in through her socks. He laughed at her.

'You're a disaster!'

'Ahhh! Give me your socks!'

'No.'

'Give me your socks!'

He stepped in the same pool. 'Shit! That's your fault!'

They took off their socks and threw them into the sea and dried their feet on Oisín's jumper.

'Fuck it, I liked those socks!'

'They were the same as all your other socks!'

He picked her up and lumbered over the rocks towards the water and she screamed in fun and then out of fear, 'If we fall we'll smash our skulls, Oisín!'

When they got to the edge of the water he put her down and tried to teach her how to skim stones but she couldn't learn and began giddily hurling them out as far into the water as she could, and she kissed his cold bare chest because she was wearing his jumper now.

They were shivering all the way back on the Dart and didn't talk much. They tried to warm each other's feet with their hands.

When they got back they took a warm shower together at Helen's, whispering like bold children in case someone walked by and heard them. He grew hard from the sight of her naked with the water and suds running over her round breasts and down between her legs and she kissed his mouth and touched him a bit to tease him and stepped out of the shower. He groaned and turned the shower to cold before stepping out. Then they ran back to Helen's room in their underwear, her wet hair dripping all over the floor and Oisín's hands cupped over his crotch, covering what was left of his erection. They pattered as fast as they could so that no one would see them, trying not to skid on the wet lino floor.

They made love in bed, looking at each other, kissing each other's faces, whispering sex talk and love talk in the twilight beneath bed sheets. When Oisín closed his eyes at last to sleep, she said, 'I love you Oisín,' whispered it close to his hair so he could feel her breath, her kiss at his temple. Then she fell asleep too.

I love you.

That was true. Whatever happened now, that was true.

nine

I DIDN'T go to the Health Centre. Instead I made an appointment with a different counsellor, one called Siobhán. I'm going to try it again, telling the truth this time, because I don't want pills. Not yet. Once you go into that land, I bet you never come out. They just block the paths, you see, that take the information from your eyes to your brain. They just make you blind. They wreck your liver and turn you yellow. Particularly lithium. Helen told me that. Her dad takes it.

Siobhán has also got impeccable nails. They are French manicured, so I know she gets them done. I have formulated good answers this time.

'Why are you here?'

'Because I'm having very bad nightmares, and my own thoughts are deafening and I feel sad all the time and panicky and I'm hoping that if I talk about things then I can sort a few things out in my head and not have those dreams any more.'

'I see.'

'Isn't that what dreams are? Things that haven't been worked out?'

'Oh. Well there are a lot of theories and nowadays it's hard to know what to think. It is impossible to gather empirical evidence on these things. Freud, of course, would have said that yes, you can, in fact, interpret dreams and heal the patient that way, but that's not really my discipline.'

'Oh.'

'Most people don't buy that any more. Tell you what, why don't you tell me a bit about you and we'll go from there. Your family?'

I'm trying this time, really trying, but it is just too boring. What I do, though, feels useful. It feels like the real reason I came was not to tell my story at all. I need to tell Helen's story. I want it heard. I want this woman to understand the story of her source, her heart, normal and dull as it may seem, because Helen would never come here and tell somebody her story like this. Helen doesn't even know her own story. I want this woman to see Helen.

I know from spontaneous little statements that have spilled forth every now and then over the years, details she needs to tell, like the colour of her daddy's pyjamas one morning when he was happy and laughed at her joke.

'Knock knock.'

'Who's there?'

'Orange.'

'Orange who?'

'Orange you glad to see me?'

They were green like hospital scrubs and the front was buttoned up wrong. When he laughed her daddy threw his head back and she could see his hairy belly.

In his way Helen's daddy loves her. He loves her as well as he can with the things that clamp his consciousness and make him a danger to love. I have met him, a grey man with sad dog's eyes and faraway feelings. I know the story of her daddy and her mammy and of everyone who should have loved her, and I want to tell this woman their stories so that she can see.

'My dad's not well.'

Helen's daddy is not well. He is separated from the world by a film of grey cotton wool. Behind it, he bumps lower and lower to worlds that are unbearable, where the ground always opens. There is no bottom to this world. I say that to Siobhán.

'The thing that makes him like this is not him. The thing is an evil thing.'

She takes a breath to speak, to explain that they taught her at college about depression, and about that word 'evil', but then she glances at the clock and thinks better of it.

Not very fashionable, I tell her, but there is no other word for this thing that inhabits some bodies until it breaks into the soul when he's not watching. It rises and falls, wave upon wave. Each splash is a promise that it will rise again, it will never be exorcised and its final rise will be its victory, it will claim him in the end with an overdose or a jump from his office window. That's its promise.

'My daddy is very rich …' There is an evil that blossoms in prosperity. Pain struggles to maintain its status quo. During the war, only those with very good reason killed themselves. Only those for whom a horrible death was inevitable.

'Sometimes,' I say, using Helen's head-tilt and quizzical voice, 'it seems like it doesn't matter what state the world is in, pain seems to maintain a sort of … status quo.' I enjoy this idea – it seems holistic – and I wonder if maybe the selfish lifestyle is right; maybe we should all just enjoy our relative goodness against things we cannot change. Keep your own soul safe, it's all you can do.

'How many children are there?' asks Siobhán. My descriptions are good and she is enjoying the story now. I wonder if she's guessed it's not mine. 'There are six of us. I'm the eldest.' As for Helen's mammy – but Siobhán looks at the clock.

'I don't like to interrupt you, but we've already gone over. I have someone coming in at three. I'd like to talk about your mother too though. If you want to make another appointment I'm here on Wednesdays and Fridays.'

When I get home Helen is sitting in the kitchen, blowing on freshly painted nails and gazing at the fish. The bowl is on the table and they are swimming quickly up and slowly down, puckering at the surface of the water where Helen has sprinkled their food. My own nails are ragged from abuse and I decide to get a manicure, even synthetic nails or something, when I get the chance.

'You want a cup of tea, Helen?'

'No. Where were you?'

'I went to the counsellor.'

'Oh. Any good?'

'No. She was all it's hard to know what to think nowadays, like I'm interested in her post-everything crisis – Helen, do you think there is a link between postmodern thought and psychosis?'

'Dunno. You should look into it …'

She is bursting with something, the dimples irrepressible in her cheeks.

'Cassy I really like Oisín.'

I don't want to hear it, but she starts to tell me anyway. She doesn't need to. With her eyes, and the sex tingling around her like perfume, she says it all.

YOUR LOVE comes suddenly and unexpectedly. You fought it half-heartedly out of fear, then gave in to it.

It is the silly things: the way he pronounces 'th'; the warm down at the back of his neck; when he shaves and misses three long strands clinging to his cheekbone. When at last he lays his head on your shoulder instead of holding yours to his, and you know that he trusts you, and you want only good for him. Only beautiful places and healthy meals and warm beds and jokes and kisses for him for the rest of his life.

Your love is a series of images: spilling coffee on his duvet. Knowing he is watching you dress. Feeling happy and naked. Winter sunlight on his back and bum. Jumping on the bed and hitting your head on the lampshade. Laughing.

It is a feeling like forgetting, like falling asleep. Your mind has turned to bubbles. Love makes every moment precious and fleeting. Love is missing your lectures for one more kiss or five more minutes to talk about nothing, wearing his T-shirt for two days while he is gone for the weekend, flushing as you piss so he doesn't hear you.

And fear. Fear and the ancient knowledge that this is not something you have earned.

ten

YOU CAN'T FIND any clean knickers and he raises an eyebrow in a way that makes something in you leap. 'Go out without them,' he says, and you laugh and continue to look. At last you give up and, as you reach the door, enjoying your nakedness under your tracksuit bottoms, he yanks a very short skirt from your wardrobe and throws it at your head. 'No,' he says, 'wear this.'

You go to the Student Union shop together for milk, which was the plan, and then he wants to go somewhere else, to lots of poky little shops that you have never been to before. He walks you into a shop that sells comic books and *Star Wars* models. There are some teenage boys there. As you leave he whispers that you have probably made their day and you think how crazy lust is, that it can make a man think everyone else wants you too. He fingers the end of your skirt. You walk through an alleyway with no shop doors, only a high, narrow window at the back of a hairdressing salon. He thrusts his hand under your skirt, and in his touch you feel how lovely the curve of your bum is. He pushes you to a wall, presses himself into your buttocks. He is out of his trousers already, stiff and hot against the yielding fat of you. You can see the top of someone's head through the small window, hair-dye and foil in it. 'Feel that?' he says, 'That's for you. You make me so hard, your perfect little ass …'

On top of you, his eyes shutting and opening, gaze moving all over you, he looks as though he doesn't recognize your face. His jaw is clenched. Your fingers are locked but he detaches one hand and puts it around your neck as you both move towards climax, four fingertips beneath your ear and a thumb pressing above the collarbone. You stretch your head back. As you come he brings the other hand to your throat, pushing on your windpipe, stopping your breath, his hands trembling with arousal and something else, something new: his eyes on your eyes but not looking. You don't recognize him and you can't speak – *Who are you? Who are you? Who are you?* – and you're afraid of choking and your blood pumps faster like a loud passing train and you must like it because you come in waves, in platforms, up and up and up like a rising fever, and you shudder and moan and push into the mattress with the back of your heels.

At the end of the bed the kitten kneads the duvet with its claws, and purrs.

You must like it: his face like the face of a sleepwalker, his grip stopping your breath. Is he imagining he is murdering you? Is this what sex is like? He comes but it isn't enough. He stays hard, pushes deeper in, spreading your lips, hitting the cervix, teeth locked, jaw set, trembling, and his hands, wet from sex sweat, still pressing into your neck. His clenched teeth are moist. His lips are cracked and drawn back like a growling dog's and he pushes in and in, determined: 'I want to make you come again.'

He watches you undress for him, pumps himself slowly. You think he will plunge into you, hold your wrists and fuck you, looking at your belly and your breasts. Wordlessly he takes you by the hips and turns you over, holds you in a handstand position on the bed. You know how ugly you must look, your breasts flopping towards your chin, your chin doubled by the position. 'No Oisín, stop.' But he holds you like that, 'I just want to try something', and begins to lick you. It makes you pity him. He can never do much for you with his mouth. You can tell he doesn't like it. Maybe you taste funny. Something about the position creates a vacuum and your vagina fills with air. 'Put me down, Oisín, come on.'

'I just want to try something,' he says, 'Fuck Helen can't I just try something?'

You see how fervent he is with desire and you think, 'That's for me,' and you are grateful, and he pushes into you, in and out and it makes a squelch sound because your pelvis has filled with air and the top of your head is pressing on the springs of the bed and you feel heavy and clumsy as though you might fall soon and he keeps pushing in – and then he stops and lets you down. There is a loud sound like a fart as the air comes out. He sighs, 'I just wanted to try something.'

You sit naked on the bed, waiting for him to kiss you, make love to you, but he's not turned on any more.

'Gotta go baby,' he says in a voice from a Hollywood film, kissing you on the cheek. 'I have work in an hour, want to pick up some stuff at my place first.'

On top of him, touching yourself. He likes that, told you to do it; 'Baby, perch on my cock and touch yourself, baby.' Then you pivot around so your back is to him, your bum at his eyeline. *He will like this*, you think. He reaches forward, puts a hand on each shoulder and pulls them back gently.

'Keep your shoulders back,' he says, 'you're hunching – doesn't look nice. That's better. That's sexy.'

'Tell me you love me, Oisín ...'

eleven

HELEN'S CURLS were spilled over the pillow. He knew she was awake from the way she was breathing.

Before they'd fallen asleep last night he'd heard her murmur, 'I'm never alone with my body any more.' He had kissed the back of her head, and fallen asleep. She didn't say it like a complaint. Why would she? Why be alone with the protrusions and orifices that are so obviously meant to fit with someone else's? After all, women never appreciated their own breasts, did they? That's why lads made that joke, squeezing their imaginary tits. *If I was a bird I'd be doin' this all day, that's all I'd need in the world. Me and my knockers* ... That's what Oisín felt now, in a different way, *Me and my Helen.*

Come to think of it he had been neglecting the lads lately. They were starting to notice. The last email from Aengus said: 'Here's some barely legal pussy to brighten up those student days. No word from you in an age. Too good for us losers now ur a trinners head. Trinners 4 winners eh man?'

Helen was becoming his girlfriend now. It had been three months and Oisín had grown used to her body. The first sensation of the day was her skin against his lips and hands, her scent, the familiar shoulders, the wispy ringlets. They were what he looked for on waking.

Without warning she sat at the edge of the bed and stood up. Her sudden nakedness, free from all ritual, her breasts and arms and bum lifting themselves unceremoniously out from the covers, up from the bed, shocked him a little. Usually Helen lay in bed with him first, she kissed him when she woke up, and they touched each other. Usually he got up before her and she was half-dressed when he came out of the shower, or she got into the shower with him. He had never seen her so brashly naked before, her legs, her sleep-creased breasts, that little triangle neither asking for sex nor inspiring any sort of arousal; fleshy and functional. He had never seen her naked before unless he was about to make love to her, or had just done so. Separated from him like that, her body repulsed him. He thought: *She shits, she pisses, I am only one part of her body's many activities*. He felt betrayed. To remedy the situation he began to pump his morning hard-on a little. He groaned to let her know he wanted her, though for the first time, he didn't. She turned. Her soft face made that question mark she could do by arching one thin brow, and he stopped. She knew. 'We don't have to have sex all the time. Go back to sleep.'

He must have looked hurt because she came over to him, sat on the bed, her bum near his face. Something he had noticed before was that her bum had little red dots, like goosebumps, though it didn't feel bumpy. 'You're my man,' she said. He closed his eyes. She kissed the lids, then his forehead, 'Go back to sleep, baby.'

When he felt her lift off the bed again he opened his eyes a little and stared at the wall, hearing her move around his room. What was she doing? She didn't usually behave like this. *You're my man.* Maybe he could like that. *I'm your lady, you are my man.*

He heard his wardrobe door open and peered over the duvet. It was the door with the mirror on the inner side. She was standing in front of it in the neutral pose of a dancer: feet slightly apart, hands by her side. She was looking at her naked body, at the neck, the sloping shoulders, the belly. The belly. Sex and piss weren't the only occupations of a pussy. There was a Polish woman who lived in the flat opposite his, with two men who Oisín thought must be brothers. Her belly had swollen suddenly and she began to waddle. He felt terror whenever he saw her coming. She had been such a hotty, with such a smooth, tiny waist. It was monstrous, pregnancy, the way it could transform the body so suddenly, the way it destroyed the very sexiness that made it possible, and that looming threat to burst the woman open at the end.

They seemed to like it, women, they seemed to think it made them powerful. On the bus people got up for them and they plopped themselves down with their thick ankles, stroking their bumps with pride. *If I was a woman*, thought Oisín, *I wouldn't make such an exception of myself just because I got knocked up, I'd stand on the bus, I'd get on with it, and I wouldn't make men feel bad about being men.*

He watched Helen watching herself, evaluating her body parts the way girls can. If he were to look at himself in the mirror, he wouldn't be able to say, *this thigh is good, this bit here ought to be underplayed with suitable clothing* … but women could do that. Always, thought Oisín, if a guy got a girl naked, he would find that she had some flaw that she knew about, a floppy belly that she had somehow managed to hide with the large breasts she pushed into his face, a flat chest that she had padded out with a special bra. Even in bed, even after she knew the truth was up, she would still pose as though he were a camera. The fat ones took cock between their breasts so that the guy forgot about the belly, was grateful for it even, for facilitating such expansive cleavage. The ones with no breasts perched on top and swung around so the guy could see his cock sliding in and out of them from behind, and all he could think about was their tight little asses.

Helen tilted her head and put a hand on her abdomen. It was obscene, this privacy in his room, with him there, this communion with her own body. It was rude. She was taking him for granted. She thought he was all hers, *her man*.

In revenge he thought of the letter he had received last week from Petra. She was coming in six weeks to see him, she'd said. He hadn't replied because he wasn't sure what he should do now that all this stuff was happening with Helen.

Petra had sent him a picture of her breasts and torso with him fucking her. She had bought a disposable camera on her last trip to see him, and she had asked him to take photos while she took him in her mouth. While she bent over and he entered the second place where no man had ever been, she had said in her manly German accent: 'Photograph you focking me in de asshole,' and he had. The next day she had handed the camera to him while she sat on top of him, the way he had shown her, and rocked herself back and forth until she came.

He had never taken sex pictures before. It made him uneasy but he felt a little sorry for Petra, having taken her virginity, and he didn't know how to say no. She had taken the camera home with her. She sent him a single picture in every one of her letters, and usually he jerked off once to it, then placed the photo and letter in a shoebox along with the other ones. Filthy photographs and girlish letters, written on pastel-coloured paper. She wrote in brightly coloured biro, sometimes with a different colour for each line, pink, then purple, then blue; little doodles in the margin to illustrate what she meant. Beside the sentence, 'I didn't mind that you were so grumpy. You are cute when you are grumpy,' she had drawn a little picture of an angry face surrounded by love hearts. The letters were full of phrases unnatural to her language, 'I miss you, honey.' Where did she learn a phrase like that? He hadn't even wanked to the last photo yet. He had slipped it and the half-read letter back into *A Very Short Introduction to Critical Theory*.

Helen had turned around now; she was looking at the reflection of her back and her bum. She had a hand over one breast, plumping it up so that the image reflected in the mirror implied that her breasts were rounder, fuller, higher than they really were. Red filled Oisín's stomach. There was a reason, he thought, that literature showed women as artsy and manipulative. Look at her, watching herself, posing for herself, pretending things. There were plenty of women with better breasts, plenty of women he had made love to, nipples he had licked; who did she think she was fooling?

She pinched her own hips and wrinkled her nose. Then she did something that made him love her again. She stuck her tongue out at her reflection, and closed the wardrobe door. She walked back towards the bed and he closed his eyes. 'Baby, I'm going to shower,' she said.

YOU USED TO take stock of yourself when you woke, run a hand over your head, your breasts, your armpits. You used to smooth your palm over your abdomen, your crotch, the back of your neck. It was a way of feeling yourself placed in the pace of your life, remembering who you were and where. Sometimes you would watch your hands, the way babies do, entwine them above your head or trace patterns on the low ceiling. Now when you wake he is already on you, cupping your bum, your breasts, a large hand wrapped around your thigh.

In the mirror you look older. The morning after you first made love you turned to him with your face blank for perusal, 'Do I look different?' and you giggled. You have always had cherub's lips. This morning you can see that they are thinning, or perhaps it's just the mood you're in.

Once, when you went to buy mascara in Brown Thomas, the lady tried to sell you a thing called 'lip freeze'. She said that as you got older your lips would just get thinner and thinner. That day you felt pretty and invincible, you had your glow on and everywhere you went men glanced at your blue eyes, your luminous blonde head. 'Lip freeze'. That was a marketing ploy, fear mongering. You had some good years left in your face. This morning though, it looks true. Everything is growing looser, flabbier, becoming less valuable. For a few days now, you have been gripped by a sort of panic after making love, a sudden sense of something wasted. Every time you have sex with him your pussy gets a little looser, you can feel it. Pussy is his word, part of your sex language. You never used that word before him. This morning you have woken without the sweet, murky veil of love. But the other thing is still there – that engulfing desire for him, or the desire, at least, to be wanted by him.

You turn around to look at your bum and back in the mirror. You have a nice bum, a good waist. If you angle your arm a certain way and turn your head back towards the mirror, you look as though your breasts might be larger than they are. You have been waiting for your breasts to get bigger ever since puberty. You remember the excitement when those few downy hairs began to sprout, and a hard little ball under each nipple. What kind of body would you get? What kind of breasts? The things your body decided to do now would affect you for the rest of your life. You would become a beautiful woman, or a plain woman, or, the ultimate fear – you wouldn't become a woman at all. You would be like the sexless little bird woman who taught gym. You did all right out of puberty, considering the vast possibilities.

Oisín is asleep again.

This morning your own face – with the little laughter lines, the gradually thinning lips – is making you angry with him. You close the wardrobe. You'll have a shower.

BEFORE LEAVING for the bathroom she kissed his forehead again. She didn't usually do that. She was annoying him this morning. When she was gone he picked up *A Very Short Introduction to Critical Theory* from where it lay closed on his laptop, and slipped out the photo. Petra had beautiful round breasts with brown nipples. He remembered them bouncing up and down when he had taken the photo. He reached under the covers and fingered his foreskin. Then he swapped hands. He spat into the hand that had been holding the book and began to move it slowly up and down. He thought of Petra's rosy little bum hole, the way she had bent over so willingly and spread the cheeks for him. Helen had never done that. He had never even thought of doing that to Helen. She wouldn't like it. She would probably cry again and make him feel like a monster.

Petra's breasts were better than Helen's. It gave him pleasure to think that. Was her pussy tighter? Hard to remember. It was easier to remember what girls looked like than what they felt like. He tried to tell himself that he would rather have sex with Petra right now than with Helen.

He wanted to have a proper wank over Petra but he couldn't come like this, with Helen in the next room. He closed the book. He made his way to the bathroom door and watched Helen shower there, a blur of pink behind the water and glass. He got into the shower too and they made love silently.

He planned it while he was inside her, looking at the tiles with his hands around her wrists, his cheek against hers, the water running over their backs and anger in every thrust, with every thrust wanting to undo the quiet power Helen had gained over him, making him want her like that.

As they were getting dressed he handed her the book with the photo still in it. Making his voice sound as casual as possible he said, 'Read this for your essay. It will help.'

'Oh,' she said, 'I've read it.' Her cheeks were pink from sex and the heat of the shower.

'Read it again. It's good. It will help.'

Even as he pushed the book into her hands, Petra's naked breasts glowing between the pages, her pelvis waiting there with him inside her, waiting for Helen's soft eyes, her shock, the fluttering and crumpling she would feel, the hot face, pounding ears, he thought, 'But I want you.'

twelve

AFTER WE BROKE UP it wasn't just Brian that I missed. It was them too, the artists. While I was with Brian I was someone to know. The artists called me *honey* or *darling*. They touched my hips and kissed my cheek. I was someone who had a place at the after-show parties. I had plenty of brunch dates with arrogant and unusual people, the striking kind, people who give the impression of being famous even if you don't recognize them. I was privy to an exciting underworld where everyone was broke but lived in a sort of feline leisure. There was always wine and good coffee and gourmet food for us. That was simply the world we were in. It was what we felt we deserved.

For a few months after the split I still held these brunch dates, meeting the artists at my regular place, Café Rimbaud, an Italian café with a French name where they served excellent coffee. *Your office* – that was the joke – *I saw you in your office with Jo Reilly this morning*. It applied to everyone about their regular haunts, *Butlers is Bridgeman's office, she networks between ten and one ...*

Café Rimbaud was famous for the authentic rudeness of the waiters. There was a mahogany barista area and an assortment of elegant tables and chairs that must once have belonged to various grand houses. The effect was that of a pirate home, a shanty place built from a plundered colony, abandoned big houses, collapsing old money. Introduce an artist to the place and they'll say, 'Oh, how *bijou*. Mismatched chairs. Fant*aaa*stic!' There were three types of customers who frequented the place. The first were the wealthy businessmen, their bronzed daughters, trophy wives and mistresses. They were trying to be knowing: 'This is where the artists hang out. You know those paintings that we have in the dining-room? Well that painter lives around the corner and he's always in here. You can see paint under his fingernails.' Then there were artists and writers. There was always some half-famous Dublin playwright sitting at the one of the tables outside with pillar-box-red lipstick or a distinctive hat, musing alone over a glass of house red in the early afternoon. The third were Arts lecturers from Trinity, along with the most promising of their PhD students, talking loudly about Foucault. It was a trendy place to be, probably still is. I haven't been there in a while.

This was the place where I had my brunch dates with people whom I think of now as Brian's groupies, or 'colleagues' if I'm feeling kind. Back then I saw them as mutual friends.

I would order a croissant with butter and jam, and it would arrive without butter or jam. I would order the butter and jam and when I was halfway through the fatty pastry, butter would arrive; white continental butter that wouldn't melt. It lumped the dough and tasted like nothing. I would order jam and another Americano and by the time the coffee arrived with a little pot of jam on the saucer, the croissant would have been eaten. Whoever I was with would say '*Fantastic*, isn't it? So rude. Very Italian. They just don't give a shit. When I was in Rome …' It was fantastic coffee though. Fantastic. That was indisputable.

I thought I was the more interesting half of our couple. I was brighter, more entertaining, a better listener. I saw more of the friends than Brian did, my company was more sought after, but I was always 'Brian Durcan's partner, the young one he left his wife for. Stunning.' At these brunches I would talk with Brian's colleagues about their work, sharing ideas and so on. The fact that I didn't paint or take photographs didn't give me less authority on the subject, in fact, it made them more comfortable discussing it with me. I was not a rival.

After we broke up I felt as though I were in a sort of limbo. I didn't even know whether it was real, the break-up. Pain emanated from me like a bitter but intriguing smell. I began to talk about the relationship. The artists wanted details. They wanted dirt on Brian, sex stuff, but the pain was blinding, I couldn't think properly, I couldn't tell well-structured anecdotes. Gradually they stopped contacting me, stopped answering my calls, and I realized that the reason they had continued to meet me was that they thought this was a temporary split. They thought I was still in the loop. When he began to take a tall black girl with him to openings – a slender Somalian actress with the shoulder blades of a panther – it was clear that we were no longer a couple on a break, and I was no longer someone to know. The mutual friends, as I had considered them, would be turning their attention to her now, having brunch with 'Brian Durcan's partner, the actress, the one he left that model for. Stunning.'

Their rejection hurt a lot more than I had expected. At first I had been so aware of the superficiality of it all, I had engaged with their talk in an effort to be polite to Brian's friends, but somewhere along the way I had fallen in love with them, with that whole self-contained world where mismatched chairs were charming and installation art was serious and vague lives like theirs were at the centre of everything. It was like a second childhood, the smallness, the fiction of it. They had become home.

The last meeting I had was with Matilda – Tilly. She arrived late, out of breath, lugging a potted tree. 'It's a Japanese red maple. Isn't it beautiful, Cass? So rich, like? That colour. It's for my piece on Nymphs ...' Tilly was from Cork. She had buck teeth and bulky bones. Her hair was bleached to a watery orange and roughly chopped like the hair of a TV self-harmer. She was ugly, and the hair was designed to make a feature of this ugliness. That day she was wearing striped tights and a vintage blouse with shoulder pads and pearl buttons up to her chin. She had large, protruding ears that added an endearing childishness.

At that time she was photographing pubescent children through the dappled light of leaves, and painting fairy wings onto the prints with real gold. She had recently received an arts grant, which accounted for the good mood and the purchase. She pulled out the cast-iron chair opposite me – a piece of Victorian garden furniture, I think – leaning in to kiss me on either cheek as she did so.

What betrayed Tilly's image, that well-honed sense of pride in her aesthetic wrongness, was that, up close, it was possible to see that she was wearing the subtle, laboured make-up of a woman who hates her face. The hollows were expertly lightened, the eyes widened with natural brown shadow, the cheekbones faked on with expensive bronzer. A flat mole by her mouth, which might have been cute, might have been an ironic sort of beauty spot, was thickly daubed over with skin-coloured paste. She was wearing a perfume that smelled like sweets.

'So,' she stroked my cheek. 'Poor petal. How are you doing?'

'Fine,' I said, 'fine.'

'What are you doing with yourself now, Cassy? I hate to think of you all alone out there in the world. Do you have friends?'

I opened my mouth and closed it again. Was she clearing something up? Had she been sent as a messenger on behalf of all of those I considered mutual friends? Had I been harassing them with brunch invites? Did they have a meeting? I didn't have friends. I thought *they* were my friends. I don't know how I would have answered had we not been interrupted by the maple tree. It toppled towards us, its crimson leaves spiking my head and spreading their colour over our table. She was right. It was a beautiful thing. It would be wonderful to be the one to plant it somewhere, I thought, pack the earth around it like some act of half creation. I tried to straighten it but we were sitting outside. The wind had suddenly taken up. The tree was in a light plastic pot, hardly large enough to fit the trunk. It toppled the other way, dusting black compost over the ground. Tilly sighed, straightened it, and held the bark close to her face so that the canopy of leaves made a headdress that gave her the look of an ancient fetish. She really was a bizarre thing to look at, Tilly.

'I suppose you have your college friends. What are you doing these days?'

'College.'

A dark waiter with a V-shaped back picked his way over the spill of compost, disgust on his face, as though smelling something vile. Tilly turned a knobbly finger in the air in an attempt at elegance. 'We'll order,' she said.

The waiter turned around. He had very high, thrusting cheekbones and a strong chin, and looked as though he might be wearing eyeliner. 'Yes?'

It was a miraculous achievement on Tilly's part; usually they ignored you until they felt like serving. There was a sort of authority in Tilly's bizarre looks. No one would be that brazen about their buck teeth unless they had reason to be. People thought she must have been an intellectual or a famous person's child. The waiter attended our table with much more haste than if I had asked. I didn't order a croissant, because she only ordered an espresso. This was to be a quick one. Time with me was no longer an investment. Our coffees arrived promptly. I was still formulating an answer to both of her questions – who my friends were, what I was doing – when I spotted Paul's long neck, a cerise silk scarf, a little hat with a feather. 'Yankee Doodle', a rhyme I had not heard in years, began to loop in my head. He clocked Tilly with a nod and a side-grin. But not me. I gave a little nod but no, definitely not me.

'Hello my little siren.' At first I thought Paul was being nasty to Tilly. He had applied for the same arts grant. Whenever he talked about her he dismissed her art, calling it 'fantasia crap for paedos', commenting publicly on her ugliness. He had explained to me once that because he was gay he had licence to bitch, being neither a sexual rival nor a prospective mate. I used to defend her. Paul and I had become close friends, I thought, but now he was ignoring me outright. He approached the table, kissed Tilly noisily on each cheek.

'Oh, hi Cassandra.' He said it as though he had just noticed me.

'Hi.'

'What are you doing these days?'

I don't know how I replied. I remember the coffee. It was perfect – bitter and smooth, with creamy spume, and it stayed hot through all of this. Paul sat inside, where he was meeting someone. Tilly downed her espresso like a Sambuca shot and clanked a two-euro coin onto the table.

'Can I leave that with you Cass? I need to talk to Paul about something. Take care. See you soon.'

'Yes …'

Tilly wasn't listening any more. She was lifting the pot to her chest as though burping a baby; the tree wagged over her shoulder. I still hadn't quite got the message. I was straining my head around, trying to catch her eye, 'Yes, let's have dinner next week or something.'

'Next week's not good,' she said, 'but soon, yes. Good to see you. Mind yourself.'

It was only a small americano but the coffee seemed to take forever to finish. 'Yankee Doodle' played around and around. I watched the table, tried to make a fish skeleton from a maple leaf that had fallen there, but failed. They weren't that sort of leaf. *Yankee doodle went to town a-ridin' on a pony, stuck a feather in his hat and called it majagory.* Were they really the words? 'Majagory' wasn't right.

It was impossible to get the waiter's attention to ask for the bill. I was tempted to shame them both by going inside to pay, walking past them, walking out again, the better person. But I was stricken. I didn't feel better. I felt like nothing. What *was* I doing now? Who *were* my friends? Helen. That was it. There wasn't a single other person. I left the money on the table and walked away.

Yankee doodle went to town a-ridin' on a pony, stuck a feather in his cap and called it macaroni. Macaroni. Not majagory.

The break-up nearly killed my grandmother. She had loved Brian instantly on the basis that I loved him and that therefore he must have been worth something. She had invested a lot in him. She had accepted his greying hair, his tendency to kiss my neck with my grandfather in the room, his unwillingness to earn a living. She had defended me when my aunt had called me cheap for moving in with him.

'Well what do you expect, Hannah? Two young things like that, and when you like each other? Well there must be something wrong with you if you do not want to spend all evening together isn't it? They have just red blood, both of them.'

While Brian and I were living together my grandmother used to arrive at our flat – Brian's flat – with a basket of treats: homemade fruit cake, organic coffee, Italian ham. She would never stay long. Her presence was never an intrusion, even on our odd little bubble of a world. She has a rule, and that is never to interfere in someone else's relationship. Nurturing it doesn't count as interference.

She tells stories to back this up: a young man whose mother wouldn't let him marry a Jewish girl because she thought the girl wore too much make-up. He ended up marrying a plain, Catholic woman who had a string of affairs. In the end the humiliation killed him. 'You should have seen that man,' she would say, shaking her head. Another one was about a young woman whose mother wouldn't let her marry a poet because he was too poor. The poet became very famous, and the farmer that the girl was forced to marry drank all his money and ended up selling the farm, piece by piece. The girl had ten sons one after the other, all over ten pounds with farmer's hands. On the tenth, she died in childbirth.

What my grandmother really meant by these stories, I think, was that no one should ever leave anyone they love. That makes perfect sense, in theory, but Brian, love for Brian, consumed me, and what I learned was the truth of that awful cliché Mr O'Hara wrote on the board in school, 'Happiness writes blank.' He was looking at Helen as he wrote it, blushing, and she blushed, and the rest of the class wanting to puke. And I thought, what wank-talk. I get it now though. Brian was an artist. He was incapable of the blank of happiness. The pleasure of his life was found in the tug between elation and hell. Without the hell he wouldn't have known who he was.

We would be having a beautiful morning, eating pancakes and drinking coffee on the balcony, watching the sun rise, and me trying not to ruin it, when Brian would say, 'Isn't it a pity that this is an illusion, our love? This sense of common understanding, this apparent need for each other?'

He thought it was still intellectual to deconstruct everything. He would launch into a monologue about the transience of love. He had been to a conference on an Arts Council bursary about it. Love lasts four years, he would say, chemically it lasts four years, then it's just a matter of falling in love again or finding someone else or pretending. 'Which will we do, Lol?'

That was the name he gave me when we first made love. He had whispered it against my cheek with his big hands gripping my shoulders and waist. I had the feeling of being covered by him completely, as by the many suckered fingers of an octopus. 'My little Lolita.'

There was never any deviance from that nickname. I used to envy other girls when I heard their partners call them baby, or lovebug, or pushky-bunny. Most of the time he treated me with an odd mixture of resentment, desire and repulsion, disallowing that thing I called romance, and that he called kitsch. I loved him utterly. Sometimes, if I was lucky enough not to be noticed, I would watch him contemplate something before he photographed it. He would frown when he was working in a way that let me know what sort of child he must have been. His gaze was like a tongue, licking every crevice, taking in every subtle texture, every change of temperature depending on where the light hit. That's what I felt like when he first photographed me: like I was being licked. That is the party trick of the self-regarding: they can make you feel as though their consideration might transform you, like love, into something sublime. When I watched him work that miracle on someone else; some other face, some piece of household equipment, gracing it by virtue of his gaze – by virtue of the miraculous transfer of reality into art, the play of light on that dark strip waiting behind the shutter – with an importance beyond its station, I was overcome with a desperate need to say those words, *I love you*. Or to touch him calmly on his thick back, breathe the smell of his hair and say, *mine*.

I used to remind myself of how it began, how much he wanted me then. I was still too young to understand that there are so many ways to want and that his desire had very little to do with me. I would whisper it in his ear as we made love. 'While you watched me undress,' I would say, 'what did it feel like? Did you ever think you could touch me, did you ever think you would be pulsing and throbbing inside me like this, your big, hard, hot, fat …' and he would say in that high, weak, desperate, about-to-come voice, 'No I never thought … my Lol, you are impossibly perfect. Watching you sit there, your naked spine, your taut virgin tummy, your skin, your …'

The impression we gave in public was a little off. It was not uncommon that at an exhibition, or post-exhibition piss-up, a woman would whisper enviously, 'Brian has been talking about you all night, my god that man adores you …' Later on in the evening a man would crack some joke about how lucky Brian was, and what was his secret? I suppose I dressed up for these evenings, floated about as though oblivious to Brian and his desire for me. I suppose I was a catch. At home it was different. I was like a puppy, irritatingly zealous. I was always having to be brushed off and patted down or thrown a bone. 'I'd love an ice-cream,' he would say, and I'd be off to the Italian ice-cream shop with his coat thrown over my nightdress. There was something missing from us as a couple, I knew that. All our conversations were like a college tutorial, theoretical and self-conscious – all words. There was a level of communication we simply couldn't reach. I would disperse his brooding black moods with an insistent blow job, having no other access to him. At night I often lay facing his back and, despite my own resolve to say nothing, whispered, 'Brian? Do you love me?' at which he would pretend to be asleep, or laugh, or say: 'What do you mean, Lol? What is love?' or he would begin to shout at me, 'What more do you want from me? I can't hug you all the time! I left my wife for you, I pay your rent, I don't sleep with anyone else, ANYONE ELSE! What do I need to do?' Again, the only way to end this rant was a blow job.

The best thing about us was when we were making love in unlikely places: the theatre, on the abandoned set of *Salome* after the audience and the performers had left; behind a screen at an exhibition; in the open-windowed toilets of a train rattling through Tuscany. This gave me the impression that we were in love, so desperately needing each other's bodies, so defiant of all the artsy trappings that made up our world. But without them we were nothing at all. Without them we only had each other. A fuck-you to that world was, to me, like a declaration of true love. When we were out in public I was calm and as near to happy as I could get. Then I could believe in our love for a while, because everyone else did.

I tiptoed about his moods. If he was having a bad day I had a heavy lump in my tummy until I had fixed it. There were days when he was plunged into depression like a black liquid, swallowing black, seeing black, crippled by a private hell that used to open up in him. It was one evening, after he had had one of those days, that I left. Thick wrinkles had descended over his eyes like the frown of a bulldog. He had tied my ankles and painted a black eye onto my face, a bloody scar over one breast, and photographed me sipping tea in an armchair. I had been posing for hours, cold, with him complaining that the photos weren't right, that I wasn't sitting the right way, that he was shit.

'I'm shit, I'm shit. I'm getting old, going blind …'

Finally I made it better by telling him to tie me to the bed, that this might work better as a sequence. The whole idea might read better, I said, if the woman was photographed in a lot of different settings. He took some photos there, but he still wasn't happy. I needed to do something.

'Oh God,' I moaned. 'Please, Daddy, let me kiss your cock!' He looked at me, raging that I would take his artistic block so lightly, but the lump already swelling in his trousers. He could never resist sex. That is what made it seem impossible that he could have been faithful to me. I began to roll my tongue, purr, talk in that Eastern European accent that he found such a turn on: 'I vant tho sock urrr coch, plis, oh leth me …' I strained away from the bed, as though I were dying of thirst and his crotch contained the only drops of moisture. I took him in my throat, which is hard work every time. You learn how not to gag, but that doesn't mean you don't always feel like gagging. My hands were tied and it was difficult to balance. After he had come he was calm and sleepy. I kissed his flaccid penis, 'Brian, untie me.'

He did, and I got up. As I was nearing the door he grabbed me, turned me over, and pushed himself, hard again already, into my bum. That is something else I never really got used to. Then he was spent and lay panting peacefully on the bed.

'I didn't like that,' I said.

'What?' He swatted the air sleepily, as though I were a fly preventing him from rest. He was in no mood for this, 'Oh for fuck's sake Lol. You were the one … I just wanted to photograph you. You were the one. Don't be a baby. I'm tired.'

I was determined to keep him in his better mood, proud of myself for dispersing his bad one. I could make him happy. I *could* make him happy. After cleaning up his semen in the bathroom, resting my shocked bowels a bit and brushing my teeth, I went for a walk. He would be hungry when he woke up. We would have a good evening, I was determined. He was my man and that was my job and I couldn't bear the unhappiness that seemed to settle on our home for no reason.

I went to his favourite restaurant and asked for take-out. The dark, round main waiter said the chef would do it for me, though they didn't usually do take-out. He said this as though 'take-out' were a dirty word, a hideous concept, like instant coffee, and I should know better. I think he liked me though. I intrigued him: the skinny girl with the older, fatter man. The waitress who served me was the same one who always worked there and always treated me with the silence and knowing of a servant who has been solicited by her mistress's husband. I got him spinach and ham ravioli, with the sauce and pine nuts on the side. I got myself tagliatelle with broccoli. He loved their ice-cream. It was home-made Italian stuff and didn't have as much cream as normal ice-cream, which meant he didn't wake up with sinus pain. I should have got the ice-cream in tubs but instead I got it in cones and hoped to rush it back to the freezer before it melted. I paid with my debit card. There would be money going into that account in the morning from my grandfather for college books and food. I resolved to take some cash from Brian's wallet to pay myself back, or to pay my grandad back.

The journey back didn't work out as I had planned though. It was a Wednesday evening but for some reason Temple Bar was full of stag parties. Overweight men sweating drink, tops off, toppled about the street. There was hairy, tattooed flesh everywhere. It was a battle to get back to our flat. By the time I arrived one of the cones had been so crushed that I had thrown it out. There was ice-cream all down my fingers. It had made the handle of the take-out bag too soggy to hold so I had to carry it by the base.

Brian was up when I got in. He was just out of the shower and walked, wet and naked, into our kitchen, where I was washing two plates for our dinner.

'I got take-out.'

'What did you get?'

'Ravioli.'

'Oh.'

'Do you not want ravioli? I can swap with you. I got tagliatelle with broccoli.'

'I just don't feel like pasta.' He slapped his hairy belly, and it wobbled. 'Too starchy.'

There was dried melted ice-cream in the crack of my elbow. I remember that. It was pink and there was fluff stuck to it. The heat rose to my face. I was going to cry.

'Don't do this,' he said.

'I got ice-cream too. There's one in the freezer. The other one broke.'

He opened the freezer and let out a bellow. It took me a moment to realize that it was laughter, not anger this time. It could have gone either way.

'Lol! Lol! Is that what's all over your hands? Ice cream? There's some on your arm there too! My silly little Lol! I don't even like the strawberry!'

'I know. That one was for me. Yours melted. I told you ...' I was crying now.

'Lol,' he said, 'Lol, I don't need food, look, I'm a fat old sod as it is! Come here!'

I was hungry, but he began to lick my arms, my abdomen, my groin, 'Tell me I'm the only one who's ever done this.' This was something he said a lot, our sex talk.

'You're the only one who's ever ...'

'You're my girl, my best girl aren't you, Lol? You're my best girl.' I was weakening now, with his tongue inside me, hungry, ready to fall or faint: 'I'm your best ...'

Afterwards we lay in bed. My hunger had disappeared, left unattended for too long. It was after midnight by now, bedtime anyway.

He held my hands, kissed each fingertip, 'My perfect Lol. My perfect girl. Look at all your perfect, long fingers, one, two three, four five – all there!'

I felt the heat flow out of me, as though her ghost had put a hand on my head. Had I ever told him that? The way she used to kiss my fingers, keep me in bed with her all day. Maybe. It didn't make a difference; he was her incarnate regardless. He was as impenetrable as her and my stupid, eager, puppyish love was running off him, would keep running off him like water over oily feathers. He was as incurable as her, as incapable of care, or even of looking at me. When he had fallen asleep I packed a few things – I realized there wasn't much that was mine at Brian's flat – and left for my grandparent's house.

My grandmother's reverie for love came from the fact that she had found it at seventeen and it had taken her from a claustrophobic home where, as the eldest girl, she cooked and cleaned instead of going to school, and into the exciting life of my grandfather's attic room. They had survived the war together, the confusion of it, the instability of it, the fuddle and shifting of rights and wrongs, the pervading, constant fear for your own life. My grandfather was the love of her life. For my grandmother, love, for both sexes, was the ultimate goal and the ultimate achievement; without that, everything fell apart. For her, my mother's failure was in love. She had chosen the wrong man, or failed to keep him, and her bad motherhood was merely an extension of that.

Brian was not an escape for me, though. I was not running from a home, a mammy and a daddy and a set of moral codes, but searching for it. For my grandmother, freedom was the goal, an opening out from the ideas of her parents, but all I wanted was some of those rules, constraints, some idea of order, some daddy to pat my head. He was just like my mum though, a child himself and unfixable. I know all that, all the things Amelia would have said to me if I had told the truth to her.

What my grandmother said to me, the night I turned up on her doorstep with mascara on my cheeks, semen in my pants, and a backpack, was: 'Well, who is right for you then, Cassy? Who will love you my darling? You will need someone to love you.' My grandfather said nothing. We read together the next day as we used to. Two days later though, he interrupted the dinnertime quiet with, 'I have been thinking Cassandra – Pouske and I, we were actually through a lot you know? When I think on it … but I think we were all right. We could come through it, because we were together. You can come through a lot if you are together.'

I try to finish up these thoughts before I get up this morning, so that I don't carry them around with me all day. It is nearly 2 PM, though. I need to get up soon. I suddenly see my life the way an old person might see their last years: a dragging on of time after the real living has been done. No one knows whether I get up today or not. It makes no difference.

It was not gentle and good the way some love looks, but at least with Brian I was living, I was feeling things. And little details, like what we had for breakfast, mattered.

I remember the number. I call him and hang up and then I call again. This time he answers quickly.

thirteen

OISÍN WAS WALKING Helen to college. It was one of those clean, mild mornings when the fresh air itself seemed rested, happy to brush his face and fill his lungs. She was wearing kitten heels and walked awkwardly in them, making an uneven clacking that echoed on the concrete, bounced up the walls, petered off down the empty street. They were passing a strip of sex shops with blacked-out windows. This street was always empty during the day but for a few straggling drunks or the odd junkie heaped in a shuttered doorway.

Her slender, wobbling ankles made him want to carry her, scoop her in his arms the way they did in old movies, swing her around, kiss her, dance with her. Now that she had slipped the book into her bag all his feelings of irritation had faded. Once the threat had been set in motion the terror of losing her came roaring through. He had heard of men who liked to watch their wives strip for other men. This was something like that. The threat heightened his arousal, put her back out into the world of the uncertain, the world where she was only a hope, her worth set alongside that of other prospects, her value weighted by the possibility of loss.

They had settled into something now. Perhaps that's what had happened this morning, the realization that they were settling into something. She should have been making him strive harder for her. He wondered how he could explain that to her.

'Baby, I'm not that great, you know.'

She laughed, 'I know.'

'I mean don't be too nice to me baby, okay? You have to make me work harder for you. Ask me to do things for you.'

'That's bullshit. I'm not playing games with you Oisín. You should be glad I'm not playing. It's too early in the morning for that stuff. You're annoying me.'

That expression didn't seem to suit her. *Bullshit* was a word that other girls used, Dublin girls. He imagined her saying that in a group of students, all with the same peroxide hair, the same skinny jeans and boots. He would pass the group and think she was just another Dublin girl. Is that what she seemed like to everyone else? Another girl. Is that what she was? Was this all a mistake, this assumption he had made, that Helen was somehow better than any other girl?

Outside the little world of Helen-with-Oisín and Oisín-with-Helen, they didn't really know each other at all. The version of his childhood that he had given to Helen was true, but it was not the same as the equally true versions that his family had, that the lads had. The events he told her about – that time he fell off his bike, that girl he had kissed when he was eleven – the events that seemed significant when he was with Helen, meant nothing when she wasn't there.

Other events took on a different meaning in her presence. The way he had lost his virginity at thirteen, at the back of a nightclub to an older girl he had met that night, who had an older boyfriend who might beat him up, seemed sordid and pathetic when he was describing it to Helen, like something he needed to be rescued from. With the lads it was a funny story, a heroic story, even. He, the youngest, was the first to do it. The guy, the boyfriend, worked in the pharmacy, and sometimes he went in and bought johnnies off him. The lads would wait outside and watch.

He was only Oisín-with-Helen when he was with Helen. They did not go to parties together or know each other's friends. What, for example, would Helen think of the lads? What would she think of Petra? And what would he think of her friends? Who were her friends?

There was Cassandra, an old school mate who was with her the night of the gig. She was in some of his classes. Once Helen had said: 'I wish I was tall like Cassandra. Isn't Cassandra beautiful? Sometimes I don't even hear what she's saying when she speaks, I just look at her face moving. She's addictive to look at, like a kaleidoscope. Her face keeps changing as she speaks, even her eye colour changes.' He had nodded, but actually he didn't find that girl attractive at all. There was no mystery about her body, no sense of anything sacred, anything to be discovered. There would be no point in sleeping with her, nothing would be revealed, nothing conquered. It wasn't even like a normal unattractive girl, like Sharon, where he couldn't picture her boobs, where curiosity spurred him on, where there was at least a sense of revelation, achievement. With that Cassandra girl you knew exactly what her breasts were like, she practically told you. The way she talked in his 'Genre and Gender' class about the female body, as though it were over-priced merchandise, as though she knew the value of her own pussy and tits and they were only for fools. He could imagine her laughing at a man's erection, laughing and saying, 'What? For these lumps of fat?' holding her perfect breasts roughly, one in each hand, like two pieces from a box full of hundreds of the same fruit.

She reminded Oisín of one of their neighbours at home, a fat woman who had eight children. She would leave them all in the house and pop in to Oisín's mam with biscuits or a stale cake. She had been beautiful in her youth and now she put no value on beauty any more. She had let herself go, she had surrendered any notions of her body as sacred. She belched and scratched and made jokes about her weight and about how long it had been since her husband had given her a good time. That sort of thing made Oisín's mother uncomfortable. His mother didn't talk like that. Her body was always strapped in, covered. She had had an operation in Dublin last year which she never explained and they don't talk about, but Oisín saw her bra once by accident. He thought it was his laundry that was in the machine, but it was hers. One cup was padded all the way through.

His mother gave the impression of having nothing under her clothes, of having more clothes and cotton wool and clean bandages and face creams. His mother was not one of those women who forgot to flush the toilet.

That was something he didn't like; girls who forgot to flush the toilet, or girls who let you hear them piss. He had told Helen that he didn't like to hear her piss and now she flushed the toilet loudly at the same time, the same way that he did. He didn't think he'd be able to piss with her in the flat unless he was running the tap or flushing the toilet at the same time.

He had been angry with Helen last week. She hadn't wanted to make love all day and afterwards he knew why. He went into the toilet and the bowl was streaked with shocking red, a little disc of heavy blood settled at the bottom. He had planned on leaving the blood there, marching her back to his flat, standing beside the toilet bowl pointing and saying: 'What's this? What's this Helen?' forcing her to feel the shame that she should have felt for herself. He couldn't bear to leave the flat without flushing it though. He was cold with her for a few days after that.

She thought it was because they weren't having sex and made numerous blow-job offers, which he accepted without gratitude. He wanted her to ask him what was wrong so that he could tell her and watch her face cringe. How could she have forgotten something so obvious? She wouldn't let him touch her when she had her period, not even her bum, but she could forget to flush all that bright blood down the toilet?

He was glad this sense of peace was restored between them now. They were walking side by side without speaking. Sometimes these were the best times. Her heels clicked, her ankles wobbled, her little bum moved under her swinging skirt. He loved her.

The shrill ringing seemed inappropriate. It was so unexpected, so unfitting, that he didn't recognize it as his own.

'Are you not going to answer your phone?'

'Oh, didn't realize it was mine! Ha!'

It was a foreign number. Blood rushed to his ears. He felt the reality of what he had done, giving Helen the book with Petra in it and what that might mean. It was Petra calling. Of course it was. He pressed the 'silence' button, 'Missed it.'

She stopped and turned to face him. 'What's wrong?' He wanted to keep walking but she put out a hand to stop him, 'Oisín what's wrong?'

'Nothing, baby.'

'You're upset. I've upset you. Has the phone call upset you? Who is it? Is it your mum?'

'Why do you have to go on about my mam? Jesus, leave my mam out of it.'

'Out of what?'

'What's your problem? We were having a nice morning, baby, why do you have to do this?'

She turned and kept walking. He walked beside her. When they reached college he realized that his face was sore from screwing up his brow so much. Their neighbours at home, a nice old couple, used to mind him sometimes while his mam cleaned the house. They called him a worry wart because he frowned so much as a child. His mother didn't like the familiar tone the neighbours took.

'Kay. Well, thanks for walking me.'

The panic was still pumping through his ears. He clung to Helen's waist. The warm, comforting rush of all those sex hormones filled his pelvis.

'Hey. I love you. You know that?'

'Why do you say that in a Hollywood accent?'

He grabbed her and thrust his tongue down her throat, squeezing her bum, concentrating on the feeling of her breasts squashed to his chest, her lips, trying to savour the closeness of her body and measure the value of it – did he want this? How much? He kissed her for so long that he thought he felt her pulling away from him. He imagined her opening her eyes as he kissed her, looking at her watch. He stopped and smiled, kissed her nose.

'I'm just grumpy. I'm a grump. My neighbours at home used to call me a worry wart because I frowned so much!'

His phone began to vibrate in his pocket. Could she hear it? He flicked the tangled ringlets back off each shoulder, took her face in his hands and looked at her with all the love he could muster. Her eyes were very blue today. It was the necklace she wore: aquamarine, it brought out the colour. 'We cool?' She nodded. He kissed her again, 'God you look so hot, baby. See you later.' He squeezed her bum ceremoniously, a half-joke. She walked towards the Arts Block.

'I'm finished at three. Meet you in mine?'

'Yep. You're a hotty, you know that?'

He was doing it again, that thing Helen called his 'Hollywood accent': a slight lisping of the Ts, 'hoddy' instead of 'hotty'. He couldn't help it sometimes. When he was younger he wanted to be Marlon Brando. He had practised his voice in front of the mirror and incorporated it into his own speech. He had hoped that the accent would seamlessly merge with his own and he wouldn't be able to help speaking like that. Then he would remind people inexplicably of Marlon Brando, they would say, 'Gee, you remind me of someone … Marlon Brando! Dunno what it is about you …' That's what had happened, the accent had become part of him, it manifested itself particularly when he was self-conscious or flirting. No one ever said he was like Marlon Brando though.

Helen turned, grinned and rolled her eyes, spun around on one heel and walked slowly away. He watched her little bum wiggle under the skirt.

He waited until he was out of Front Arch before looking at his phone. Three missed calls. That must be Petra. He was on his way to a call shop when it rang again. She didn't say anything. For about a minute all he could hear were her ugly sobs. He was afraid to say her name in case it was someone else, in case, impossibly, it was Helen.

'Em. Are you okay?'

'*Ushin*? It's Petra.'

'Petra. Are you okay?'

'Oh I am very glad that you answered Ushin. I am very disappointed. I …' She began to cry again. It was a deep, messy, coughing cry. He imagined snot.

'What's the matter Petra? I'm sorry I haven't had time to reply to your letter – '

'You have been very busy at the Uni, I know. I anderstand. I …'

'What's wrong?'

'The flights. They are more expensive. I have not enough money. The prices go up when you wait too long … I have not saved enough you know? I have been warking only two days per week at the ice-cream café …'

Here was Oisín's escape. The little dilemma was cleaning itself up nicely now, at least for the moment. She couldn't come.

No problem. No excuses for Helen. He could explain that photo somehow, undo the mad act he had committed that morning, give himself more time with Helen. He thought of Helen kissing him this morning on the forehead like a mother and suddenly that gesture that so irritated him at the time took on a sacred quality. Who else would kiss him like that, as though she knew him and loved him anyway? He loved her. He would retrieve her, it would be okay. The image of her walking away, the lovely little round bum, was still fresh. It was all his, that perfect curve under the skirt, beneath her panties. He felt an urgent need to feel her skin again. With Petra still heaving on the phone, he glanced back down Dame Street to College Green at the huge clock above Front Arch. Four hours and forty-five minutes. Then he'd be making love to Helen again.

Why then, even as he was thinking what a relief it was that Petra wouldn't be coming, what a lucky escape it was, did he say it? Maybe it was the noisy crying. It was like an attack, the harsh 'huh huh huh', the hysterics invading this soft morning. He wanted it to stop. He saw no other way back to conversation and off the phone. Maybe it was because he wanted to be a nice guy.

'How much more is the ticket?'

'One hundred euro and four, you know, I have not the money saved ... I miss you so much, hüny.'

There it was again, that inappropriate word, 'honey', pronounced like something heavy and smothering. God, he wanted to hang up.

'Text me your bank details. I'll put it through.'

fourteen

I AM MEETING Brian for coffee this afternoon. I don't even play that game where I pretend to try to persuade myself otherwise. What else will I do with my afternoon?

When I see him sitting on a plush black sofa waiting for me all I feel is shock: the small shock of recognition. This is the kind of quiet hotel café where people conduct short business meetings and I feel out of place.

'Hi.'

'Hi, Cassandra.' He kisses me on the cheek like an associate, 'I was here early. I ordered a drink. Would you like one?'

'Yeah. Okay.' Then I remember what a bad idea that might be, 'Just a coffee actually.'

'Which? A drink or a coffee or both? You can have both.'

'A coffee.'

'You're sure you're not going to change your mind about that? I don't mind either way but it's just if you keep changing your mind I don't know what to order –'

'Yeah. A coffee.'

'You really haven't changed have you? First you want a drink and now you want a coffee. I just don't want to order one thing and then have to cancel when you change your mind.'

'A coffee is fine.'

He orders me a double espresso in a large cup with a jug of hot water and a jug of cold milk on the side. I had forgotten about that. That is what I always ordered when we went out, my quirk, a little feature of my protectively fashioned self.

At first, before I began to build my circle of brunch friends, I was looked at by them. It wasn't the men, they weren't that interested. It was the women. Older women – other models or artists at opening nights and launches – would whisper, 'That's her. You think she's really over eighteen? Do you think she's pretty?'

They were divided on whether I was the fool being taken advantage of, or I was using him to get ahead – as though that was the kind of world we lived in, as though I'd be with him if I could have helped myself, as though art or modelling were the kind of worlds I wanted that badly to get ahead in. Those were women I would have liked to be friends with. I was very lonely then. I would have liked to rest my head on those women's shoulders and cry and tell them: 'No, I'm a child. I don't even like coffee.'

One night we were at the theatre. Brian knew the set designer and a lot of the actors. There was a lock-in at the theatre bar. I had seen her in the audience: a tiny little woman with black hair and a black dress and ankles a man could snap with his fingers. I kept my eye on her, and afterwards she moved like a fairy between all the actors. She knew them all and seemed hungry for acknowledgment. She was smoking through a cigarette holder. The way she turned her delicate wrists filled me with nostalgia. I shadowed her all night like a girl with a crush. I wanted her to see me, to like my dress, to look at me and say, 'I understand just how you feel,' to call me 'baby' and tell me I was beautiful. When at last she looked at me, her gaze skimmed my narrow frame. She turned to the woman beside her. 'Jesus, do kids these days really think that's sexy? Anorexic chic? I would have thought Brian Durcan had more taste …' I cried in the toilet. It was as though my mother's ghost had walked in through the walls and hit me in the mouth, or worse, she hadn't bothered to hit me, she had looked at me and spat in my face and gone back to bed.

Brian is looking at my lips. He has put on weight. His arms have softened. His eyes are bloodshot. I could never tell whether he was good-looking or not. It was all about the pheromones and the role-play with us. It was all about what I could be for him, how young I could feel.

He licks his own lips before he speaks, 'So what's been going on with you?'

Suddenly I am the one being looked at. Suddenly he is utterly exempt from any scrutiny. What's been going on with me? What have I been doing? How do I account for the last two years? How do I account for ending up back here with him, with a knife still twisting my heart and my bowels, slashing at my knees?

'College. I've been in college. Doing some modelling for money … My grandad died last week.'

I realize suddenly how true that is. I had hardly acknowledged it. The rhythm of my life hasn't even stuttered. It's the first time I've said it. I haven't even mentioned it to Helen. I didn't even say it to that counsellor with the manicured nails.

'Oh, I'm sorry.'

'No it's fine actually. He got sick a long time ago, just after you and I broke up. He was in hospital for nearly two years. On machines. He couldn't speak or eat or recognize us or anything.

'I'm surprised at how easily I'm taking it, actually. Maybe I never really loved him after all! Ha!'

I have no idea why I'm laughing. It's not at all funny. I can't stop. The laugh isn't mine. It's the sort of laugh other women have, older, phonier women. He laughs too, but *at* me. He knows me too well. He knows how weak I feel suddenly, how lost. 'You look good Cassy.' I laugh again. I sound bitter. He shrugs tolerantly at my belligerence, licks his lips again.

'I got a room upstairs. I'd like if we could talk more privately, you know? I feel exposed here.'

It didn't occur to me that he would do this. Not so quickly or so openly. How naive of me. That's why we've met in a hotel. Of course.

The coffee churns my stomach and shoots around my bowels almost instantly. I use the bathroom before going upstairs. I take my time, use a 'feminine freshness' wipe, check my face in the mirror.

There is a vending machine beside the hand-dryer where you can get condoms or sanitary towels or disposable toothbrushes with miniature toothpaste. I can assume he's carrying a condom. I put two euro into the slot and press the button for the 'minty fresh kit'. The little cellophane package lands in the delivery drawer like a miracle. I'm surprised it worked. The mini-toothpaste is so cute that I decide to keep the tiny tube as a souvenir. The bristles of the toothbrush scratch my gums, but I am grateful for the minty freshness. This is humiliating enough without having coffee breath.

Upstairs we try to make it like it was before, but it feels all wrong and I cry and he clasps my face into his neck and kisses my hair and continues pumping. I was wrong; he doesn't have a condom. I wonder if he is still living with that actress, whether he does the same things with her, and whether the inside of a black girl is pink like me, or darker.

He turns me over and I look at the wall, his hands gripping either side of my buttocks. I do not recognize his grunts. This is not the way I remember it. The wallpaper is the colour of butter with blue *fleur-de-lys* printed on it. I have decided not to let him come inside me, because the morning-after pill makes me very sick for weeks and I have an essay due in a fortnight. The decision should make me feel modern and empowered. In the fifties women had no such choices, but I don't feel like a member of some sisterhood. I have never felt more alone. That's another cliché: lonely whilst engaging in one of life's most intimate acts. I am ashamed of myself.

I haven't been able to think about my grandfather's death since it happened, but now I can't help it. My grandmother opening the door to me, her old body lit with grief. 'We were trying to contact you, Cassandra. We couldn't contact you.' She said my name over and over, as though I were the only one who understood, as though I were the only one who could bring him back. She was wrong on both counts.

I couldn't conceive of the sort of grief that poured from her. She clung to me and wept loudly, with no shame. How, at her age, did she have the energy for such grief? How, after so much loss, did she have the courage to rage like that? How on earth could she possibly still believe that life should be fair? The effort it must take to love like that, all these years, on and on – how is that possible? She roared in my ear and I had an image of her as a girl, giving birth to each of her lost babies, a roar full of power and submission. I thought of her in prison, dividing the newspaper-toilet-paper between her fellow inmates, her jaw clenched against the stench, waiting patiently to be acquitted, confident – even then, amongst all that chaos – that truth meant something. Her discovering my mother's body in that bed while I still stood staring at the window. The silence. The scream that never came. The scene she never made. And her hands that night, younger then, shaking a little, passing me my hot chocolate and saying, 'Life can be very difficult', as though that fact were acceptable.

That was a misunderstanding on my part. She never accepted it. I knew that when I heard her cry for my grandfather. She didn't say 'No no no.' she knew by now that those words couldn't change anything. She must have believed, stupidly, that in the end there would be peace for her, and happiness. As she clung to me I suddenly felt how small she had become. She had always seemed to me like a large woman, sturdy, with well-set hips, someone who could lift me in her arms even now. She clung to me and wailed and shook and I could feel the ribs in her back and I was proud of her for having the courage to rage. I had never felt such love. For that reason I wanted her to cry in my arms forever.

When I can't stand it any more I pull away and finish him off with my mouth. The taste of my own pussy is sweet and tangy like melon – then I open up my throat and take him deep; tongue all over his balls the way he used to like it.

fifteen

YOU ARE GLAD your strange mood has cleared. Silly Helen, worried about your lips thinning, your pelvis loosening. How could you worry about things like that when you are loved? Isn't this what youth is for?

You're a hotty. The way he says it, so silly, so boyish. The demands he makes are so simple. Be pretty and good-humoured. That's all it takes to be loved. It floods you with warmth. You grin, spin around on a heel, look back over your shoulder at him. You see yourself now like a slow shot from a film: your face and hair lit white by the morning sunlight, your eyes, the round of your bum – *your perfect little ass*, that's what he calls it – visible under the frivolous pink skirt, and his desire, the desire of the audience, waiting for you as you skip away to your lecture.

'Body *and* brains,' Oisín would say, 'What a fox!' Going to college is a big deal where he comes from. They think it's for clever people.

You are a little late for the lecture as it is but you pick up a latte in the Arts Block anyway. No one notices if you are late for these lectures. It's a large lecture hall.

The lecturer is young and good-looking and cocky. By the time you arrive there is a projection already on the wall: THINKING OUTSIDE THE BOX. There it is: that image of yourself as light and beautiful tripped up already, that sense of failure gripping you by the throat. He is given, this lecturer, to setting the whole class a psychological test that they take themselves, and then telling them what the result means about them. You invariably come out as small-minded, conformist, stupid, and always a typical product of a typical middle-class youth. You are trying to enter quietly. The door thuds closed, muted by that felt stuff that lines the walls. Two heads turn and then face back to the projection. You are looked at and ignored at the same time, and you feel how silly you must look, Helen, in this short diaphanous skirt, like the clothes of a fairy, or someone beautiful.

You want Oisín, who doesn't care if you are stupid or whether you think outside the box, who likes you in frilly things, who thinks you are wacky because you take cinnamon in your latte, and prefer your pancakes with just butter, or pull down his jocks in an alley and give him a blow job right there. As soon as you are with him again you won't care about things like this. 'You're a loco lady!' he will say, crossing his eyes and spinning a finger beside his temple, 'Can't think outside the box, eh? We'll have to do something about that. I have just the cure …'

The exercise has already been done and the lecturer is giving the result. It is literally about thinking outside the box. There are nine dots beneath the lettering, making up a rectangle. They form a box. That's what you immediately think of, a box, because that's one of the words on the wall. The task was to connect all the dots by drawing four straight lines and never taking the pencil off the page. The lecturer shows the class what should have been done: it's a triangle with a line through the middle. It is very easy to do, but only by going outside the confines of the nine dots, only by ceasing to think of the rectangle as central, by not assuming certain rules. The 'box' is not a box at all; the space around it is a free-for-all. He asks how many students got it right, and four of them lift their hands.

A new projection is put up. You take this opportunity, while the lecturer is standing admiring his slide, to sit down quickly. Your bare legs seem inappropriate suddenly. You're not even wearing tights. You sit with your knees slightly apart and feel how near to naked you are.

The lecture is hard to follow. It's about how there are always rules created by society, how language shapes our thoughts and we cannot think beyond language, how we are products of this language, even our morality, even our rebellion. You are not sure how it all fits together, or how it fits with the box exercise. Perhaps it is just for his own amusement that the lecturer gives you those exercises.

You thought this was a psychology lecture, but the word 'postmodern' keeps coming up, 'the postmodern era' and 'Derrida'. They are phrases from your critical theory class, from the English course. Derrida? You understand the theories of all these people, once you can get over the bad translations, Cassandra says, they're really not that complicated. But you can never remember who thought what. Wasn't Saussure the one with all that language-creates-meaning stuff? *Derrida and différance.* What does that mean again? Usually you wouldn't bother trying to follow the lecture. You would take notes and figure it out later, or ask Cassandra, but you have vowed to make more of an effort in college from now on. You glance at the foolscap of the boy beside you because he's writing fervently and you assume he's following this, but he is actually drawing eyes all over the page. If you can just figure out what Derrida is about you'll be back on track. There's that book Oisín lent you to help with the essay. The boy sees you slip it out of your bag, and snorts disparagingly. It is a shameful thing to have that book, *A Very Short Introduction to Critical Theory*. It is akin to being caught with York Notes in your bag. *A Dummies Guide to University*.

You open it on your desk, scanning the index for Derrida's name. Didn't he have a first name, this Derrida?

'Excuse me,' the lecturer is thrilled. He has been expecting this. He is ready to show his authority.

'Please don't read a book during a lecture. It's rude. It's insulting. If you find me that uninteresting you can leave.'

He doesn't pause long enough for you to explain. He goes on and on and you gape at him. You can feel your face reddening. The boy beside you has stopped drawing eyes. He is staring ahead so as not to embarrass you any further. You are grateful for that. Your eyes are stinging but the lecturer goes on: '... I don't take a roll call so you don't need to come unless you are interested in listening. I would like if you left now.'

The lack of any name adds to the humiliation. He doesn't know your name, of course, there are too many of you and it is not that sort of lecture, but it humiliates you, that implication that you are not Helen, but *you*. You plural and singular. 'You' means nothing. All it means is 'Not me'.

You expect him to carry on with the lecture now, but he doesn't. He keeps looking at you. The only escape from his gaze is to get up and leave. You don't bother packing your bag, you just tuck the foolscap and the book under your arm and grab it by the handle. When you stand up you can feel the exposure of your knees again. As you leave he resumes the lecture.

Outside the door you stick in your earphones and head straight for your room. When you are wearing your earphones you don't meet the eyes of the people you pass. Cassandra says it's anti-social, but it's a way of making the overcrowding bearable, a way of creating invisible space.

You don't know what you feel like listening to so you select 'shuffle' and listen to whatever the iPod chooses to play.

Oh girl look at yourself what have you done? What have you become? – a woman's voice, singing high, excited and free, percussions bashing in the background and an electric guitar. It's The Cardigans. You don't remember downloading that. The lyrics seem quite fitting to your current disgrace.

You will resist the temptation to call Oisín and meet him early. He is already sure that you are too eager. What was it he said yesterday? Something irritating. You were going down on him. You're very good at it now. You said, 'God, baby I love you, I love your perfect fat cock,' partly because it was true, and partly because you have heard more than once that what men really want is for their penis to be idolized, and because the words 'fat', 'hot' and 'big' all have the effect of boosting his arousal instantly. He bent down like a benevolent lord, his face contorted by pleasure and pity, saddened by some mortal's foolishness: 'Save some love for yourself, baby.'

Save some love for yourself? You laughed at him but now you wish you had stood up off your knees and looked at him straight, so that he could see who you really were, not a fool besotted with him.

'Oisín,' you should have said, 'please don't speak to me like that, as though I am a child. It's not as though I don't have choices. I choose to love you. To love: that is worth something to me. You make your choices, I'll make mine.'

Why didn't you say that? He doesn't see that part of you, the part that is strong and open-eyed. Or is it really there, that part? Maybe it's just a fantasy of yours, that noble Helen, seizing life, throwing herself into the fire of love. Perhaps you are just what he sees, Helen.

You go back to your room and get into bed with *A Very Short Introduction To Critical Theory*. You will find out who Derrida was; you will not be disheartened.

You open it right on the page and a shock of adrenaline whooshes through you. It's you and Oisín: you on top – his favourite position – your hands on his torso, your neck arched back in pleasure, and his beloved abdomen, the little curls on his chest and around his pubis, one strong arm in frame, a hand reaching for your breast. You can remember and anticipate that touch, warm, the way it makes you melt into sex. Your breasts are impressive, much better than you thought. In the darkness of the photo the nipples look brown. When did he take that? How did you not know? It was a morning. There is a crack of light bursting between the flimsy curtains, sending a thick yellow beam at the lens, cutting off your face with an explosion of light, splattering your shoulders with blue blotches. It was taken in his room. He should have told you he wanted a picture and not taken it in secret. You are glad there is some evidence of your youth. You follow the curve of your waist, your body stretched upwards as though in celebration, a swell in your thin abdomen where he is inside you, your labia.

It's only then that you realize it is not your body. The vagina in the photo is waxed or shaven to some strange design. Bald with a little patch of hair like a Hitler moustache, the bare lips squashed outwards. There is a letter with the photo, written on pink paper and folded four times.

sixteen

WHEN I get back to college I need company. I want the feeling of coming home. I can still taste Brian and my own cunt. I sit at the kitchen table and watch the fish. They are each floating at either edge of the bowl, releasing a bubble every now and then, darting suddenly, only to rest some more beneath the surface of the water, and push out another bubble or two. I don't rinse my mouth.

Helen's door isn't locked. Her room is empty.

I lie on her bed which smells of sex and of Helen's perfume and that grease she uses to separate her curls.

Her room has a dressing table, which mine doesn't have. I look in her mirror and see how old I am now, at the age of twenty-one, and I realize that it's too late to ever be young, and too late for me ever to get it right. I could spend my life untangling the past, unearthing the dead, moment by moment, but I will never find my way back to the start. Time will keep chugging ahead while I rummage in memory, and I will get older and older. On the dressing table there's a letter in an envelope, addressed but not stamped. A German name – Petra – and a German address. I didn't know she had a friend in Germany. The envelope has not been properly sealed.

Helen's handwriting is perpendicular and unmistakably feminine with orbicular vowels and accurately placed dots. She wrote the letter with slow deliberation. What I don't understand about the letter is the affection she has for the other woman, the sisterhood she has found in being fucked by the same man.

'I know you didn't know about me,' she wrote, 'I didn't know about you either. I am writing to you because I know you will understand. You love him too, so I know you can understand ...'

Helen is garrulous sometimes. I can't let her post this. I could tell her that I found a letter on her dressing-table, addressed and enveloped, that I posted it for her. I could replace it with a sheet of blank foolscap, folded four times, and seal it so that she won't know.

When Oisín comes in I'm still on Helen's bed. He gets a fright when he sees me. I intimidate him. From the first time we were introduced I have known by his eyes and the way he takes his hands off Helen when I enter a room, that he is frightened of me. He glances at my nails. I had them done after meeting Brian. It was just a fancy because I didn't want to go home yet. I told the girl to do whatever she liked. They are acrylic. Long, stupid-looking red things glued on in a nail bar. She drew Asian-style flowers on two of them with silver. The girl told me off for not using a cuticle cream, gave me a loyalty card and told me to come back in five weeks.

'I had them done.'

'Oh right. Do you know where Helen is?'

'She has class till three. You can wait for her in my room if you like. How did you get in?'

'Cahill was coming in.'

'How are you, Oisín? We never talk ...'

What Helen does not know, is how to see into people. I can read the way they tick. I know that what this boy wants, and what he thinks he wants, are two different things. What he thinks he wants is a virgin with angel curls, shocked by his virility, desperately passive, but what they want, boys like this, is for someone to smack them like their mammy never did. What they want, really, is leather trousers and a whip and someone to dress them down.

He deliberates a little in Helen's room before pushing my door, peering in and entering softly like a frightened puppy. Once I have him in my room I don't bother with conversation any more. I press my new fake nails into his scalp, and nip his ear. Then I trace patterns on his back with them, slowly, lightly then harder, as though I want to pierce the skin. I lie him down and kneel on both shoulders and pull my thong to one side and tell him to push his tongue inside while I run my fingers from the base of his cock over the top, parting my fingers to simulate virgin pussy, and down the shaft again. The trick is to turn your hands around the shaft as you do it. Constant motion in two directions. That's the trick. I take it down my throat once, just to show him I can deep-throat, gently tugging his balls, massaging the ridge behind. A lot of men don't know that. It was Paul who told me. A lot of straight men don't know the pleasure to be had from that line that runs from balls to asshole.

Then I stop. I rest my lips on the top and flick my tongue and purr, so he groans for me to take it and I won't.

I spin around so I am straddling him, my neat, clipped pussy hovering above the quivering knob-end, and watch him writhing there, lips wet, wincing with arousal. I won't let him yet. I wait till

I'm about to come. I make him watch me touch myself but I don't let his hands near his own red, pulsing cock. Every time he tries I grab his wrists and pin him, licking his nipples, tweaking them with my teeth, rubbing my cunt along the shaft until he's whimpering with the pathetic helplessness of his own arousal.

This is not like fucking Helen. It is not like fucking the sweet, stupid German girl. He doesn't feel powerful now.

'Oh, Jesus,' I say, husky-voiced now, a voice Brian liked: Marilyn Monroe meets Medusa. 'It's so fucking huge and fat. I bet you'd love to push it inside my tight little pussy ... I bet I know what you'd love more. I bet you'd love to tear into my ass with it.' I take the pulsing tip and press it to my asshole so he thinks I'll let him. He relaxes into the bed with relief and breathes out. 'Thank you!'

I push on it just enough to give him a taste, make him think I'm going to sit right down on it, as though I'd let him impale me. Then I shake my head slowly and smile at him in a way that draws a high, wavering moan out of him. I touch my own nipples and pretend to enjoy it. Then I take it in for less than a second, squeezing my pussy around it, and slip a finger into his anus. I know just the spot. I massage it lightly. The mouth drops open. Round eyes. He didn't know he had that there, that bundle of nerves. He comes in one long, shuddering anticlimax. He thinks he knows what it's like to be fucked now. He has no idea.

As he pulls on his trousers he says quietly: 'Hey. You're the girl in the A|wear catalogue, aren't you? You'd hardly recognize you. The hair is different.'

It's only afterwards, in the shower, that I realize how much cum there was. He is younger than Brian, I suppose younger men have more. It glugs out in three lots, dribbling down my leg to the ankle, and suddenly I realize that I have not won. Despite my intentions, which were to violate him, I feel violated.

seventeen

OISÍN HAD pulled it off after all. He had arrived at hers early, slipping in with one of her housemates. By the time she returned his encounter with Cassandra was over and he was sitting on Helen's bed.

Helen didn't greet him when she came in. She didn't kiss him. As soon as she saw him she glanced at her dressing-table where there was a mirror. He liked this little vanity in her; that she cared how she looked for him. Then – it was something about the way she parted her lips and gulped a breath – for a flash he thought she knew what had happened in Cassandra's room, for a moment he thought she just knew. People can know things. It happened. He knew it did because once he and Helen had dreamt the same dream at the same time. He had woken up to tell it to her and she had told it to him. Women could be so close, Helen and Cassandra had known each other for so long … what if all the while it was happening she knew? What if she could just feel it?

He hadn't had time to think about it himself. It had happened to him. She had done it: Cassandra. He hadn't planned it. He hadn't wanted it. He felt completely uninvolved in the crime.

Helen fiddled with the things on the dressing-table, some pens and foolscap, and put on some bright pink lipstick, which somehow made her upper lip look as though it were shadowed with a faint moustache. She sat down beside him on the bed, and smiled. He touched her waist with one hand and with the other he pulled her closer, breathing her sweet, milky smell, pushing her teeth apart with his tongue. He kicked the door closed. When he parted her legs she kissed his earlobe and whispered, 'Make love to me, Oisín.' With every thrust she used her shins to push him more inside her. He could feel the little balls of her heels pressing his buttocks. He fucked her with all the intensity of the shock, the humiliation of being fucked by Cassandra. He fucked her as though to cleanse himself of the monstrous bitch by fucking something beautiful, sacred, loving.

Afterwards, when Helen had gone to make sandwiches, he had rustled quickly in her knapsack, found the book and removed the photo. He was amazed at how simple the damage control was, how he had failed, despite himself, to rupture their love.

In the calm aftermath of sex, the photo, because it had lost its only power to arouse him, seemed ludicrous. It seemed ludicrous that she would even have been jealous had she found it. Sex itself seemed a ludicrous thing to do with anyone but his girlfriend, who loved him. That swell under the skin, the shaven flesh of those lips. He had always heard that Germans were into hairy muffs, but maybe Petra had heard that Irish boys weren't. He would have to deal with Petra. He would not let some fuck-buddy mess this up for him. Just because she thought he owed her, just because he had taken her precious virginity.

He booked a special-offer weekend break at The Radisson in Galway. Petra would be pleased with that. He rang and told her as though it was a surprise he had been planning for a long time.

He told Helen that he was having a lads' weekend in Galway. She frowned but he kissed her and smiled, 'Baby don't be silly. Lots of the lads have girlfriends. It's not that type of lads' weekend!'

The only danger was that Petra wasn't able to transfer the flights to Galway. He met her at Dublin airport. Of course she wanted to go back to his flat. She loved his flat. 'It is so *Ushin*. Exactly the home you should have. I can see you in everything here.' Having her in his flat though, where Helen slept so often, would have been a betrayal. He felt he would be caught that way. Petra would leave some sign of herself, perfume, or a German condom wrapper or something. Galway was different. Galway was none of Helen's business. They took the bus from the airport to the Bus Éireann station and from there to Galway. Altogether the journey took them three hours. She complained of needing to piss the whole way. She didn't say 'piss' though, she said 'pee pee', which repulsed him.

Travelling always made him restless. He was horny by the time they got there, which was just as well. He had almost forgotten the pleasure there was in fucking someone he hardly knew: the wonderful isolation that there was in it; the privacy of his own arousal. He had no idea what Petra was feeling and he didn't care. All the same it occurred to him as he removed the brand-new underwear – transparent pink bra and thong, still smelling of shop – that Petra might not have had sex since he last boned her. That he was her first and only.

The room was spacious and clean with a wide bed. The weekend package had cost him seven hundred euro, including meals. At reception he had tried to look as though he was used to this sort of thing. He had leaned against the marble reception desk, his arms folded beside a bowl of limes. He felt like a phony. He was probably doing something wrong. The receptionist was a hotty from Eastern Europe. Her hair was unnaturally white-blonde and her eyes were a little bloodshot from trauma or exhaustion. The hair was eerie. It was cut to her jaw, completely straight, with a fringe that boxed her face like a gift. She was like the sexy mad girl in a movie.

'Thank you very much.' His voice came out all wrong. It was the voice of Marlon Brando again, deep and mumbly. He smiled and winked as he took the room key, smacking a five-euro note onto the reception desk. The receptionist raised her eyebrows and grinned, but she wasn't flirting, he could see that. She was laughing at him.

As he went up with Petra in the glass elevator he watched the foyer shrink away; the fountain in the middle, the leather couches where couples lounged and read the paper, the vast, clean marble floor.

After sex with Petra he took a long, powerful shower. There were four towels each in the bathroom, a shower head the size of a beach ball and a deep, broad bath. A sign said to leave the towels on the floor if they had been used and needed to be cleaned. He took an uncomfortable pleasure in doing this. Imagine doing that at home, expecting his mother to bend down and pick them up. He never would. He looked at himself in the mirrors. There were two, a normal mirror and then a smaller, magnifying one on the end of an extendable wire. He hated the sight of himself with wet hair. It made him look weedy. 'I'm a good guy,' he thought, 'I'm a good son. I'm nice to my mam. I'm good to my girl. Galway is none of her business.'

There were two soft porn channels in the hotel room that you had to pay for. There was a thirty-second clip before the sign went up asking that they call reception and give their credit card details, but Oisín and Petra flicked between the stations for half an hour, taking in the thirty second clips. One channel was of a man wearing a devil mask entering two different women in turn, one blonde and one dark. They were both dressed in lacy slips – one white and one red – and tied with ropes to a church altar.

The other channel was tamer again, a man lying down, a woman kneeling on top with her curly black pussy in his face. He was licking and they were both groaning. The camera took in every angle. Petra had never seen porn before so she giggled and wanted to play out the scenes, but Oisín didn't like girls sitting on his face.

'Do you ever watch pornography?'

'When I was younger.'

A massage each was part of the package he had bought. Oisín gave his voucher to Petra and she exchanged it for some other treatment. While Petra was down in the spa he rang Helen. He missed her, he said, but he was having a great time with the lads. Her voice sounded as though she might burst into tears so he got off the phone as quickly as he could. She loved him too much; he was beginning to feel that. She was giving him too much.

The weekend went off quite well, even though the weather was bad. They walked on the cold beach and ate nice meals in the hotel restaurant and Petra told him about herself. 'Me, I do not think money is important. One must do what makes one happy in life. My *Vati* keeps a job he hates. All for money ... Me, I prefer paper packaging to plastic, you know, it is easier to recycle ... Me, I think travel is so important for the mind, you know? The piple who do not travel are ignorant, you know? I can see that from the piple at in my Uni.'

He went with Petra to the airport on Sunday night. She kissed him and said, 'Oh I will miss you hüny. Dis was perfect.' He would have to clear things up before he saw her again, or next time she came over she'd be wearing a wedding dress. He'd compose a funny email to the lads about her: the hot-but-scary German girl who was big into porn.

The journey from the airport to Helen's house was too long. He had never missed her more. It seemed impossible that he would really see her soon, touch her. She seemed like a fantasy. He had showered before they left the hotel room so that he wouldn't smell like perfume or like sex. They texted each other for the whole bus ride from the airport.

'U on ur way?'

'Yeah can't wait 2 c ur cutie face.'

'U want dinner? Got steak.'

'Wow i missed u baby!'

She had bought fillet steaks and pressed chili and cracked black pepper into them. They were frying in butter by the time he got up the stairs, the smell filling the tiny kitchen. There were roast potatoes as well, with salt scrunched over them, and fried onions with sage, and broccoli, which she made him eat because she said it was full of antioxidants. She said this cautiously, and he knew she was thinking of cancer and his mother.

He wanted to make love to her as soon as he saw her, but he was afraid he wouldn't have enough cum after the weekend, and she would know. Anyway it made it all the sweeter to prolong it, to sit eating the fortifying steak and anticipating her naked skin, her taste, that thing she did with her tongue as she went down on him. She had bought dessert, expensive stuff from Marks & Spencer. He was full, and anyway he couldn't hold out any longer. He pulled her pelvis towards him and whatever it was that their bodies did to each other happened again: a magnetism, a feeling like falling into something wonderful, sinking into each other, fainting and running at the same time. He could feel her body become softer, more malleable. It was the effect he had on her. Her pupils widened. He began to open the belt on her jeans, and she flinched. He touched her chin.

'What's wrong, baby?' She didn't answer. Her eyes were wide and moist.

'Are you worried about Galway baby? The lads are good guys. We didn't do anything dirty you know. We met some girls but I said, why eat hamburgers when you can have steak at home?'

She smiled but still she wouldn't look at him. All he could do was keep kissing her and then inching the belt of the jeans open slowly. At first it irritated him, but then he began to enjoy the game. It was like seducing her for the first time again. She wanted it, of course she did, he could tell – he could almost smell the wetness of her pussy – but she was shy for some reason. It made sex an achievement and he liked that. He pulled her to him and growled in her ear: 'Oh baby, you're so fucking hot do you know that? Don't do this to me, I missed you so much.' He was starting to sweat. The intensity of his own arousal, his own urgency, surprised him.

'I love you, Oisín.'

That was all she said, over and over in a high, trembling voice. He got her into her bedroom and managed at last to pull her T-shirt off. Down on his knee he pulled down her jeans. He didn't particularly fancy going down on her – he was too tired – but it looked like he would have to work for this one. He slid a hand over her taut abdomen, over the familiar curve of her perfect ass. The contours sent a wave of crippling pleasure over him. His temples were throbbing. As he reached her panties she held his hand firmly, stopping him from taking them off. 'Oisín.' She put the other hand up to his face and made him look at her. 'Look at me. I love you. Do you understand?' He nodded. He was going to blow in his jocks if she didn't let him at her soon.

'Baby, I love you too, you know that. I want to make you feel nice baby, please.'

She was wearing new underwear. White and lacy with little pink strawberries embroidered on them. The bra made her breasts look bigger than usual and the panties were the type he liked: little shorts with the curve of the bum peeking out.

He looked up at her and smiled, 'Are these for me?'

'It's all for you baby.'

He used one finger to pull them down. He loved this moment, the moment when he saw her pussy, waiting for him. But it was different. There was a little patch of hair and then bare lips. They looked long and dangly. They were red. There were small scabs along the more delicate parts and a few lone hairs here and there that were too short for the wax to take. It reminded him of a pubescent beard with pimples. 'Baby what happened?' She didn't answer. He touched the tender sores, pulled back the lips and saw that the damage was inside as well. She stood facing ahead with her eyes shut, her hands in his hair.

eighteen

I WATCH the streets rolling by, empty except for an Asian man with a loudly whirring pavement polisher, an immigrant hired by the state to pick up chewing gum and crisp packets, and wash the footprints off the brickwork. He must hate this country.

I catch my reflection in the wing mirror of the taxi and wonder why anyone would pay to let them take pictures of this jaded face.

The driver is full of chat but it's too early. I feel ill. I had a stale croissant for breakfast and some strong coffee and they're both sitting stagnant in my tummy. I'm too tired to digest them.

I think it's imprudent to give a model a call time of 5 AM. It decreases her chances of looking attractive. It wastes money on concealer.

I say this to the make-up artist, who is hungover and old-school camp. This kind of man makes me anxious to impress. I want him to like me because if he doesn't he will talk about how ugly I am with the other models. He will make me feel like shit. If he really doesn't like me he will make me look like shit too. I have ten minutes to struggle against the early morning crankiness and build up a rapport. Self-deprecation is usually the way to go, or at least the only thing that has ever worked for me. I don't know how to make friends at a shoot. It is a theatre of insecurity in here – the men who hate their gayness so much they parody themselves, hanging their hands as though their wrists are broken; the girls whose bodies are betraying them moment by moment, all the time wrinkling, growing dryer, greyer, fatter. In the make-up chair I look at my reflection mockingly. 'Lots of Touche Éclat please!'

Touche Éclat is a miracle concealer thing, particularly useful for photography. All the make-up artists I've met claim it as their secret. It deflects the light so that if you put it under your eyes and on your cheeks everything glows and the flaws are blurred. That is what most beauty products are; an attempt to deflect and conceal. The word 'enhance' is nonsense.

The make-up artist rolls his eyes and opens his mouth in mock-horror. 'Oh sweetie!' The smell of alcohol from him is enough to make my head throb like a drum. His voice is so loud, so high. His eyes are dancing and his skin is ruddy like a child's. 'No, no, no! Who told you to use Touche Éclat? It is really so over-used! Really, people think it covers anything. Well sweetie – it doesn't.'

He looks me earnestly in the eye when he lands the final affirmation. Only he is standing behind me so he is looking me in the eye through the mirror. It's disarming really, all this reflected directness. He is holding the make-up brush like a cigarette, 'Oh sweetie!' He touches my cheek as though it's dirty, 'What – is – THIS?'

In a sudden wave I feel nauseous. It's a kind of sickness I have never felt before, like the worst hangover I have ever had. I cannot talk or move. I stare at the mirror but I can hardly see for the nausea. It has overcome me completely. This sickness has gripped me by the stomach, the bowels, the throat. It is even in my ears. The thought of speaking makes me want to vomit. He goes on though. At first I am not sure what he is talking about and then I realize. Sometimes I get pink blotches on my cheeks. He touches them again.

'Oh sweetie – what night cream are you using? This must be product build-up.'

'I don't use ...' I really cannot speak. This is not in my head. I am ill.

'You're pale sweetie. Have you been to bed? This is the problem with the industry, you know? The girls destroy themselves ...'

I vomit. It does not resemble the coffee and croissant I had for breakfast. It does not resemble half-digested food at all. It is a colour I have never seen before. Luminous yellow liquid that just keeps coming out. It tastes like acid.

IN THE MORNING you wake very early. You can hear Cassandra rushing out to some modelling gig. You know that's where she's going because you hear her in the shower room and she spends a long time with the water turned off. That's because she is shaving. She has to remove all body hair before a shoot.

You lie on your side with Oisín at your back and face the curtain. It is still wonderfully black outside, and very still. No wind. You have been crying in your sleep and your body aches. Either that or you are getting the flu.

When Cassandra has left you get up and go into the kitchen. You haven't the energy to make a cup of tea. You fill a glass of water and sit by the window, looking at the darkness, waiting for the day to start.

THEY MADE ME go on anyway, they put me in different poses, moved the big white things around me to reflect the light. It was a fashion shoot intended to advertise clothing but we were half dressed, myself and this other girl, and they kept putting us in lesbian poses and asked us to part our legs a lot. Strange thing about it is that there were no straight men in the place. There was no one there who found any of it sexy. I fainted. It was the movie kind of fainting: swooning and falling down and all. When the hair guy sprayed some product all over my head I vomited again. The product smelled so bad that before it was even out of the bottle I had keeled over and then when he sprayed, it started heaving up out of my gut; that yellow stuff. When I fainted for the second time the other model stood up and shouted at the photography director.

'She needs to go home, Shea. I'm not going on with this. She's unwell. She needs to go home. Get her a taxi. Get Allanah to come out instead. She's not working today.'

They did what she told them. She was very nice, holding me by the elbow, stroking my hair. She behaved older than she looked. As she helped me into the taxi she whispered gently, touching my crispy hair: 'Chicken, is your period late?' I couldn't answer. I couldn't think. It seemed as though even thinking might be so much of an effort that I would vomit again.

'Put that in your bag. Four doses. I always keep them with me. They won't prescribe them. How late are you? If you've only missed one it should work. One should still work but if it doesn't, if it hasn't worked within three days take the rest of them all quickly. You're so young, chicken. You really are. Take them soon. Don't think about it.' It was a little silk pouch that felt as though it had sheets of hard, bumpy plastic in it. Each sheet contained one pill.

The taxi can't drive into Front Arch so I tell him to let me off here. I can't pay him, but he says he'll get it off the company. As I get out he tells me to eat something and look after myself. He must be someone's daddy. Usually I'd be jealous, wish he was my daddy, but I haven't the energy this morning.

When I get in Helen is sitting at the table. I fall down again when I see her and she makes me a cup of coffee but the smell of it makes me sick. She touches my cheek. 'Why are you crying?' I don't think I am crying, not really, I feel too sick to do anything, but every time I vomit the effort pushes tears out. Helen is kneeling down by my chair, looking up into my face: 'Cassy, what's happening?'

I don't know what's happening. I feel sick, that's all, but the way she says it – 'What's happening?' – shoots panic through my limbs. Something is *happening*. Everything hurts, my hands and legs and head. I need out of this body. 'I need to lie down Helen. I'm not well.'

She helps me into bed and it all seems unreal, this sudden infirmity. I am not used to being ill. I lie very still, because any movement sends a wave of nausea through me. Helen sits beside the bed dumbly. I want her to go away but I don't want to be left alone either. It's getting brighter outside. Helen is still and I can feel her wanting something from me, which seems ridiculous, the state I'm in.

'Cassy?'

I grunt but it takes huge effort and shoots another rush of sickness through me.

'Cassy, I don't know what to do. I'm – I don't know what I'm going to do, Cassy.'

I squeeze my eyes against the queasiness and the light from a lamp. I can feel the sickening heat off it. It's on my face, making me sicker. 'Can you turn off the light?'

She switches it off and we are silent in the dark. After a while she stands up and kisses me on the forehead. She must think I'm asleep because she doesn't say anything, just closes the door gently behind her.

HE FELT the weight of her sinking back into bed beside him. Her body was cool, as though she had been out of bed for a while. Where was she? He didn't remember her leaving. He rolled over and curled an arm around her to warm her up.

'Oisín?' The sound dispersed into the morning darkness like breath. Her words were barely audible, the blackness already absorbing the sounds. 'Why do you love me?'

He stayed lying on his side and opened his eyes in the dark. He was too tired for this. Should he make a joke or massage her ego gently? His voice was croaky and slow, unwilling to wake.

'Let me see. One: you're hot, foxy. There's foxy and there's cutie. You're foxy. Two: you're kind and cool and you have a nice laugh. Three: you give great head.'

She punched him gently, whispered, 'Asshole,' and they made love reluctantly. Just before he came he made a mental check: yes, they had remembered the condom. Then a moment of terror when he realized that there had been no pause in their daily lovemaking for months – how many months? Two at least. At least. She hadn't had a period since that time she left it in the toilet.

HE MISUNDERSTOOD. He thought this was some self-deprecating gesture, fishing for an ego boost. He misunderstood you completely. What you mean is, 'Why are we together, you and I? Why do you love me instead of someone else? Why do I love you?'

nineteen

I HAVE very bad cramps like period pains all day. My abdomen starts to tighten at intervals and it hurts. I run a bath, swishing fistfuls of salt into the water before I step in. It happens. It is not as painful as it should be, if this is what I think it is.

The blood comes in black balls that disperse to impossible fragments. Red filigree spreads through the water. It is curiously beautiful, moving gently outwards and upwards in other-world slow motion. The blood-lace caresses my skin like a million tiny, loving fingers.

I remember something I must have heard somewhere about hot water being bad for the baby. Maybe I knew that when I ran the bath, but I don't think so. I never really believed in this pregnancy anyway. I don't know if that model's pills made a difference. I think this would have happened regardless. I cannot imagine myself with a pregnant belly, with something kicking inside me. I cannot imagine that I have enough life in me to sustain someone else's. I am no mother. Then again, some non-mothers have children anyway. Some bodies are full of paradoxes.

There is no baby, at least no baby I can discern, but I am very weak and faint and do not look very hard. It occurs to me that I am in shock. I feel very, very sad.

I become quite ill, and bleed like this for over a week, lying in bed or sitting by the kitchen window. I do not go to lectures. Helen isn't around much.

So that's that. You may as well never have been, little baby. You may as well have been a phantom. I hope your tiny life was okay while it lasted. I hope we had something. I hope it was happiness you felt, or comfort at least, in the dumb gloop before thought.

Goodbye. I will only say it once. I have no room in me for any more ghosts, so you will have to be satisfied with this one goodbye. My scare, my slip-up, my something to love. Goodbye.

twenty

OISÍN'S COUSIN was getting married on Sunday so they were going to Clonmel for the weekend. Tonight he would take Helen out in the town and introduce her to the lads he grew up with.

She had spent seventy euro on a new outfit for the wedding last week. It was a sixties cut, zooming out at the waist instead of brushing her ass the way modern clothes do. He didn't like it. She looked silly in it. He didn't say that, but he let her know by his reaction. Thankfully, she had put it by her bedroom door in its bag with the receipt. Instead she packed a sexy dress that she owned already. It was brown and blue – tight, with a frill up the side. He loved that dress, she knew that. The first time Oisín had seen her in it he had closed the door, pushed her onto the bed, and made love to her. When she had lifted the dress to take it off he had said, 'No, baby, keep it on. Tell me to stop, that I'll crumple your dress ... say, "Oh no stop – you'll crumple my dress!"'

He loved the feeling of the material; cool and heavy. He had grabbed a handful of it, bunching it up over her ass, and it felt like liquid in his fist. While he was in her he thought how it must feel to have a sleek body covered in that rich fabric and decorated with frills. He imagined the significance it must give her flesh; the knowledge she must have of her own body's loveliness, being fucked in that dress. Not for the first time, he envied women their easy beauty and all its trappings.

They would be staying with his family in Clonmel. It was a four-hour bus journey from Dublin. They sat at the back of the bus and shared a two-litre bottle of berry-flavoured water and a packet of Fox's Creams.

AS SOON AS the bus pulls out of the station you need to go to the toilet, but you remember him complaining about an ex who kept whinging that she needed a piss for an entire bus journey, so you don't mention it. He doesn't like the idea of you weeing anyway. He wants to read the paper but you're bored of your book and keep trying to distract him with anecdotes about bus rides of your past. It's no good though. Even the story about when your school bus blew up doesn't really get much of a reaction.

THE BUS was stuffy and the man in the seat in front of them smelled like dog. He didn't notice until she pointed it out, and now he couldn't keep from smelling it – that oily terrier smell. Oisín just wanted to read the paper. It was the *Tipperary Star*, which his dad sent every week, and always questioned him on, and which he never read. He wanted something to talk about with his dad. There was an article about a guy from Tipperary who was making it as an actor, but he couldn't concentrate on it with Helen looking for attention all the time.

He began to wonder whether this was such a good idea. He wanted to show her off to the lads. They'd clock her slender legs, her round breasts, her perfect, pert little bum, and they'd slag him in a West Brit accent, saying, 'Fine little poshy you got for yourself there in *Trinners*.' They'd see how she looked at him and they'd know she adored him. They'd notice how good his hair looked and how much he'd filled out and they'd know he was happy with her too. He wanted her with him this weekend and didn't like the idea of leaving her behind in Dublin, but he saw suddenly how disastrous the evening might be. The lads wouldn't know how to treat Helen and she wouldn't know what to make of them.

There used to be some girls who hung out with the group intermittently, but they had grown up now, and got jobs and husbands. The only girl who hung out with them now was Eoin's girlfriend, who was sound-out and didn't mind lads' talk. She never made a nuisance of herself unless it was to drag Eoin home if she thought he was too drunk, and she was usually right. The girlfriend's little sister came out occasionally too. All the lads fancied her. Helen might get on with the sister – maybe he'd ask Eoin to bring her along.

It was possible that it might come off all right. Helen might drink and smile and try to fit in and not take anything too personally. He wanted her to have a good time though, and he found it hard to envisage that. He tried to imagine her chatting with the lads, laughing. Would she laugh with them? That was his favourite thing, when she threw her head back and laughed.

There were no windows on the bus. There was only a small strip of glass where the windows should have been. Helen kissed his cheek and he felt nauseous. She held his hand, which became clammy, and flicked restlessly through a magazine. He had to resist the temptation to whip his hand back and dry it on his jumper. She offered him a biscuit every few minutes. It seemed clear to him now that there was no way she would swill beer and laugh and allow him to let off steam with the lads. There was no way she'd get the lads' sense of humour. He should have thought this through.

YOU STARE OUT at the smooth black road, the spindly shrubs haggard with exhaust soot, and try to feel okay. You kiss him. He kisses you back but you feel worse because he doesn't really mean it. You try not to seem too needy. You try to remember that he loves you. You offer him another biscuit.

His father is waiting at the station. You realize that you already had a mental picture of his dad, constructed out of Oisín's anecdotes: a darker, hairier version of Oisín who flew into vicious rages. Something like Orson Welles, some dark soul. It is hard to marry the real man with that image. His nose and belly are very large and round. His tiny eyes squint behind glasses. He reminds you of a toy clown one of your sisters had as a baby. It was weighted at the bottom, and rocked back and forth if you pushed it. He smiles vacantly. All he says is 'Well', and 'Good'. He utters these words at regular intervals without being prompted, a sort of verbal tick. You are not sure whether a response is required. All the blood in his body seems to be concentrated in his thick fingers and red nose. He blinks a lot, slowly, as though it pains him. Oisín doesn't resemble him in the slightest.

In the car on the way to Oisín's house his dad asks you questions. He has a very thick accent and you find it hard to understand him so Oisín answers for you a lot. They are questions about college and about how many siblings you have, what schools they go to, and what your father does. He seems pleased with the answers. The eldest of six and a convent boarding school. It must sound very Catholic. Then he turns to Oisín, 'Well?'

'Good now,' Oisín replies in a voice you don't recognize, 'Tippin' away. College is good. Goin' good now.'

'Good,' his dad says, and then after a pause, 'Well.'

You listen to the radio for the rest of the journey, though that too is indecipherable: a crackling buzz, a man's excited voice, a Gaelic match or a horse race or something.

Oisín's mother doesn't get up when you enter the house. It's a small house, impeccably tidy, but dirty. A carpet flat and glossy with grime, and the whole house smelling of people, stale cooking, sweaty clothes, shoes. Oisín takes you into the television room to meet her. She smiles with her lips closed, and says quietly, 'Hello, Helen.' You are very aware that she makes no gesture to touch you – to shake your hand or kiss your cheek. Her hands don't move. She has the same colour eyes as Oisín, a long face, and long, silver hair. There is a look of disappointment and surrender at the corners of her mouth. She looks sad even when she smiles. You want her to like you. You say hello and she nods again, smiles again, and stands up. There is no warmth in her. You cannot imagine her giving someone a hug. You imagine her hands must be cold and smooth and disinterested, the way a competent nurse's might be.

Despite her coldness she is kind to you and makes you smoked salmon on soda bread and tea. Oisín's father stands by and watches you eat, beaming, proud of the offering. You get the impression that smoked salmon is what they give to important guests. Oisín is very quiet. He eats the salmon and bread with a lot of mayonnaise. His mother asks you about college and tells you about an art exhibition she saw last year in Dublin, or rather, tells you that she went to an art exhibition and that it was good. She doesn't really describe it in very much detail.

You brought a very sexy red top that shows your tummy, but you are not feeling brave enough to wear it tonight. You slip on a black Rolling Stones T-shirt that you brought just in case, and wear it with those jeans he likes your ass in, the ones that pinch your pouchy. 'Pouchy' was a word Clodagh in school used for her fanny. 'Fanny' was a word Lauren used. You don't know them any more, Clodagh or Lauren. You are miles away from who you were then. The school is closing down. They have no money or nuns any more. They are selling up and the nuns are moving to the sister school in France. You received an invite to a closing ceremony. You would like to go, to show off your boyfriend and the fact that you are still here, pushing along through life, and not a virgin any more. Cassy doesn't want to go though.

As you are putting on your jacket Oisín smiles: 'The Stones? Do you even know one song by the Stones baby?' Could he be sneering at you? But he likes that. He likes when you are a bit silly. He couldn't be sneering.

As soon as you walk into the pub you realize there will be no dancing tonight. His friends are a lot less attractive than you had imagined. The rough bad boys Oisín had occasionally talked about are a little geeky. There are three of them. The first one he introduces you to is older than you or Oisín, a little wrinkled, with a receding hairline, but he is dressed like a teenage rocker: studded leather wrist-bands, tight jeans. He scans your body quickly, as though appraising you. You can't tell whether he finds you attractive. That makes you uneasy, not knowing. 'Kev man this is my – this is Helen. Kev's a rocker.' So he must be the musician, the leader of the gang, the ladies' man that Oisín told you about.

The second one has long ginger hair sleeked to his head, and very bad acne. His girlfriend introduces him: 'I'm the long-suffering girlfriend,' she says proudly, raising her eyes up to heaven.

'This is Aengus.' She gestures towards him with a thumb, and he nods at you, rolls his eyes at the girlfriend; a dogged performance. You get the impression you and she will stick together for the night. She makes a star with her hand, 'Five years!' she says, as though it is a debt.

The third of Oisín's mates is hunched over like an old man. He has long hair too, and it dangles down to his chin in oily clumps from around a small bald patch. He looks like a flasher and doesn't talk very much. 'And this bugger is Denny,' says Aengus, 'he's a poor old bugger, don't mind him if he tries to cop a feel. He's a poor old bugger, aren'tcha Denny?'

You want them to like you but you have no idea how to achieve that.

Oisín is different now. He hunches his back more. His voice is deeper and louder, his words all swallowed inside, as though he doesn't really want them heard. He looks like he might punch someone, or as though he wants people to think he might. In fact the pose makes him look weedy. You have never considered that he might be weedy.

They sit around a bar table and drink a lot of pints very quickly. You sit between Oisín and Denny – the one with the bald patch – and laugh when they laugh. You try to make eye contact with Oisín, but he doesn't see you. Then you try to exchange something with the 'long-suffering girlfriend' – a look or a word, but she is looking at her boyfriend, blank faced. The corners of her mouth are turned down like an old woman's, making little sags where spit might gather as she ages. Two more men arrive. They talk about things Oisín has never talked about with you, bands you didn't know he liked, and MTV videos, which you didn't think he watched. Mostly though, they describe previous nights like this, how drunk Denny was and how much he puked.

Oisín's face is fixed in a growl. He looks like a different person. You want to wave, you want to kiss him, shake him out of this trance. 'Hey!' you want to say, 'It's me, Helen, it's me, you like me, remember?'

A plump girl with dimples is sitting at a table nearby. The lads make jokes about her having a face like Kirsten Dunst and tits like Jordan, and you are not sure whether they are being cruel or kind. Then one of them, Aengus, the one with the girlfriend, says: 'Oisín was rootin' her for a while!' Oisín says nothing. Under the table you try to slip your hand into his but he pulls away. 'Biggest fuckin' disappointment of my life, man! Lousy lay! Two weeks I was rootin' her, and it didn't get any better ...' Then he opens his mouth and a loud fake laugh you have never heard before rolls out.

SHE SAID she wasn't drinking. He didn't see that one coming. There was no better way to lose points with the lads than being some precious princess on a detox. He was trying his best, making an effort to pace himself with his own pints. She was humiliating him. She looked at him as though she had never seen him before in her life, as though they had not eaten ice-cream in the bath together only the night before, as though she wasn't in love with him, as though she had not been excited about meeting his family and his friends. She sat tight-lipped, giving a cold, fake laugh when the lads tried to include her. He had told the lads she couldn't get enough of his dick. She was making a fool of him.

Oisín drank heavily and began to slur his words, to lean all his weight on her shoulder when he spoke to her. He knew he was pissing her off, but he didn't care. She was behaving like a stuck-up Barbie – backing away from his beer breath and disappearing all the time. She went to the toilet a lot, or outside 'to take a call'. He had a laugh with his mates despite her. They talked about the craic they had last New Year's and about Kevin's plan to play his songs at the strip club. 'It'd be cool man! Imagine, the girls dancing away to the music, smoke machine in the background and me givin' it socks, man! They'd make money sellin' tickets, and I'd get loads of people in to hear my music. We could sell CDs from the bar!' Poor Kev – his plans never worked. He was a good guy though. He had a FÁS job at the homeless centre. Girls loved when he said: 'When I'm not making music I work with the homeless.'

Helen took his hand, and kissed it.

'Did you ever go to that strip club?'

'No, baby. Never.'

The lads laughed. He should have known she'd ask that question. All girls were the fucking same. It was well after closing time and Byrne was being an asshole. 'Lads! Out! Or I'm not letting you in any more!'

Aengus patted Byrne on the shoulder, squinting at him through puffy beer eyes. 'We're going man – we're going!' The girlfriend clung to his arm, tugged him out the door. The lads were the most regular of Byrne's customers though, there was no way he'd bar them. A wave of nostalgia crashed over Oisín. No matter what happened the lads would always be here, drinking themselves stupid and talking shite on a Saturday night. He loved the lads. He wouldn't give them up for the world, and certainly not for a bit of pussy. Helen had gone off again. Kev fumbled with his pocket under the table and took out a little plastic packet, 'Hey, hey Oisín man – I got some yokes, you want one?' It had been years since Oisín had done ecstasy, except the herbal stuff in Amsterdam. The lads were back into it though, he knew from Aengus's emails, but the truth was it fucked with Oisín's head a bit too much in ways he didn't like.

'No man. My bird ...'

'Oh sure, okay man, no worries.'

Shame licked at his ears. The lads would think he was pussy-whipped by some stuck-up poshy from Trinity.

He found Helen at the front entrance, Denny leaning on her shoulder, talking close into her face, and her leaning away. Just before they saw him he heard what Denny said.

'So I hear Oisín popped your cherry? Yeah, you look real innocent but I bet you're a minx in bed …'

He went home with her instead of going on to the late club with the lads. She might be behaving like a cunt but she was the best ride he'd ever had, and he had introduced her to his mam. He didn't want to lose her, not yet. They made crisp sandwiches together in his kitchen, trying to be quiet so as not to wake his parents, and she seemed okay again. She kissed his cheek.

'Baby did you tell Denis I was a virgin?'

'Denis talks shite. Don't mind him.'

They switched on the TV but there was nothing much on. He always switched on the TV when he got in from a night out in Tipp. The low buzz, the fuzzy picture, and that damp, worn smell of his parents' couch – years of bums and feet – reminded him what it had been to be a teenager and not to have anyone to take to bed with you. It reminded him as well that the lads were there for him then, and would be for years to come, that it was Aengus he had run to after scoring for the first time. Aengus, a face thick with acne and bum fluff, who had whacked him on the back and said: 'Fair fucking dues to you, man!'

Helen laid her head on his lap. She fondled his crotch a bit, kissing his belly. She wanted to suck him off, but he pulled her to her feet. It was 3 AM. Helen's lips were puffy – they always went puffy when she was tired. He was the only one, perhaps, who knew that about her. Suddenly he stopped disliking her. He kissed her lips. He never wanted to feel angry with her again.

'You know I love you?' She nodded.

'Let's go to bed. Dad always wakes me at eight in the morning! For mass. He'll wake me extra early because of the wedding. He'll be up at sunrise, shouting.'

He laughed but she just looked at him.

'They're good lads you know. Kev is alright. He helps the homeless.'

He kissed her goodnight when she was tucked into bed in the box room, went into the bedroom he had slept in since he was three, and closed the door. He had the room to himself; his brothers weren't coming up until the morning. He could hear her sobbing through the walls. All women were the fucking same. He texted Denis:

'Wa d fuck u say 2 my bird I'm in d dog house now ur a wanker hav a gud 1!'

twenty-one

I MEET BRIAN again today. I had planned to tell him about the pregnancy but I know as soon as I see him that I can't. We have a drink first, downstairs. I have a gin and tonic, and I don't worry too much about looking graceful as I drink it. He peers into my top and I wish I wasn't wearing a padded bra. He grins at me. How stupid. He knows every inch of my naked body. What's the point? He says there's a recession coming. He was always telling me there was a recession coming, that the Celtic Tiger was toppling.

'I'm not worried about it though. What happens to the artists in a recession, Lol? Not that much you know, because we never did ride the tide of Capitalism.'

Upstairs things go pretty much the same as last time except that he's more aggressive, flipping me over and lunging into me from behind. How strange that this really is how babies are made. I can't stop thinking about our baby. It was only a speck though, a plunge of blood, a hormonal shift. I feel foolish for thinking a word like 'baby'. Even more foolish for thinking 'our baby', particularly as it might not have been. It is more likely, in fact, to have been Oisín's, unreal as that encounter now seems. I feel like some sort of lunatic, as though I have made it all up. No one else knows. It might as well never have happened.

I know anyway, what Brian would say if I told him, and I know what he'd say if I cried about it or used the word 'baby'. He would talk about the Church state, the national consciousness. He would laugh about my convent education and call me a fucking Catholic.

My mouth is so dry that I keep reaching down beside the bed for my bottle of water while he's pumping. I bleed a bit. I'm still not right after the whole thing. He doesn't mind blood. He used to like my periods. Today he is still there when I get out of the shower. He asks if I want to go for lunch and I say no, I have to get back to college. He makes a stupid comment about me watching my weight and he can see my ribs, and we separate with a peck on the cheek at the corner. I realize suddenly that I don't love him any more. It is a new thought and it hurts more than the longing I used to feel.

I walk back to college watching my shoes squash the damp filth on the pavement, pink and blue and yellow paper sticking to the concrete, gathering in the crevices; sodden confetti from a town wedding.

I want to love. I want my heart to stay open and bleeding for the world. I want to stay young, to hold on to the last traces of earnestness; even if that means being foolish, because once I lose that, once everything becomes sardonic, once I am grown up, nothing will matter as much. Moment by moment my heart is turning old and leathery. I am getting over this, all of it. I can feel it all seal over like a scab. In a few decades I'll die with watercolour feelings.

When I get home one of the goldfish is lying on the stones at the bottom of the water. The other one is puckering at his head, thinking he's food. I fish him out with the smallest of Cahill's assorted-sized sieves and flush him down the toilet. Then I sit on the floor in my room and cry for the dead fish and his unfeeling, un-remembering survivor.

twenty-two

HELEN NEVER told him she was rich. He knew she was posh, all the Trinity girls were, but he didn't know she was this loaded.

They had taken the bus to Wicklow town, and then a taxi to Helen's house. It was a horrible trip. Cassandra came along. She was wearing red underwear. He could see the bra through her white T-shirt. When she leaned into the taxi her top rose, showing the red lace string of her thong. She had no boobs anyway, and a concave stomach. Too skinny to be sexy. He wasn't attracted to her. Even now, after fucking her that day, the sight of her left him cold.

The three of them sat together on the bus along the back row of seats. He hadn't spoken to Cassandra since that day. *You're the girl in the A|wear catalogue.* He had taken the poster down the following day. Helen must have known it was Cassandra all the time. She never said anything about it.

The incident seemed to have no impact on Cassandra at all. Afterwards whenever he saw her, and whenever Helen mentioned her name, he felt ill and began to sweat. But she continued to treat him with the same disdain as she always had. Even the way she ignored him if she bumped into him and Helen in the kitchen or the library wasn't any different to how she had always been with him. She seemed so unaffected by the incident that he sometimes wondered if it had really happened.

On the bus Cassandra didn't talk much, but she cast a humourless shadow over the whole journey. He felt that everything he said would sound ridiculous in her presence, every gesture of affection he made towards Helen would feel like a lie.

The trip began with Helen trying to chat, but Cassandra was quiet. Oisín gave a clipped response to all Helen's babble so that she realized how much she was annoying him and put on her iPod. She was getting better at knowing when she was annoying him. Then he opened a packet of Tayto. Helen wrinkled her nose. 'Oisín, please. The smell is disgusting.' He watched her upper lip curl a little as she said the word 'disgusting'. He laughed at her: 'Euw. Excuuse me *madam*.'

Cassandra just shot him a look like a threat and he closed the crisp packet. Then Helen moved to another seat because she said she could still smell them. Precious bitch. A shock of hatred flashed through him, a sudden, pure emotion, sensual as pain.

He opened the crisps and ate them, Cassandra sitting prim beside him, her cropped hair curving around her head like a helmet, those harsh cheekbones glistening, nostrils twitching. Could it have been a warning, that look? No. She was like a mother tiger with Helen. She wouldn't hurt her by telling her something like that. That's why she hated him – because she thought he hurt Helen. She thought he wasn't good enough. *Fine*, he wanted to say. *Fine. I'm not good enough ... Who is?* She hadn't told Helen, he was sure of that, and she wouldn't tell her. He wondered if Helen would believe her anyway. He hardly believed it himself.

The sound when he munched on the crisps was too loud. No method, not closing his mouth, not chewing more slowly, would make the crunching less offensive. He wasn't trying to be polite though. He relished Cassandra's repugnance. He would like to fuck her properly once, he thought, see the changes in her face and body as she came, expose her like that. He would pump cum all over her prudish little face then stand up and walk away, throwing her knickers back at her, spitting at her. He would like to call her 'woman' and make her suck his cock, atone for whatever she had done to him that day, making him lick her pussy like that. He would fuck her in the ass and undo all of this, undo Cassandra's straight back, her stiff hair, undo Helen's curled lip, her disregard. It was only with Cassandra that Helen was this way, that she was this person he could so easily hate.

Cassandra was reading some book. She was ignoring him completely, but Helen, a few seats up, was leaning her face against the window, her eyes squeezed shut, clutching her stomach as though the smell of crisps was really inflicting some dreadful pain on her.

He became intensely conscious of the eating process. The chewing turned the crisps into a doughy ball, butted about by his tongue. Then it was swallowed down, moving from his throat to his stomach by the contractions of his gullet. The over-flavoursome powder on the crisps and the salty smack of MSG sickened him, but he forced himself to the end of the bag, crumpled it in a fist, and licked his fingertips.

It was a bumpy ride. Helen stayed in her seat up the front. He could see the back of her head, her ringlets bopping with the bumps of the bus. She had put away her iPod and curled her knees up to her chest. It was three o'clock when they set off and even though it was March now the evenings still darkened early. He spent the journey watching the coach windows turn from white to grey to blue.

He carried Helen's bag from the bus to the taxi, while she sat in the front passenger seat, massaging her temples. Helen directed the driver to a giant cul-de-sac that ran down a hill. Each of the houses was different: different shapes, different bricks. They were all huge, like embassy buildings. Some had tall security gates and tall trees. Others had low walls and no gates at all, so that all their splendour was on display. He noticed the taxi-driver fiddle with the meter as they passed a tennis court on one side and a Rolls-Royce on the other. Oisín snorted. If he had that kind of money he wouldn't spend it on a Rolls-Royce. What a waste. There were much better cars out there for that price. He didn't say anything though, not with Cassandra there and Helen in this contrary mood.

Her home was down at the bottom of the cul-de-sac. A huge stone boulder at the foot of the drive said 'The Elms', the carved letters designed to imitate Irish calligraphy. The house itself was set atop a mound of gravel and greenery and half-concealed behind trees and shrubs in blossom. Only the top of the house – a muddle of peaks and chimneys – was visible from the road. A rockery garden was built into the sloping lawn: stone orbs, various flowering shrubs, and an assortment of ponds linked by a trickling stream.

The driver stopped at the open gate. Helen didn't move. 'Would you mind driving up? We have loads of bags …'

Oisín breathed deeply. He reminded himself that it was Cassandra who made him hate Helen. He tried to remember that he liked her. He tried to remember that feeling it gave him when she giggled. The driver didn't answer, but turned the wheel emphatically and they crunched up the slope to the house. On the way up they passed under an iron arch with some sort of pink-flowered creeper growing on it. Big, loose blossoms dangled over the car, trembling from the vibration of the motor.

When they stopped at the front door Oisín glanced at the meter. The journey had only taken fifteen minutes but it said thirty-five euro. He reached into his bag for his wallet but Helen touched his hand in a way that made him want to smack her. 'Don't be silly, my dad will get it.'

Before he could answer, a woman with a huge arse came bounding towards the car. He could see that it was huge even from the front. It swelled out from her sides and inhibited her walking. What made the rear so absurd was that her shoulders were narrow. Her cheeks and neck weren't even chubby, but her thighs were thick. She leaned forward as she ran, the way he had seen ostriches do on nature programmes. Her face was not unlike Helen's but there was something a little crazed about the eyes. They protruded a bit, as though there wasn't enough eyelid. She was much younger than Oisín's mam. She kissed Helen briskly and then put an arm around Cassandra.

'Hi! Hi! Hi Cassy, love, how are you sweetheart? You skinny bitch, look at you! So you're Oisín! I'm Helen's mammy.'

Oisín saw Helen flinch at the word 'mammy'. She had told him she didn't get on with her mother. As she spoke the mother fumbled in a black leather bum bag with silver studs on it. Then she turned her head towards the house and let out a roar: 'Emmmm-maaaaaa! Tell Daddy, Helen is here! We need money for the taxi!'

A bony girl with lank hair came out of the house in a baggy jumper and pyjamas and handed fifty euro to the taxi-driver without looking at him. Then she kissed Helen on the cheek, gave a weak wave to Oisín and Cassandra, and disappeared back into the house. The driver didn't argue. He lifted the bags out of the boot silently and got back into the car.

Hands on massive hips, the mother looked Oisín all over. Oisín wanted to glance at Helen's little bum. He wanted to make sure it was still there. Was this what Helen was destined for? Would her bum spill out, when she reached thirty, into a blubbery ring around her? He smiled and stretched out a hand. He was trying to look boyish. 'Hi, Mrs O'Brien.' He wanted to say something snappy, something witty that would make him seem familiar with this sort of wealth, but he could think of nothing. He felt betrayed by Helen. She must have been shocked by his parents' small house.

She must have thought all kinds of things that she never said. If he had known she was loaded he wouldn't have brought her there, put her in that pokey spare room, let his mam serve her discount smoked salmon as though it were caviar.

Helen's mum gave a shriek of laughter, throwing her head back. 'Missis O'Brien … Ha! Call me Trina!' Her hair was not Helen's halo of ringlets, but it had a bit of a curl in it and it was blonde too. It was hard to tell how blonde though because the hair was wet. It was cut into a youthful bob. She really was very like Helen. Or rather, Helen was very like her. The similarity was obscene, as though her likeness to Helen, coupled with the deformity of the swollen arse, was a gesture of mockery.

'Anyway,' said her mother, 'I have to get dressed so you three can look after yourselves can't you? Helen, put Cassandra in the attic room. You and the boy can't sleep in the back room because Mary and Denis are in there. I told Tatiana to put sheets on all the spare beds, so sleep wherever.'

She was just out of the shower, dressed in a long, baggy T-shirt and towelling slippers with the name of a hotel on them. The hair dripped steadily onto the T-shirt. It was the smell, Oisín decided – that disgusted him. It was the smell of her warm, fat, just-scrubbed body and some other lingering fragrance, like cooked fruit. It was her posh-totty soap, or skin polisher or whatever people like her used. She had no trousers on, just the very long T-shirt. Her legs were swollen, the skin dry and flaking with pink spots and blue veins. His own mother would never have greeted people in that state. She turned and disappeared back into the house.

The three of them carried the bags in. There was classical music playing from invisible speakers. The hall was huge with a marble floor and high ceiling. Portraits of Helen's parents and five sisters hung everywhere: studio photos with everyone standing like figurines and raising their chins slightly. There was one he liked of Helen when she was a toddler. She looked like an angel:

huge eyes, sprigs of curls filling the frame. There was a baby on her lap. It was newborn with a scrunched-up face and scrunched-up hands and a mass of black hair. Helen was looking at the camera as if to say, 'What?'

Glass doors on either side showed two immaculate rooms. Those rooms lead to other rooms, connected by more glass doors. To the left was a room with a marble fireplace and a coffee table that might be an art piece of some sort: a naked iron woman holding a slab of glass. It was the type of thing that belonged in government buildings and posh hotels. The room had deep, plush chairs, couches of the same fabric as the curtains. To the right was a room with a piano, a harp, and a dining-table. He had never seen a harp before. It was bigger than he would have imagined a harp to be. Messy oil paintings hung on the walls. The hall branched into a staircase on one side and a kitchen ahead. The staircase lead up to more than one floor, you could tell just by looking at it, and by the light pouring down from a high skylight.

Helen didn't dally in the hallway. She didn't give any commentary, even when he raised his eyebrows at her as if to say, 'What's all this?' Cassandra didn't react either. Maybe she was loaded too.

The two girls dumped their bags in the hall and went into the kitchen. Oisín followed. There were several foreign women milling around, preparing food. They looked at the three students with irritation and returned to their work, except one of them, who stretched her arms out and smiled. Helen kissed her. 'Hi Tatiana!'

'Helen how are you, darlink? Cassandra, you have come too!'

He felt vaguely jealous. How come Helen's servant knew Cassandra? Helen never told him she had servants. He didn't know they still existed. Then a squat Asian woman with a giant salad bowl in her arms elbowed Helen.

'You can't eat this stuff now you know? This is for the party. Your mammy told us no one is to eat it until the party.'

The kitchen made him uneasy. It felt like another world. The light was evenly dispersed, as though each reflective particle was suspended at equal distance from the other. He looked up to see what sort of light fittings were giving that effect. The entire ceiling was glowing from strips of pink light. The lights were set in a thick, clear glass ceiling. Up through the ceiling he could see the landing above, and another glass ceiling above that one.

YOU CAN TELL Oisín is annoyed with you for something. His jaw is set in that harsh line. You send Cassandra up to dump her stuff in her room so that you can be alone with him. You still feel queasy, but it's easing. All the same you are glad that Oisín is carrying the bags. First you look for a room to stay in, opening doors and inspecting the beds for wash-bags, books, a pair of pyjamas to mark it as taken. Oisín follows you, lugging the bags from room to room.

'But which is your room?'

'Oh, I slept in the back room for a while, then I moved to the yellow room, then back to the back room. But while I was in secondary school I slept in that room there at the holidays.'

His eyes slide around the sides of your face, they don't meet yours. You grab his hand and kiss it, and you know what a strange gesture that is, and how useless. It's with your skin that you know each other though, and you urgently need to remember. You need him to remember. Something is slipping; you are losing something. It's this house. You hate this house. Your sisters hate it too. When you were stoned one night last summer, you and Emma and Carla, the three of you sat in the kitchen and talked about burning it down, the whole house. You really meant it that night. All three of you meant it. You would light a match to Mammy's recently done seventy-two thousand euro kitchen, starting with the 'Family Organizer' on the wall. The flames would soar upwards in exaltation, blackening all the glass ceilings, the fresh paintwork, the new tiles, until everything trembled and shattered with the heat. Up with the house would go your childhoods, the fake versions and the real ones, the violin lessons, the maths grinds, the carefully planned meals cooked and frozen by staff under your mother's supervision. Up in flames with the wedding photo in the hallway, of your slender mammy and your frightened-looking daddy before all of this began, you and all the babies, before all the money came building up, and the au-pairs and the staff and the home improvements. The blaze would lick at the six studio photos of each of the O'Brien girls that are hung in ascension along the staircase, marbled backgrounds, French plaits, airbrushed noses, all would be blacked out by the blaze, glass splitting, paper melting, those faces shrinking out of being.

Oisín takes his hand back and kisses you coolly on the cheek. It's this house and Mammy. It was stupid to bring Oisín here. Somehow, you will lose him here, Mammy will make him go away. She can do that in a look. Because Mammy, and only your mammy, knows what you really are, and in her gaze you become just that.

AFTER HE HAD spent ten minutes following her like a lap dog, she found a double bedroom at the back of the house that was free. Oisín dropped their bags at the foot of the bed. Everything in the room was matching. The curtains and duvet had a bright, splotchy floral print on them. There was a border running around the room with flowers of the same colour and the same water-paint effect. They were made-up flowers: petals like poppies but in bizarre colours with fluff of some sort bursting from their centres. The furniture looked antique. There was a double bed of carved mahogany with a mahogany side cabinet by each pillow. A mahogany table stood in the farthest corner beside a mahogany wardrobe. The table had a mirror attached to it, built with the same wood and flanked on either side by two smaller mirrors on hinges. There was a cushioned stool at it. The floral pattern reflected out of the mirrors from various angles. On each cabinet was a lamp with a pleated shade made from the same material as the curtains.

'That's freaky! Everything matches!'

She grinned and nodded, rolling her eyes, 'I know. It's Mammy's idea of decorating!'

He was disappointed. Ever since arriving at the house he had felt an intense urge to insult her home. Her attitude to her own house, though, was that of an outsider. She seemed to have no loyalty, no attachment. She didn't even have a bedroom in the house. She didn't care if he hated it.

Helen sat on the bed with her arms behind her and made fuck-me eyes at him. It was her way of calming him down when he got worked up, but now that look made him tired. He didn't feel comfortable having sex in this big house, with people milling about everywhere. Didn't her parents mind them sharing a room? He hadn't met her father yet. He couldn't imagine what he was like. The mystery made him anxious. Helen began to remove her shoes. 'I'm going to have a shower.'

When she was down to her bra and knickers he turned the key in the lock. She leaned back and parted her knees. He shook his head. 'No. I'm just locking it 'cause I don't want any of your servants walking in while you're changing.' He was sure this would hurt her – his tone when he said the word 'servants' – but she still seemed unperturbed. She laughed and rolled onto her tummy, so that he stood looking down at her slender back and buttocks. He had to resist the impulse to smooth a hand over her back, to trace the journey it made, the way it tapered in at the waist, the small of her back with that transparent covering of hair and those two little peaks at the pelvic bone, the cheeks of her ass pushing through the pink panties. He could see the shadowy crack through the material.

'They're not servants Oisín! Tatiana and Kitty have been helping here for years. The others are relatives of theirs. They're just helping to get things ready for the twenty-fifth.'

'Couldn't your mum do it? You have lots of sisters, couldn't they help? It seems like a lot of fuss for a wedding anniversary.'

She shrugged, and removed the rest of her clothes.

'There're lots of people coming. My family are lazy. What do you want me to say?'

She walked into the en-suite bathroom, leaving her knickers in a twisted cord beside her shoes. There was a little white discharge mark on them. He hated the way she did that, walked about naked even when they weren't fucking. He hadn't decided on how to tell her that. It made him feel less of a man, it made him fancy her less. That was it. How could he explain that?

He didn't go in and take a shower with her. That's what she expected him to do. Instead he leaned on the windowsill and looked out onto the vast back garden. He would show her the knickers when she got out. He'd tell her the sight of the discharge made him want never to go down on her again. He'd say it as though he was joking, but it might make her less cocky.

The garden was the size of a field. There were fruit trees and exotic plants, some sort of wooden building that belonged at a health spa, and a paved area with a huge outdoor table and chairs, and a built-in barbeque. In the middle of the grass a huge canvas tent was being erected. He looked for someone who might be Helen's Dad: someone directing the men, or helping them, but all of the men were dressed in paint-splattered work clothes and steel-capped boots. Beyond the garden was a field with high yellow grass, a cloudy pink sunset rolling along the horizon. He opened the window and let in the pecking and clacking of the workmen. The cool air moved against his cheeks. *I want to cry*, he thought. He was hungry though. The crisps from earlier kept exploding back up his throat in little parcels of cheese-and-onion-flavoured air. He had forgotten his toothbrush.

Helen came out of the bathroom warm from the shower and completely naked. She stood behind him and pressed herself against his back, her hand creeping towards his fly. He moved away and pulled the curtains over.

'Helen, do you want those men to see your tits? Is that it?'

She fell back on the bed as though she had been thrown. 'They're not looking. They're busy building the marquee.'

She rolled onto her front. His own arousal bored him, but he put a hand on one cheek of her ass and kneaded it slowly. She drew her legs under her and raised her bum towards the hand like a nuzzling calf. The angle opened her cheeks out a little and he could see her clean pink asshole. It was still raw after that Brazilian wax ordeal, but the little sores had healed up. He wanted to lick it. Her hand was moving slowly between her legs. She was massaging her clit with one finger. He was hard already, his cock out. She whispered something in a soft, high, baby voice. He leaned in closer so that his face was next to hers and clenched one of his hands over one of hers. Her hand was so fragile, so easily crushed. 'What, baby?'

Her cheek felt cool and he realized that his was not. He was sweating and trembling. She said it again, but still too quietly.

'What, baby?'

'Fuck me?'

He breathed out slowly. Not since his first time had he felt such disempowering arousal. He was suddenly aware of his jeans around his hips. The buckle of his belt dangled forward, cold against his thigh. She was making a fool of him. He slapped her ass and drew back from her. 'Not now baby.'

He wanted her to beg him. He wanted her to cry and ask him why he didn't want her but she didn't. Instead she slid her own fingers inside herself. One hand was on her clit and in her pussy, the other moved over her bum and slipped a pinkie into her asshole.

Oisín was leaning back on his hunches now, watching, his cock pulsing like a sore thumb. She moaned. It was a high, twangy sound, like a parody of pleasure.

He walked into the en-suite and closed the door. She stopped moaning instantly.

There were four toothbrushes on a glass shelf over the sink, still in their packets, and pink toothpaste that smelled like disinfectant lying open beside the taps. He opened one of the toothbrushes and used the strange paste. It made his gums tingle. Then he took a short, cold shower.

HELEN PUTS ME in the pink room at the top. It has a sloping ceiling with a skylight facing the bed. This is where I always used to stay if I went home with Helen on bank holidays. Helen hates her house. She used to want me to go home with her all the time. It wasn't because she wanted to see more of me. She used me as armour. For me though, it was always an adventure going to Helen's. Her mother's cruelty, her tantrums, the anonymity of cleaning staff wandering about the place, amused me. I never understood why it damaged Helen so much. Her mother's expressions of dislike came in little outbursts. They were hateful – that's the only word for them – but so petty that I never saw what was so disastrous about them. One mid-term break we got in to find that the drawers in Helen's room had been emptied into the middle of the floor, the books and keepsakes washed off the shelves with a swoosh of her mother's hand. A little ceramic cherub had lost its wings. They lay in jagged white fragments amongst the books. Helen sat down on the floor and cried. I didn't think it was such a big deal. I folded her clothes and put them away while she sobbed. Then her mother came to the door.

'I couldn't bear to pass the door knowing the shit-heap that was in here. I made a start on it. I emptied the rubbish into a pile. All you have to do is sort it out. And don't make Cassandra do it for you. She's not your skivvy, just because her mother is dead, are you Cassy? You're not Cinderella.'

She thought this would embarrass Helen, this lack of sensitivity. Rudeness is a sort of weapon Helen's mother uses against her children. She farts at the table. She used to tell us to watch how she could eat an entire packet of caramel hobnobs in one go, filling her mouth from the packet and then crunching down on the whole lot, bits of biscuit flying like sparks. The other thing she would do was spray canned cream into her open mouth and swallow it down defiantly. With her mouth still full of cream she'd answer her daughters' repulsed faces by quoting the tin: 'zero-fat!' If there was any reaction at all on Helen's face her mother would imitate her, pursing her lips and sticking her nose in the air. Helen, she said, had been a little madam since the day she was born.

The other thing Helen's mum enjoys doing is making sex jokes about Helen's dad not being able to get it up. It was a regular thing when I used to stay here. She would gesture to his trousers: 'I'm telling you Cassandra, it's been a while since that old boy's been in action. What with all the medication he's on for being such a bloody loony!'

Helen's dad rarely speaks. He is handsome and tall but with the sort of face that betrays nothing. When she spoke like this he didn't even go red. He didn't even flinch.

Helen didn't see her mother all that much though. It's a huge house. Staying here was a sort of all-expenses-paid hotel with the slight drawback of an angry woman bashing about determined to make Helen's life less pleasant. We were kicked out of our rooms by Sally around noon every day so that she could make the beds and pick up our laundry. Our holidays here were spent avoiding Helen's mother. We had to. Helen couldn't stand to be in her presence. She would visibly shrink when she was in a room with her mother, and a prickly heat rash would appear on her arms and thighs. Her mother was always slamming in and out of the house with painters and builders and gardeners. There was always work being done. When she was called to the phone by 'the help', she would say, 'Look, I'm very busy. I have six children and a house to run! Make it quick!'

Sometimes we would spend the whole day in Helen's bed, watching TV and eating snacks, only leaving for an hour while her room underwent its daily clean. They have a pantry full of goodies that her mother keeps locked, but Tatiana used to let us in to get treats. If someone rang for one of the sisters you never knew whether they were in the house or not, it's so big and sprawling. If you didn't wander into the kitchen around dinner time Tatiana would go and look for you, and if she didn't find you Sally would put the dinner in the fridge. If we were hungry Helen would ask her daddy for money and we would order pizza or wander down to the village and eat in a restaurant called The Stables. Even so, if Helen's mother got it into her head to have it out at Helen, she would think of any reason, and she would track us down.

The incident I remember most clearly was when she pulled Helen out of bed at four in the morning by the scruff of her neck. I was sleeping in Helen's bed. We had fallen asleep watching a *Friends* box-set. I followed as Helen was shoved down three flights of stairs and into the wide hallway.

There her mother stood over a little pool of foaming vomit and screamed for a good forty-five minutes. 'You sick little bitch, you asshole, you prissy madam, you ugly little skank …'

The gist of it was that Jed, the ancient Labrador, who had been a Christmas present from Santa when Helen was nine years old, had been vomiting regularly at times when the staff were off. Helen, apparently, had never taken true responsibility for her own dog and was a prissy little bitch and could damn well clean it up herself. The dog was ill and had been whining at night, which was waking Helen's mother, and why should she be up when Helen was sound asleep because of Helen's fucking old bastard of a fucking shit-heap of a dog? Her accent began to shift into one I didn't recognize. She had moved up in the world, Trina, her father was a farmer who had become rich suddenly when she was a girl, and then she had married Helen's father, who does something I don't understand with money and property and makes a fortune.

She began to address me.

'Why on earth are you friends with someone like Helen, Cassandra? You have no idea what she's really like. Since the day she was born she has done nothing but take …'

Then I was treated to an in-detail description of the stitches Helen inflicted on her mother, the taut stomach that the pregnancy destroyed, the un-shiftable weight she had been carrying ever since.

'And you have no idea Cassandra, how I loved that child …'

Her attacks always ended like this, with a profession of unbearable love. I always thought Trina's behaviour towards Helen was that of an unrequited lover. There must have been some sort of love behind the will to torment Helen. It was a sort of attention-seeking, a way of staying present in her daughter's life.

These incidents didn't affect me all that much. I loved staying at Helen's. It was totally different to my grandparents' house, where my every move was monitored, where we read together in the same room, and lunch and dinner were served by my grandmother promptly at one and at six. At meal times my grandfather would ask me what I had done that day, and I was at pains to make it sound like time usefully spent. If they noticed that I was still up at ten reading, my grandfather would say that really it was foolish to stay up late reading because your brain was getting too tired to work properly, and my grandmother would gently suggest that I had a good sleep, and I, totally incapable of willfully displeasing either of them, would switch off my lamp.

I lie on the bed and look up at the setting sky through the skylight. I like being in this house again. It fills me with a sort of nostalgia, a familiarity that gives me a sense of belonging. The room still smells the way it always has: sweetly, of straw for some reason.

I'll have to start getting ready though. Opposite this room, through a wide landing done up like a girly den – pink sofa and wall-mounted TV – is the bathroom where Helen and I first shaved our legs. I walk across to it and look for a toothbrush. I didn't bring anything like that. It's a well-stocked house in that regard. There are three new toothbrushes by the sink, Molton Brown shower gel and shampoo, and some sort of anti-ageing facial wash.

I open the window and lean out over the garden. The air is heavy and dark. Breathing it is like taking a long, cool drink of water. A marquee has been assembled on the lawn, and there are workmen in overalls climbing about, stringing up tiny lights that twinkle like millions of stars. It's only then that I notice the yellow Post-it stuck to the windowsill. There is a smiley face on it, and a little note:

Hi Cassandra! Have a good time. x Tatiana

twenty-three

WHEN HE came out of the bathroom, Oisín found Helen sitting at the mirror wearing a dress he had never seen her in before. It was the colour of wine. There was no back. Instead the dress was held on with a thick ribbon that cut red lines over her cream back. The nakedness went all the way down. It stopped just before the crack of her ass.

'Where did you get that?'

'Are we fighting?'

'No. I just asked you where you got the dress.'

'Sorry. I thought you were angry with me for something. I've had it for years. I wear it for all these sort of things. I got it made for my pre-debs.'

'It's sexy. Stand up.'

She smiled and slipped on a pair of high, green satin shoes that were under the stool. She stood and turned to face him. The dress was heavy and shiny. It was a corset on top, with the silk ruffled on the torso. The ruffles tapered into a peak at her abdomen, as though pointing to her pussy. Then it fell straight to the floor from her hips, with a lighter, see-through material over it. It pulled in her waist and pushed her breasts up.

'Your tits look amazing.'

She didn't conceal her disappointment. The heat rose to her cheeks as she looked down at the cleavage. 'They're fake. I have these gel pads in. You can't wear a bra, obviously ...'

She gestured over her shoulder to the strap-revealing back. There were mirrors behind her and on either side. She looked lonely, standing there with her back to herself, waiting for his verdict. The colour of the dress made her skin look translucent and emphasized the colour in her lips and cheeks as though she were burning with passion. She looked like a woman. He loved her again suddenly and wished he hadn't said it. 'Baby, you look so hot! Okay, *now* I want you to take it off ...' She grinned and shook her head, 'No way. It's impossible getting it on and off. Today was the first time I got it on without help.'

She sat down at the mirror and began to apply blobs of yellow cream to her chin and forehead. She had never done her make-up in front of him before. She had applied lipstick in the morning and things like that, but she had never done the whole thing.

'Do you think my suit is okay? I didn't know this was such a big party.'

She nodded. 'Dunno. I suppose so. A suit is a suit, Oisín. I dunno.' She was putting something else on now, something white under her eyes and under her eyebrows. Then she brushed brown powder under her cheeks. He had no idea make-up was so complicated.

He got dressed quickly. He didn't like being naked when she wasn't, and he hated the sight of his flaccid penis lying off to the side like that. Then he sat on the bed and watched. Who was she doing all this for? Surely it was cheating – fake boobs and all this make up? How come women were allowed to do that? As a man he could see that a girl was wearing make-up but he still fancied her because her eyelashes looked long and her lips were red. If he wore make-up under his eyes to cover up the dark circles no one would take him seriously. And women had no scruples about strapping on fake boobs and taking them off once they'd got you into their beds. If a man took off his shirt to reveal arm padding he'd be a laughing stock. It must make women feel powerful to know all those tricks, to build another face onto their own, to transform their bodies. He would like to know what it felt like to be inside that silk dress. The fabric would be cool and soft, wrapping lovingly around every curve and dip of the waist and abdomen. That must be why it made Helen glow like that. No one could help but feel beautiful, lapped all over by that precious fabric. It must make a woman feel powerful to walk into a room and know everyone is gazing at her wiggling bum or her naked back, to know she is setting off all kinds of involuntary chemical impulses.

Helen turned to him and made a kissing shape with her lips, 'Do my lips look any bigger? I'm wearing this new stuff, "Fat Lip". It's meant to puff them up.'

She ignored his silence, turned back to the mirror and continued to plump her lips using pencils and paints and lube. The result was obscene. Her lips were just right as they were; any bigger was ridiculous. All the fake shadows and shine made them look like cartoon lips. Still, the thought that they were Helen's lips but also different to Helen's turned him on. They belonged to him, those fattened red sex organs. He could fuck those lips if he wanted to. He knew what they looked like naked.

'Okay, don't take it off. Leave it on.'

'Hmm?' She had forgotten what they had been talking about. They had been in silence for so long. 'The dress. Leave it on. Tell me not to fuck you and I will anyway. Tell me I'll crumple your dress.'

Still facing the mirror, she looked at his reflection and laughed. On either side, her profile laughed too. Then she got up and approached him slowly. She put her face very close to his but she didn't kiss him. She smelled different. It was some other perfume. It wasn't girlish like the stuff she usually wore. He looked into her pushed-up breasts, and kissed the part where they met. He could feel the warmth from her body on his face. She grinned as though what she was about to administer were not pleasure at all but some atrocity, and began to open his trousers. It was not a gesture of affection, she was proving something. The trousers were cheap. He had never thought that before. He thought they were a bargain but they weren't. They were cheap. They were thin and unlined. The threads all hung loose inside and scratched his skin. When she undid the catch they fell open and he pushed them down until they dropped to his ankles. She kissed his abdomen and then drew little circles with the tip of her tongue around his navel and downwards. His cock was against her face. He hit her cheek with it and she smiled kindly, but as though he was interrupting her. He hit her again and it made a dull thud. 'Suck my cock baby.'

While he came he put his fingers to her throat to feel her swallow it all in. He held her head to his crotch until he turned to a soft little slug on her tongue. He didn't feel victorious, the way he should have. Despite the continuing flush of cum, the thick hard cock, despite the sight of her dress spread like a red pool at his feet, her naked white knees, her uplifted chin, he felt humiliated. With the same act that should have degraded her, that should have made him feel like a lord, pumping all his cum down this beautiful throat, she had conquered him. Whatever unspoken, obscure battle it was that they had been having since the bus ride, she had won.

She planted a satisfied kiss on his flaccid penis. He hated being spat out into the cold. When she stood up he cupped it and pulled up his jocks. Her lipstick had worn away. All that was left was the outline of the cartoon pout under and over her real lips. What he felt, along with his defeat, was a vague sort of pity for her.

He lay back on the bed while she sat in front of the mirror again and re-applied the mouth. He rolled his head to the side and noticed that the door was unlocked and very slightly ajar. She must have left to get the dress while he was showering. He was too spent to care. He let his eyes close and that thing he had felt by the window came over him again: that, lazy, almost-pleasant desire to cry.

The three-way mirror was very unusual. He had never seen anything like it. It was like something from the Victorian age, or a fairy tale. He wondered what his mam would think of it, whether she would like it. She would be too embarrassed to sit at it like that. She would refuse to meet her own eyes.

He wished he could give something like that to his mother, some beautiful fairytale mirror that she would sit at and like her face in. She was no good at putting on make-up though. It wasn't really her. He had never forgotten her eyes the day she had collected him from school with bright candy-pink lipstick pasted across her mouth. At first he had thought it was some sort of medicated sun block. 'What's on your mouth?' His brothers were there too, but they had known better than to say anything. Instead they had looked at one another, suppressed laughter twitching in their cheeks. The lipstick really did look silly, especially as it was the only make-up she had on. It glowed against the naked, wrinkled skin. She looked a joke. His mother's eyes were the only thing alive about her. They were always occupied with something faraway. There was always something they were about to express but didn't. He would never forget the way they shrank as her three sons climbed quietly into the car. He was in the back. He watched her in the rear-view mirror. He had felt he couldn't breathe anticipating it, the flinching resignation, humiliation, even anger, all about to burst out of her. But it didn't. She rubbed her lips violently with the back of her hand. 'Lipstick. I was trying it out.' She released the clutch and then jerked the gear stick forward. The car jolted to life. 'The girl in the chemist gave me a sample. She said it looked nice.'

Helen was finished her make-up. She lay down carefully beside him, restricted by the tight dress. He rolled onto his back and took her hand. They lay like that for some minutes. Both hungry, both dressed, listening to hammering and shouting as the marquee was built on the ground outside.

WHEN I step out of the shower the atmosphere of the house has changed. I can hear the mumble of faraway chatter from downstairs, but it's calm up here in the sanctuary of the attic. I open the bathroom window to let out the steam, and watch the white haze hit the cold air and turn whiter, forming itself into slow, curling ribbons, vanishing into the night then like something frightened and alive.

Down on the grass the party is brewing. There are Russian and Philippine women rushing back and forth between the house and the star-spangled marquee with large platters and bowls. The guests have seeped onto the grass, or else they have not gone into the marquee yet. Maybe it's not ready. The men are all in suits. They look like figurines. Women who have just reached a long staved-off middle age have chosen glamour in place of sexiness, and draped their ageing bodies with layers of expensive and unusual fabrics. Even their sleeves drape. When they lift the glasses to their mouths the cloth pours from wrist to curtained waist. The glasses look fragile and precious in their colourless simplicity, glinting respectably amidst all that cloth. Many of these women have sparkling things sewn into the cloth that make them glisten in the quiet sheets of light cast from the house. They look like great sea creatures, magnificent, ugly humps wading on the surface of the lawn.

It feels as though this scene belongs to me, as though it is mine to watch: the jewel-barnacled women, the fake stars and the sad waft of expensive perfume and cosmetics and marinated chicken skewers moving sluggish through the night air. I almost feel I own it, the little millings about, the tension in all the shoulders, the sense of disappointment already tickling its way into the relief after all the preparation has been done. I almost believe that I can see through to the workings of it. Then I remember how rude that is, that it is not my party at all, it's not even Helen's party, it's her parents', and I am their guest. It took me a long time in life to realize how rude it is to stand back from something and watch it like that. How disrespectful it is, that watching, because it can rob anything of its validity, make anything ridiculous, because a person can't gaze on life like God. God infuses meaning. This sort of looking takes meaning away.

My grandmother would hate this. 'Pomp', she would call it, in honour of my grandfather, who would use just that word. I can hear the way he would say it, the thick Brussels accent: 'pomp and frrrrills'. She was invited, of course. That's what most of the guests are, people Helen's mum knows just about well enough to invite. I don't think she has friends, not really. Except maybe that couple, Mary and Denis. Helen's parents have known them since before they started going out. They are her friends, I think.

Out-of-fashion pop music explodes from the marquee. The guests turn their heads. It stops and something darker begins, something classical and dramatic with lots of wind instruments. It suits the scene well. It suits the lavish costumes. Then that stops and one of Vivaldi's *Four Seasons* begins to play at the right volume. The guests go back to sipping their wine, and begin to drift towards the marquee. The party has begun.

I go into my room and take my dress out from the suitcase. It's the one I wore to Brian's launch years ago, the one with all those marine colours, that seaweed effect.

I'm still getting dressed when Helen comes in. She doesn't knock, just walks in. She looks beautiful. She is wearing the blood-coloured silk dress she wore for our pre-debs. The sight of her face, the cheeks and lips brightened with make-up, makes me think of the word 'blossom', which is a silly word but seems apt. She looks tall in that dress. I am standing in a thong, no bra over my nubs of breasts, trying to get the dress on over my head, which is tricky because it's all strings and zips.

'I don't want to go down on my own. Oisín is shaving and Mammy keeps screaming for me to come down and meet Uncle Raymond. She says I know him but I don't.'

She helps me on with the dress. When she has pulled it down over my face and shoulders, when I have scootched it around so that it sits the right way on my frame, I look at her again. I feel grateful to be allowed to look at her when she is glowing like this. It's that thing that happens with her, that effervescence. She is as tall as me now, because I'm bare-foot and she must be wearing high heels. It feels uncomfortably intimate to be on a level with Helen, face to face, when she is beautiful like this. Not for the first time, I have to suppress the instinct to kiss her. So that I won't kiss her, I speak. 'You look beautiful.'

She smiles, 'I have piles of make-up on! I totally forgot to get something new. You think it's okay to wear this dress *again*? You think it matters? Will they notice?'

'Oh shit, I didn't bring any make-up!'

'You don't need any.'

'I do.'

'You don't. There's no one here who matters.'

I get ready quickly and don't bother with any other make-up because Helen is right, there's no one here who matters. She's right as well, to want an escort to descend the stairs with. The hall is packed. The walk downwards seems to take forever, as vaguely familiar faces turn towards us and whisper, 'Now, which one is that?'

There is muttering about Helen's boyfriend, that he is around here somewhere and he is from college. All this I gather on the journey from the top of the stairs to the bottom. Then we find Helen's sisters huddled in a corner, all beautiful in a similar way to Helen, all like sexy cherubs, but only Katie, the youngest, with that glow that Helen has. It's a freak of genetics, how the O'Brien girls turned out. Neither parent has the high, round cheeks or the ringlets. I shouldn't say they are all beautiful. Emma looks awful. She is wearing a dark, long-sleeved dress and her shoulders jut out. She has transformed into a streak of sinews, sharp edges and fluffy skin. Her face is sunken. Her ringlets have turned to drooping scraggles. Perhaps she is beautiful in a new, dangerous sort of way.

Carla and Laura have boyfriends too, and Katie has invited a few boys who are all just friends and are all pining for her. They are dreadful gangly things with puberty sprouting around their chins. Katie is fifteen. She is wearing a clubbing outfit and too much make-up. She came to the family late enough to be comfortable with this wealth. It's all she knows. She is not as serious as her sisters. Katie is the only one likely to have a free gaff and let her friends trash the house. She is the only one likely to be caught with hash or cigarettes stashed in her room. She talks differently, through her nose, doing a funny thing with her vowels, and she wears only brand-name clothes. All the same, I like Katie a lot. There is something genuine about her despite, or perhaps because of all this.

The boys hang quietly on the edges of the circle. All of the girls' boys are a sort of protection against the mother, something of their own that they can take to the party and take away again into their other life, away from Trina. The girls are excited. They are enjoying the solidarity of this, the togetherness of being in their own home full of strangers, of looking communally beautiful. Katie kisses Helen on the cheek and says, matter-of-factly, in case there is any doubt, 'You look really nice.'

Then she gives me a bear hug and so do Emma and Carla and the twins, Laura and Sorcha. They say they haven't seen me in ages and they miss me and so on. Then Katie looks over my shoulder. 'Oh shit, Helen, it's Mammy. She's already got us. You're on your own. Do you know that guy? Mammy says we know him. Uncle Raymond?'

Trina approaches us with the elbow of a heavy, bearded man in her grip. She runs a hand all the way down Helen, from under her arm to her hip, then holds her chin with her thumb and the bend of her fingers:

'You look pretty when you're in a good mood, Helen. You're dog ugly when you're not.'

Trina has an odd way of touching her girls that is somewhere between midwife and brothel keeper. Though the eldest, Helen has never learned how to deal with Trina. She shudders as her mother's hand brushes her waist, lifts her chin for her and then stands blank-faced, waiting for someone to say something. Carla, taller and a little darker than Helen, with long hair piled on top, puts her hand on Helen's arm.

'Yes, she's beautiful, isn't she?'

Trina introduces the man as Uncle Raymond, as though he is a fond and familiar relative. He says something sleazy about Helen's exposed back, and then Trina leads Helen over to meet 'Deirdre, you remember her? You knew her when you were little …'

We walk out over the damp grass to the marquee and I talk to the sisters until they begin to disperse and then I pal up with little Katie, who is ignoring the boys she brought and who used to crawl into bed with me and Helen on the mornings when I stayed, tucking her neat eight-year-old body in between us.

The boys are standing awkwardly in a corner, watching everything. The marquee is surprisingly warm. The fabric inside is a thick purple velvet, and the tiny twinkling lights lend a fairytale charm. Katie and I pile salads and kebabs onto our plates and find some chairs to sit on while we eat. Katie is comfortably getting drunk before me, though she is underage.

Where is the dad in all of this? Helen's dad, Trina's husband, Pat? I spot him standing beside the drinks table, his mouth set with a slight curl at each edge, an expression of friendly neutrality, if that is possible. If asked for his opinions on anything, Pat will shrug and shake his head saying, 'Well, you know, you can't be too extreme about these things.'

It seems to go on for hours, the waiting about, the guests approaching Katie and saying, 'Which one are you?' and 'Do you remember me?'

Some of them aren't that rich. I didn't see that from the window. Some of them are wearing cheap suits and flimsy ties, the women in high street dresses. Some of them are shocked by all this. The lavishness is as much for them as for the wealthy neighbours. Trina loves her money, and she loves to display her life like this, like something to be sold. She would love to think they envied her.

At last someone taps a glass and someone else tells the DJ to turn off the music. Denis, the parents' friend, makes a speech. It is a comical thing of rhyming couplets, with dirty bits, about Trina and Pat and how they met and what happened then and all the sex they must have had to make six children. I don't hear very much of it, all I grasp is the limerick rhythm of it, and the crude, unnatural laughter that whoops out of the guests every few lines. Everyone is grinning.

They are all taken up with this idea, the generous couple, happily married for twenty-five years and still going strong, six beautiful daughters, rich as fuck, fair dues to them, that's what everyone is thinking. Except Pat, the dad, who is still standing by the drinks table with that still face, laughing politely, non-committally, and not as loudly as everyone else. Trina is standing beside him now, holding his hand and snuggling her face into his shoulder. Trina wrote most of this speech. I can tell by the way she follows Denis's lips as he recites. As long as I have known Helen though, her parents have not shared a room. And Trina has hated Pat for as long as I have known them, calling him a fucking idiot a few times a day, a pathetic bastard, a loo-la, and he has been silent on all this for as long as I have known them, so there is no way of knowing what he feels.

All the same it is infectious. The iambic meter is like a heartbeat, lulling us into its own world. And I can see Helen thinking, 'Gosh, maybe they love each other after all. Maybe we're all happy and we all love each other after all,' and she kisses Oisín and folds his beefy arms over her bare back and raises her face to him like an offering and he grins smugly, stupidly. All the O'Brien girls do this now, cling to their men and smile at Denis and then at their parents, believing in this happiness, surprised at it, but believing in it.

The party takes off after the speech. The music changes and the beautiful daughters begin to dance wildly and jokingly. I dance too, and we're having a good time now; we are enjoying looking beautiful and carefree and silly. Pat comes over and dances too, stiffly, and smiles at his daughters; his achievement. The boyfriends and the wannabe boyfriends dance too.

We are so beautiful. Especially Helen, even though she is getting tired suddenly, around the eyes and skin, the places where her glow was a few hours ago. Even Oisín. He looks beautiful too: rosy-cheeked, young, healthy. He's smiling at her with love and astonishment and a vague, respectable sort of desire, swinging his hips stupidly. I can feel my own beauty, the way it swells under my clothes, the perfection of my body at this age of twenty-one, the perfection even of the flaws just because it is all smoothed in youth. And I think for what? What is all this beauty for?

After a few hours the guests begin to leave and Helen stops dancing and touches my elbow, 'I'm tired. Do you want to come inside?' We all sit in the kitchen, Helen and I and the other O'Brien girls, and some teenagers I haven't met before, who must be friends of someone's. Everyone's drunk, except Helen, who looks tired and happy. The boys sit outside the babble, quietly intoxicated, while the girls laugh and nibble at some leftover pavlova roll with fresh berries and cream. Carla boils some milk on the Aga to make us all Baileys hot chocolate, and then asks me to take over because I am better at whipping the egg. I love this, the girlishness, the warmth, the togetherness of it. I feel privileged to be part of it.

At the same time I want to tell them to be grateful, the sisters, because they don't know how precious this is. I feel like a sister too, and so do the teenagers. The family love this. They love this patronage, this adopting of other people. There are a few of us, 'my other kids', Trina calls them, though she has very little to do with us. It is more a case of being adopted as a sister or brother. They say things like, 'I love the way Cassy makes hot chocolate, don't you? I love the way she puts the marshmallows in and cooks them a bit …' and you get the feeling of being loved, of mattering, and are grateful for it. In this way the family expresses its abundance and its lack.

I don't know what we talk about, because I'm quite drunk now too, sipping my hot chocolate and looking at the girls, all those bouncing ringlets and the animated O'Brien eyes, all different depths of blue. Helen looks fragile, leaning back in a kitchen chair, one hand on her abdomen and the other dangling loose beside her.

The dress is losing its magic. She isn't speaking with the others. She is frowning slightly. Sorcha is saying something funny, about her mother, probably, and the others are laughing.

Helen stands up suddenly. 'I'm tired. I'm going to go up.' It is the end of some private train of thought in which she thinks we were included. She goes upstairs without ceremony, and there is a sense that the rest of us have been jilted by her. The fun is gone out of our little gathering. The boy, Oisín, hangs around a bit longer, leaning on the Aga, looking awkward with his too-long arms, and then leaves too. I want to go to bed now. I kiss all the sisters, bear-hug them all, and begin making my way through the dregs of guests that are admiring the photographs in the hallway, and up the stairs.

On the landing there's an antique grandfather clock. It's 3 AM. I actually need to be up early. My grandmother will be coming to collect me in the morning. It is typical of her. 'No, I won't go Trina, if you don't mind, it is too tiring for me, but if you don't mind perhaps I could come in the morning? I could bring some croissants. It's been some weeks since I have made a batch. I could bring the pastries if you had a cup of coffee for me? What time do you think you'll be up? Is ten too early?'

My eighty-four year old grandmother, ever-dignified, skidding about in her old Merc, coming to collect me so that I can spend tomorrow night between clean sheets, wrapped in the smell of her utility room and her care. At my grandfather's funeral she sat like a guest. It meant nothing to her, this ritual for people who don't know what life and death are really about. It had nothing to do with her or my grandfather. All the grandchildren did a party piece. My cousin played something slow and impressive on the violin. I read a poem by Goethe that my grandfather had copied for me once in pencil onto a piece of paper, about death and rest. It was in German. I didn't cry because she wasn't crying. I hadn't the right.

I am angry with my grandmother for her resilience. My grandmother, well used to mourning, administering yet more of her never-ending supply of love to us hungover shits, folding homemade croissants – a two-day process, a miraculous skill that will die with her – fixing us coffee that tastes as though she has made it, because she has something, my grandmother, a wisdom that makes everything she touches sacred, and I think, well, thanks, but what a waste, what good is all this to me when you will be dead soon anyway? Leaving only us kids with all our potential, all our future, all our waste of beauty.

twenty-four

YOU WAKE, and remember. No, you don't remember because you haven't forgotten. How could you forget when it's in your body, this knowledge? You wake and it is the first thing you know.

You're not sick from it, though there is a vague waking nausea, and a nagging need for more sleep. Oisín is curled beside you, his hands tucked under his chin, his mouth pushed into a pout, snoring mildly. He looks like someone else the way dead people look like someone else. This is not how he would like you to see him. This pose, curled like this, is remiss on his part. He has forgotten – because his body holds no knowledge in its folds, lets everything dangle outwards, shakes off memory, feels for more, retains nothing – because his body is like this, its rest separate and total, he has forgotten that he is asleep beside you.

Your nausea is like a hangover. You can almost taste it in your morning breath though you didn't drink last night. You didn't drink even a sip of wine. That's how you know you'll have your baby, Helen, because it wasn't planned at all – the not-drinking. It was a decision made by your body, your stomach that lurched from the smell of deep-fried brie and the antiseptic champagne, that is guarding that other beat in the deep red of your womb. With this haze of hormones your body protects it from you and whatever you would normally think or do. Your body, ushering you into the past already like a gentle hand on the small of your back, *make way, make way* ... You are already moving dumbly, you already feel bovine. It's your body, which has a better sense of destiny than you do, and better navigational skills, that has been making the decisions all along.

Oisín breathes in noisily and turns onto his back. Something in his dreams is disturbing him. As often happens when you wake beside Oisín, the air feels used-up and dry. He saps the moisture from a room when he sleeps. You need to open the window. You roll over and sit up, aware of your lithe body, its miraculous capacity for movement. The small of your back aches, the spot where that hand is placed, nudging you on. The dress is collapsed on the floor, the shape of you still warm in its bodice and the full skirt spread in peaks and valleys all around it. Instead of opening the window you go downstairs. You need out of the room altogether, the exhausted air, Oisín's privacy.

This house is always cold. It is too big to be otherwise. Any warmth in it feels superficial, like the sweat from synthetic clothing. Your bare feet hit the heated floor of the hall and you remember then the feeling of mornings in this house: stagnated blood in your hands and feet and that cold in your back; the plush darkness beyond the glossy black windowpanes because there are no next-door neighbours, not really. Night drags on into morning here, something to do with the house's low-lying position, but you don't know what.

In the kitchen a long-legged woman with stripy hair is tackling the washing-up. It's your mother's Villeroy & Boch. It can't go in the dishwasher. She has a high, round, denim-clad bum, this woman, and no hips. She doesn't turn when you come in and you have left it too late to say anything. By the time you reach the fridge the dumbness is insistent, pressing on your lips, goaded by slosh of the washing-up. There is a clawing in your throat, a clot in your stomach like a lie let slide. You want her to turn and look at you, and you want to say, 'Do you have any babies? I am going to have one. It's being made right now. I am a woman too.' But she doesn't turn and you can't speak.

The kitchen is immaculate already, apart from the washing-up, which is stacked to this woman's left and covers the worktop all the way around the corner. There is nothing in the fridge that you feel like eating. It all smells like fridge. Then you think 'granola'. Your mother has a new slide-out press. It works by twisting a little knob on the wall. An array of dry food glides out. The food contents are accessible from both sides, the jars and packets held in by a little railing. There is no granola. But there are Coco Pops. A bowl of Coco Pops is just what you wanted and you can't get enough. You eat three bowls, one after the other, trying not to be too loud because you're sitting alone at the new oak table that seats twelve, in the huge kitchen with a transparent ceiling, your knees tucked up under Oisín's jumper, continuously chomping while at the other end of this kitchen a woman with her back to you is washing precious plate after precious plate, and placing them in the second sink, which is a sink for rinsing, like they have on the continent, or so your mother says, and this woman is pretending not to notice you. The bowl you are eating out of is not Villeroy & Boch, so she will not have to wash it, it can go in the dishwasher. It is a plastic thing from your childhood with a faded Bosco on the inside. His hair and nose are pink. The rest of him has paled to grey.

You want milk now. A big glass of milk, which is something you haven't had in years. Another sliding press contains the glasses, and you select a dishwasher-proof one, because the thought of putting your used glass alongside all those wine glasses – about two hundred, it must be, the red ones with a little pool of water at the bottom to stop them from staining – is excruciating. It's a thick beer glass you take out, and you fill it with cold milk, but something happens as you lift it to your mouth. You let go. Then the glass is smashed at your feet, shards poking up from a pool of clean milk, and at last the woman with the striped hair turns around. Her face is older than her body. She looks Russian. She must be a friend of Tatiana's, hired to help with the party. She has a small swelling in her abdomen, elasticated jeans, an early pregnancy, and she squats and picks up the broken pieces and places them in the base of the glass, which has remained intact.

'Sorry. I'm so sorry. I'll do it,' you stoop to help but then you stop, embarrassed by her disregard. She doesn't look at you. She keeps her head down. 'Is no problem. Is okay.'

What you want is for her to look at you, but she doesn't, and it occurs to you that she is not used to cleaning people's houses and she doesn't know the way it works. She does not know how to address you. She does not know that in this house the staff and the children are comrades. She wants to be invisible and do this job and get paid. She is about ten years older than you, with bad skin. Your feet are tucked up as though too precious to touch the mess, and you watch her tidy the glass and clean the milk, you keep saying *sorry*, *sorry* but she ignores you so then you stop. You badly want to pour yourself another glass but that seems impudent.

The woman has tidied the glass and returns to the washing-up. You have to shout to be heard across the big kitchen, and you know she would prefer you not to speak at all.

'I'm sorry. I don't know what happened. One moment it was in my hand and then it wasn't. Sorry.'

She turns and looks at you. She has no idea what you said. She tries to read your face, responds with an ambiguous turning upwards of her mouth.

'I'm Helen.'

She nods, the expression still fixed on her face.

'Are you Tatiana's friend?'

'Excuse me. I don't understand.'

'Are you a friend of Tatiana?'

'Ah, Tatiana. Yes.'

'Would you like a cup of tea?'

'Ah. No thank you.'

'You are having a baby?' You pat your own belly. She smiles.

'Ah. Yis. I have another, my Nik. He is five. He is a funny boy ... He is so a funny boy. He is doing Irish dancing.' She smiles and it looks as though she might cry with the intensity of it; her little boy's loveliness.

You pour another glass of milk and drink it on the landing, sitting on the top step. All the bedroom doors are closed. Somewhere a bathroom is open, the light left on. The persistent night bears down through the giant skylights two stories up.

Oisín is still asleep. He doesn't stir when you pass through the bedroom to the en-suite. You twist the shower controls and the water jolts from warm, to hot, to hotter – as hot as you can bear. You face the gush from the faucet. You want to be cleansed of everything but this pregnancy, you want to be left clean as a pebble, hollow and smooth like the large shell they had in the fourth-year bathroom at school. It was a beautiful thing with curling ridges on the outside, but inside it was impossibly white, impossibly smooth and empty. The Sisters said that when you put it to your ear you could hear the sea. That's how empty it was. The sea echoed through it.

You will the water to do this for you. *Wash through me, wash through me. Hollow me out.* You imagine yourself glowing from the inside with all this emptiness, your blood washed pale as watered milk, a shell for other things to echo through.

You know something now, or you will know something. The almost-crying, 'My Nik'. There was a promise of knowledge in the little square of blue. Blue: Positive. You feel now that you knew the moment it happened, in the quiet after climax you could feel yourself softening, the angular hipbones losing their sharpness, tight anxiety at your heart loosening into something else. If you are ever to know your mother this will be how. But you will not become your mother, with an ass that stretches all the way around her, with that hatred that glints like evil itself, with all that flailing discontent. Maybe you will take away your mother's core excuse and cripple her. Maybe you will love and love, stupidly, blindly and perpetually, and the future will fly onwards and leave all this sickness behind.

Oisín stays asleep as you slip between the covers, naked and clean. He is curled up again, his hands folded neatly one over the other and tucked under his cheek.

You try it out, while he is asleep beside you. If it is not true it will feel wrong in your mouth. You will feel like you're lying.

'Oisín, I don't love you.'

Nothing. He is asleep. It doesn't feel like a lie but it doesn't ring quite true either.

'I don't love you.'

Nothing. Go back to sleep, Helen.

twenty-five

I AM IN my grandmother's attic amidst the stacks of boxes: records of sixty years that no one will ever have the patience to go through, bills from the 1950s with proof of payment, photos of her dead children, a yellowed lace christening gown, the programme from my mother's first real play.

I explored up here once when I was twelve. It felt like sacrilege then, fingering the things my grandmother had lain to rest. Now it feels like due respect.

The programme is printed on expensive gloss paper, cool and weighty. In the play my mother had the title role, though she was killed after Act One. There is a stamp-sized headshot beside her bio. She is wearing a black polo neck and trying not to grin.

It is pitch black up here but I know where I am from the smell of damp, packed paper, and the sense of something bearing down on my head. I am looking for my grandmother's cashbooks. She is proud of how well she survived on nothing when she first came here with my grandfather, how she never begged a penny, how she fed her husband and her children on dandelion leaves and nettle soup and pulses. Her children who weren't worth the sacrifice.

'The little boy who died' – that's what she calls him. He took a lot of her love, that little boy. She never trusted anything else that came out of her again. She couldn't feed her other babies. The milk clotted to stones in her breasts. She fretted but she needn't have. They weren't worth much anyway, the next three. My mother, the youngest and prettiest and most disastrous, always jealous of the love she wasn't given, as though the clothing and feeding and care and fussing from the dregs of a heartbroken heart – the constant endeavour – were not enough.

I need to find those cashbooks: little orange notebooks thatched on both sides of the page with my grandmother's handwriting, pink elastic bands squeezing them together. It is dark though, and all the boxes smell the same, and they all look the same: dark blocks in the dark. Then the realization strikes me like a thud on my back. There is another thing up here – my miscarriage/abortion, whatever it was. It's not gone at all. It's here somewhere in the dark, a little fishy thing with silver eyes, glinting my reflection in the stifling blind. It's in a jar of odourless pink vinegar and there is no lid on the jar. I wish there were a lid on it. I feel sure that if there was a lid on it, that thing would turn into itself and expire, but it is turning in the pickle, sloshing, watching me. I asked it not to. I told it not to. Don't I have that right, at least? To say no, say goodbye, walk away?

My grandmother is somewhere here, she is telling me off. 'We never wasted a penny,' she says, 'We never borrowed a penny …' and I need to find the cashbooks to understand and I need to escape the gaze of that dumb, determined, fish-thing with giant pods for eyes.

The little boy who died is here too: a beautiful child with warm cheeks and dimpled hands. He is perched on a box somewhere, singing himself a nursery rhyme and swinging his feet against a stack of memories. He is only an infant of two and a half, but because he is a very clever child he knows all the words and the tune. I recognize the tune but at the same time I can't quite hear it. In the same way I know what he looks like, though there's no light to see him by. He has my grandfather's eyes. None of the next three had my grandfather's eyes. He wants to forgive us all, especially his namesake, my uncle Jeff. He is glad he died in the olden days instead of living now. Two and a half years was all he wanted. He wants to tell my grandmother that, but she is too busy not thinking about it. He wants her to know that she need not regret. He doesn't want to be a man of the Celtic Tiger. Poverty, for him, and his mother's breast, and some nursery rhymes, were just fine. His life was just fine, and its end was just fine. 'Don't fret,' he wants to tell her. He is perched on the box smiling at me the way those kind of children do, those beautiful, blessed-looking children full up with their mother's love. He's smiling at me because he thinks I am someone else.

I wake to the black skylight and aloneness of this attic room. I can hear birds twittering somewhere, which can't be right. The night is still thick outside. I come out of the dream full of all sorts of shapeless knowledge, a strangled sense of having something wordless to tell. My seaweed dress is in a tangled heap at my feet. I went to bed in my thong. I have no idea how I could have slept in it. The lacy string is unbearable, chafing at my bum, and I have just acknowledged my hangover, which has been there all along through my dream, a persistent, dull pain in every part of me. When people die from old age that must be what it's like. Pain everywhere, and too tired to care. How ridiculous it is to be young and give yourself a preview of that misery. How ridiculous it seems, sometimes, to be young.

I swing out of bed into the cold of this house and root in my knapsack for the nightdress I brought. I did bring a nightdress. I have no idea why I went to bed in my knickers. I put on my nightdress now only as a sort of formality. I will have to get up and be dressed when my grandmother arrives anyway, shake off the hangover, smile at her and look happy in the mysterious way that young people look to her now – cheesy, inaccessible, saying words like 'cool' and 'kosher', words that have different meaning for her. It baffles her: I do not have a man or a child, I have nothing to love when she is gone. What am I happy about? I can't answer that, but I will bamboozle her with my smile and my prettiness and she will believe that I am really happy, that she does not need to understand. That is all I have to offer her, the promise of my happiness; the promise of my future.

I will have a little boy some day, for her. Some day I will pick up the little fishy thing, take it out of the pink pickle and nourish it into a baby. I will stop drinking and eat all the right things and I will give birth with courage. I will not curse as he smashes out of me. My breasts will flow with creamy milk. I will not call him Jeff. I will not think his life has been a waste if it expires at two and a half. I will not fret.

Somehow in the dark that really seems possible, to take it out of the pickle, and I resolve not to forget what I must do.

I lie on the covers, enjoying the cold. I can feel it burrow its way into my bones, my back, my shoulders, especially my pelvis: the place my grandmother always insists I keep warm. 'Your kidneys,' she always says – but it's not about my kidneys. It's the future in there, the pulsing uterus, the place that will carry some remedy to all her disasters. I like the terrible chill in my boy's hips, in my stunned womb, begging to be covered up, to be swaddled warm. I am proving something, letting it freeze like this.

I don't even hear him come up the stairs, but he crashes into the room, Helen's daddy, in blue striped pyjamas, a piss-horn pressing through the fly. His eyes are screwed. He is blundering, half-asleep. Man-sized blue striped pyjamas? It is as though he has been dressed up to be mocked and petted, the way people put ballet dresses on kittens and stick them on greeting cards. I have a vision of Helen's mother, ten of Helen's mother, sitting in a circle around him laughing and watching him blunder sleepily.

He makes his way towards the bed blindly, a hand supporting the weight of his crotch. I am sitting up now and he sees me, and stops, and mumbles something. I don't know what to answer.

'I'm just getting up,' I say.

'Yeah. Oh. Yeah. Cassandra. Sorry, sorry. I thought it was empty.' He turns to leave, swaying, and then stops to stare ahead and shake himself awake. I have to speak to make us less alone together. It is not natural that we should be alone together, this shadow and his piss-horn and I.

'I'm just getting up,' I repeat.

'Oh, yeah. Okay.'

'I can take my bag out, if you want to sleep here?'

'Yeah okay. I – Mary and Denis are in my room.'

I didn't mean it and I certainly didn't expect him to take me up on it. At first I don't understand, and then I get up and pack everything into my bag: the twisted-up thong, the seaweed dress. He stands, sways, and tries to keep his eyes open while he waits.

When I get off the bed he keeps standing there, his eyes closed. He looks much older than I have ever seen him. His face is wrinkled in pain and I can see, because a grey light is starting to glow in from the skylight, that the little squeezes of his eyes are pink. He looks, for the first time, like a sick man, like someone on medication. I make my way to the door and he is still standing. I put down my bag and walk to the bedside. I lift the duvet cover back, opening a place for him to climb into the bed, as though he needs to be shown the way. He gets in and lies on his back. I pull the duvet over him. Then I leave.

twenty-six

WHEN OISÍN had kissed her goodbye her eyes were blank like a doll's. He had wanted to scream, shake her, make her look.

'You're breaking up with me aren't you? Aren't you Helen?' That was what he had wanted to shout, what was tumbling on his tongue, pressing forward, threatening to leap. He almost wished he'd said it, at least then he wouldn't be left with this dumb non-feeling. But that's a silly thing to say to someone if you want them to stay your girlfriend. At the bus station she gave him her key card. She asked him to hand it in because she had forgotten to do it in the rush of packing. She had to move rooms even though she'd be back in two weeks for exams.

She brought the fish with her. He told her it would survive two weeks without food but she didn't care. She had given up the cat very suddenly. The cleaning lady took it. He didn't understand why Helen wasn't keeping it. He thought she loved the cat.

It was terrible, uprooting her right before exams, moving her to a totally new building. He thought she should complain, but she said she didn't mind. They hadn't made any future plans. When he had said he'd call her she'd nodded and blinked. She'd taken a breath to speak, and then swallowed it.

Neither of them had had much sleep in the last weeks. They had been fighting. They had been staying up all night just to fight. Often in the small hours, they had lain on the bed side-by-side because their bodies were too tired to sit, and they fought like that, each looking at the ceiling, their lips moving. Sometimes he fell asleep like that, but when he woke up Helen was still talking and crying. 'You don't care. You don't even care …'

Sometimes she put her hands over her face and wept. Sometimes she pinched him with frustration, taking a fistful of his flesh and squeezing as hard as she could, her eyes red, her lips drawn back. That was what he hated the most. He hardly cared about the pain, but he wanted her to slap him, to scream. The pinching was weak and ugly and mute.

Sometimes they became so exhausted that they made quiet, painful love then, and cried, and took a shower, and ate, but then they resumed fighting. Sometimes, even in the middle of the lovemaking she would take the opportunity to punish him. Once, just before he came she had whispered:

'So, would you like to see me fucked by those guys in your porn? One in the mouth and one in the ass … can you imagine what it feels like to be fucked until you bleed? Is that what you'd like?'

Once she had pulled her knees under his torso and tried to thrust him off her just as he came. She had whispered, 'No, no, Oisín. Please stop.' He couldn't stop. Afterwards she had rolled over and sobbed like a hurt child.

It was hard for him even to understand what they were fighting about. She interrogated him. What did he do in bed with other girls before her? Did he prefer them? Did he think about them when he was fucking her? What did sex mean to him? Did he think it was wrong, the way he lost his virginity that time; what would he tell his children, if he had them, about sex and love and what they meant?

She had found porn on his laptop. Was that when it started? After the party at her parents' house? Or maybe it had already begun by then. He remembered the evening of her parents' anniversary, the look she had given him when he came down the stairs, freshly shaven, to find her. The way she stood in the mill of wealthy guests, and turned over her shoulder, her eyes moving down his body. He had been confused then by her eyes. It was as though he were hurting her just by being. He didn't know what that look meant. He thought she didn't want him to come downstairs yet, or something. He thought there was some reason that he didn't understand, some etiquette he was unfamiliar with. But by now he was used to that look.

Something else changed that day. Was it seeing her touch herself like that on the bed? After that he understood their love-making differently. When they came at the same time he used to feel they were together then, moving higher and higher into a pleasure they created for each other. He used to look at her and feel that this was as close as they could be to each other, as close as he could be to anyone.

After that evening he watched her when she came, and he could see that when it happened, that final plane, when she opened her mouth and lost her voice and shuddered, touching herself – she never came without touching herself – when her eyes rolled back and her eyebrows raised in surprise, her pleasure was a private one. He knew now, that at that moment she moved further away from him, her head back, her eyes closed, crying out for no one, and he felt a fool.

Somehow she knew about Petra. He felt that. Sometimes he was on the brink of confessing the whole thing, maybe it would lose this monstrous power it had over them. He was sure she knew, but there was always the chance she didn't, or not quite. What he couldn't handle, if he told her, were the questions she would ask: How many times? How old was she? How big were her tits?

She asked him trick questions. Questions with yes or no answers, trapped him into the bad-guy corner and then attacked.

'Do you wank to it? The porn where the girl is being raped ... Do you get off on that?'

'It's acting.'

'Do you like the idea? It turns you on?'

'Yes.'

'Would you like to see me raped?'

'I don't know.'

'Your mother? Would you like to see your mother raped?'

It wasn't just sex stuff they fought about. She had started to ask him what his opinion was. She wanted him to account for everything he did and thought.

'Do you think sweatshops are funny?'

'No.'

'Oh. Then why did you laugh when your mates were talking about those kids in Thailand? How can you laugh?'

'What do you think about the arms landing in Shannon?'

'I don't know. Bad.'

'So why didn't you go on the protest march?'

Now she was spent. For the last few days she hadn't fought with him. She was congenial – she smiled, and cooked for him, and she had linked her arm in his when they had walked home from the cinema the night before. But she didn't laugh, and when she smiled her eyes were blank, and when he woke at night she was always awake too. That morning he had woken in the small hours to find she wasn't in bed. She was lying on the couch on her back, reading a magazine. She had glanced at him when he came into his living room, her face expressionless, and gone back to the magazine. In the early light he had found her back in bed beside him, and she made love to him like a well-practised prostitute.

The way she blinked when he kissed her goodbye … He'd pulled her to him then. He'd said he loved her, but he had mumbled it close to her face, he had growled it, he had said it in his Marlon Brando accent: 'I love yeh baby, you know thath?' He had squeezed her bum then, *squeeze squeeze nudge nudge wink wink*. Fuck. He couldn't talk to her any more. He couldn't say things like that any more. Like *I love you*. Only in a jokey way or a sexy way, not in a real way. She made it impossible. She made him embarrassed all the time now.

When she had walked away, wheeling her suitcase behind her, all he could feel was loss. He thought the word 'desperate', 'I feel desperate', and it annoyed him to be thinking words like that. Flattening everything into words. It did nothing. He watched her board the grey bus. Through the plastic window, she gave him a little wave.

Now he sat on her bed. The sag of string between its nail on the wall and the curtain rail, where she usually hung her knickers and socks and hold-ups and her hand-wash-only tops, was naked. He touched it. It felt damp. It was starting to rot. He pushed downwards with his finger in the middle of the rope to see how far it reached, and let it spring back up. He bit it. It tasted of soap and mildew. He unhooked it and wound it around his hand. She should have remembered to take it down.

Like a revelation he had that feeling again of wanting to slap her or shake her and he thought so many words that they made a din in his head. He punched the wall hard and his fist throbbed but it was a distant pain. It wasn't enough. He bashed his head against the wall but it didn't hurt as much as it should have. He cried quietly on her stripped bed. It was a superficial half-cry, as though he were crying for an audience. Slow tears and a pain in his throat. Not real crying. Not bawling or heaving. Not wailing. He couldn't even cry properly.

She had made a shabby attempt to paint over her graffiti. Now that the paint had dried the scrawls began to glow through like the shadows of thought. He would have to give it a second layer or she'd be in trouble with accommodation. He was not nostalgic, so he decided not to think about eating beans on toast in bed with her, or when he read the quotes aloud and laughed at her.

'"*Images of broken language* ..." what the fuck, Helen?' He took a biro out of his knapsack. The ink had run out but he pressed the words in, correcting her. Then he wrote 'Helen', crunching it in to the drying paint. On a clear patch of the wall he wrote it again: 'Helen'. He wanted to write 'I love you', but he couldn't. He didn't know any more. *I love you* – what was that supposed to mean? Then it occurred to him – he didn't have to fix up the wall for her. What was it to him if she was penalized? He left her keys on the bed and went to pack. He was going home tomorrow.

He was thinking about the dress even before he reached the door of his flat. He could visualize it hanging coolly in his wardrobe, its folds falling long and still. Still in the way that water can be: full of possibility. It didn't smell like Helen, but like his own clothes. She had never worn it. It wasn't really Helen's style. He knew by her face when he presented it to her, that puzzlement.

'Who do you see when you look at me?'

It had made him angry. That phrase, like a line from a pop song, that ingratitude. The dress had cost him thirty euro. A few weeks before she would have laughed if he got her something she didn't like. She would have giggled with her head thrown back and gone down on him and slagged him for days. But it had already begun by then. That quiet, measured way she had now of responding to him. Those lines like bad poetry, like famous quotes. Those crappy words.

What do you see when you look at me?

What the fuck, Helen?

It was so beautiful to touch. That's why he had bought it. The feel of it. It was thin material, nearly transparent, light as foam, slipping over his hand. It had been on a model in the window as he passed the shop and what first attracted him was the way it clung to the plastic hips and the white, shiny breasts. It had a halter neck and fell to the floor. When he went into the shop to look at it he saw that it had no back. He imagined Helen in it. Making love to her from behind. He'd hitch up the long skirt. She'd be bent over and still dressed, her back dipped like a cat's.

The leopard print is probably what turned Helen off. He knew it wasn't really her. Once he had touched it though, he had to buy it. He had never felt fabric like that before.

He didn't take the dress out immediately. Instead he sat on the bed looking at the closed wardrobe door. He knew what the garment was doing in there in the dark. It was waiting patiently, enjoying its own smoothness amongst all his bulky jumpers.

He might never fuck Helen again. He thought that now for the first time. And everything they did together? What did he have to show for it? He had loved her. He was sure of that. What evidence did he have of ownership over those parts of her, the parts other people don't see? Helen sleeping, or flinching, or her face as she comes, gripping his hand, biting his ear.

They had taped themselves once, before he went home for a weekend – no, that wasn't it. It was before Galway, before Petra came over. He had told her it was a lads' weekend. When they were making love the night before, she had said, 'Let's tape us. So you can think about it when you're away.' She used her dictaphone – the one she used for her psychology module, for interviewing parents and taping kids with lisps. He had held it to her mouth in the dark. At the time it had turned him on, holding the dictaphone to her mouth, extracting all those cum sounds out of her, putting them on record. Afterwards though, when he played it back, it didn't sound like Helen. It sounded like anyone, like any porn, or any phone sex. Just breath, and sighs, and moans, and then his cry – which sounded pathetic, weak – his cry when he came.

An idea had been forming since he left Helen's. Sharon had invited him to a party tonight. He had bumped into her last week and she had smiled pleadingly and touched his arm. She was oddly attractive with her ugly haircut and those eyes. For the first time he had noticed her fingers, short and thick like a butcher's. Her nails were gnawed to the quick. Her eyes were bloodshot and there was a ball of mascara stuck in a tear duct. Those eyes.

He had agreed to go but never planned to. He had planned to get the bus home to the lads tonight and drink and not care about Helen for a few days. But he wasn't ready to go home. Not feeling like this – pussy-whipped. He wanted to leave on a high. He wanted to arrive in Clonmel full of his wild nights at Trinners, his oats scattered. The party was a fancy dress. It would be all those drama people Sharon hung out with. They were taking over the Temple Bar Music Centre. There would be pills because the drama crowd all took pills. He was going to go. Screw Helen. Fuck Helen. He was going to go.

He still didn't open the wardrobe. High and faint, he scavenged in the kitchenette for something alcoholic to keep him weighted. There was no beer so he opened a bottle of red wine that had been in the flat for ages. He couldn't remember buying it. He sat on the couch and drank two glasses, sipping them, taking his time, holding the stem gracefully between two fingers the way a woman might. He didn't remember buying the wine glass either.

The dress might not fit him. It was size twelve, a little too big for Helen. Women were impossibly small. Imagine having shoulders that delicate. Imagine having a tiny round bum. He would look stupid in the dress. His back would be too broad, his shins too long. What shoes would he wear with it? What shoes could he wear?

He would shave first. He didn't want to look at himself in the mirror and see a boar in that delicate dress. He poured a third glass of wine and brought it into the bathroom. He put it on the toilet cistern and cleaned the toothpaste speckles off the mirror with a piece of toilet paper and some spit. He was going to do this properly.

He filled the basin with warm water and found a clean face cloth. He used that shaving cream that his brother had brought him back from Spain. You couldn't get it here. It was brilliant. He hardly ever used it because it was so good. He smoothed on a pea-sized amount and moved the razor slowly and carefully. After shaving once he washed his face and exfoliated with a milk-and-oats facial scrub that Helen had left in his shower. He looked at himself. He had shaved very closely. His face looked narrower, his eyes bigger. His jaw looked as though it were sinking into his neck. He hated that. That's why he didn't shave as often as he should. He emptied the basin and refilled it and shaved again, just to make sure. It made his skin raw to the touch, soft as a girl's. He smoothed his palm over his jaw again and again. He reached for the wine glass to take another gulp and there it was, as though strategically placed by some ghost to mock and encourage him. It lay there, knowing as fate, adjacent to the stem of the wine glass: Helen's Extra-Black Super-Lash Mascara. The tube was as thick as his thumb, silver. The screw-on top was hot pink.

He swung onto the toilet and emptied his bowels in one swoop of pain and nausea and relief. It stank. He flushed the toilet but little bits still floated on the top. It was so loose and there was so much of it. He never usually got this except if he had eaten spicy food. He took the wine and the mascara and closed the bathroom door. He needed music.

twenty-seven

THEY'RE MOVING ME to a different room for the exam period. Helen too. I haven't quite gathered why. The woman at the accommodation office kept repeating, 'It's not my decision,' and flinching as though I were likely to hit her. I didn't even raise my voice. I don't even care. I was just curious.

I'm not going to go home. I'm just going to stay here until I have to move and then move. When term ends I stay in the building, pottering from my room to the kitchen to the bathroom and back to my room. I don't change out of my pyjamas. I eat everything in the fridge methodically and without relish. I think a sort of pleasant madness is settling in me. I don't sleep very well. I am not doing enough to warrant a good night's sleep.

At last I am sick of my own smell and my own stupid, sweaty sadness. So I take a very hot shower, body brushing to remove dead skin cells, to remove four days of filthy, flaky dead skin. I want to be clean. I want peace. I want only peace. Peace. I want to forget my place in the world and be only me. I want to be good by wanting only good. I want to be good by not being bad.

But the shower is just a lot of water piped up from the tank and it runs off my skin with no apology. It is not enough.

I switch off the pump and stand shivering and naked in the hallway for what seems like a long time. There's strange satisfaction in knowing that I am alone in this big building. The thirty rooms are empty and the beds have cooled. Some are stripped and some left tossed with the powdery stench of sleep and sex settled in their folds. The heaters have been turned off. I am the only warmth. Even the fish is gone. I still do not feel clean. I still do not have peace. I want darkness now, and silence, and alone.

twenty-eight

DESPITE THE THRILL of shaving it felt horrible to be hairless under there, skin sticking to raw skin. The constant chafing. How did women do it? He wanted more wine but there was none. He had been trying to clean out the kitchen before he left, so there was nothing in the fridge but half a jar of pasta sauce which he had opened the evening before. There was no more preparation to be done. It was time.

The dress was less than he had remembered. It was cheap looking, but as soon as he felt it slip through his fingers the enchantment of the garment was back. He stripped everything off and squeezed it over his head. Luckily it was stretchy material. He wouldn't look in the mirror until he was ready. It felt incredible, his skin covered in that smooth fabric. It felt magic. He turned up the music.

The front of the halter neck fell flat against his hairy chest. The strings cut into the back of his neck. He found a vest top of Helen's. It was one she wore to bed. It was made of swimming-togs material. He put it on under the dress and made breasts with socks and toilet paper. Then he put on a pair of pink tights that Helen had. They didn't quite stretch to his crotch but it was a long dress. He was nearly ready to look. Shoes. Helen had left stringy shoes in his flat but he would never fit into them. He tried, but it was no good. The ankle strap would just about close over his ankle but there was no way he could get his toes in.

There was tin foil in the kitchenette from the time he and Helen had tried grilling marshmallows. He tore two big squares. He fetched his usual shoes. They were blank brown ones, not designed to attract attention. He put each shoe in the middle of each tin foil square, put his feet in, and scrunched the tin foil over them. Back in the bathroom he did his mascara and put Helen's lipstick on his cheeks and lips, trying not to look at the rest of himself in the mirror. He wanted to see the whole effect. He scrunched his hair with hair wax and put on a sparkly hairband that Helen wore as a half-joke. If she was breaking up with him she would have to do a serious clear-out of his flat. He moved into the bedroom, switched on the light, and opened the wardrobe door. He stood in front of the mirror with his eyes closed, the blood throbbing in his eyelids.

twenty-nine

AFTER GETTING DRESSED I strip the sheets and pillowcases off my bed and put my keycard under the naked pillow. I pack tampons and a bar of soap and a small paring knife stolen from the communal kitchen in the inside pocket of my jacket and walk out. I have no money and no phone. I can't go back. I'm not sure why I might need a paring knife.

I walk for a long time, to Rathmines, across to Ranelagh and back into town again. I have been walking all night. I have seen the beginnings of first dates and the drunken end-of-night singing as the pubs are finally cleared. 'The Fields of Athenry'. Songs of famine sung by well-fed clubbers wobbling home. I am jealous of their togetherness.

I can't stop walking.

By the time the day begins I'm so exhausted that I am separate from my numb legs and balloon head. I am pared down to my aching stomach. This is good, I think, this is how it should be. I don't know where to go now. There is nowhere I want to go, and no one I want to be with. I find myself at the little archway off South Frederick Street where the smell of rotting sick and urine smacks me so hard my eyes sting. I breathe through my mouth and I can taste piss.

There is a bundle in the corner, a person, or two people maybe, shrouded in blankets. Sometimes, in my first year of college, I left tea and doughnuts here early in the morning, my easy good deed for the day. Every time I did it I thought I was great, and I would vow to do it every morning. I sit down for a little while on the ground, and feel the stone coldness work its way into the bones of my skinny arse.

Now a doughnut would make me sick on this empty stomach. I would puke up my charity. Maybe I will try to beg some change later so I can check into a shelter. I can try out the humiliation of that. It will whittle me down, all of this, it will scrape away slowly all of the things that make me despicable. I will become earnest maybe, and humble, and good.

People like me would call this self-indulgent, but that doesn't matter. I won't be people like me any more.

At the shelter there will be real poverty, real addiction. Someone told me there are sober men at the homeless centre who dress in clean suits every morning, collect breakfast from the Capuchin monks, and trawl employment agencies. Some girl told me that – Sharon, a girl I got chatting to at a lecture last week. An insufferable do-gooder, I could tell right off. She's building schools in Thailand for the summer.

But could that be true about those men?

Perhaps I should just ask my grandmother for my inheritance. I will leave college with half a degree. I will go to India and Peru and interrail around Europe. I will do all the things I could not do if I had stayed pregnant. That plan seems no less ridiculous than my current homeless endeavour.

My bum hurts on the wet stone ground. I need to piss. I open my jeans but that's as far as I get. I can't do it – I can't pull down my knickers and piss on the ground. I button my jeans and sit back down on the stone. I have stopped feeling like I need to go.

'Very cold.' I say, to a man emerging from under the blankets, his lips black and cracked, his chin crusted with vomit. He rolls back his head and looks at me slantwise. His voice surprises me – so normal. 'Very cold?' he says, and he laughs and laughs.

thirty

YOU NEVER went back for the exams. You were too sick. You emailed the department, and your tutor. They were very nice about it. You needed a letter from the doctor confirming that you were pregnant. They said you could sit the exams in September. You stay home and avoid your mammy, who loves the idea of herself as mother to an underage mother. Even though you are not underage. Even though she was this age when you were born. Things are just different now.

Your sisters mind you. They bring you soup and run tepid baths for you and guard you from your mammy. You vomit alone every morning into the toilet. At night you vomit into a ceramic mixing bowl with blue, hand-painted daisies on the rim. You turn off your mobile phone and do not contact anyone. In the afternoons you go for long walks. Your mother comes home every day with shopping bags full of baby clothes. She doesn't know yet that your daddy has bought you a flat near college, and that this pregnancy does not bind you to her in the way she might think.

It doesn't show for a long time. As long as it doesn't show you see no need to call Oisín. You don't break up with him. You just don't call or take calls. You don't reply to emails. It's not his body that's doing this, it's not his body that knows this child. Until it becomes something he can know, something with words, there is no way of telling him. He has no way of understanding.

You know how he would put his hand on your body, like he owned you both now, the way he might press his fingers on your throat at night, driving into you, put his mouth over yours and drink the voice out of you.

Only you can feel the first movements. You feel them earlier than the books said you would, lying in bed with your hand on your abdomen. A life separate and the same, a body turning in your own.

Tumbling in the glow of its own beginnings, it doesn't know where it is. It doesn't know there is such a thing as a place or a body. It doesn't know about the space between people, the lines that separate one mind from another, its body from yours. All it knows is the thrill of matter itself.

thirty-one

NOW SHE SAYS he can visit her in her new flat. By email she says it. He wants to remember her voice. It's been six months since he's heard her voice.

Hi. exams went all right, I think. Sorry I have been incommunicado. It's all been a shock. Please don't leave any more of those voicemails. I don't need extra grief. I don't want us to go out any more. Please respect that. Sorry. I just don't. If we have a baby it means either forever or not at all, and I think not at all would be best. Would you like to come over though and see me and bump? We could talk about how we're going to do this …

He presses the bell and she buzzes him in. It's number sixteen, on the second floor. The door is on the latch and she's already sitting down when he gets in.

The flat is very nice. Sunlight washes in through the big window making everything look clean and loving. She is very beautiful; it's true about the glow. She glows. Light pumps up through her cheeks. Light plays on her hair, bounces in her eyes. She seems to have even more hair now: a big halo of blonde ringlets barely held up by something that looks like a chopstick.

And the bump is a firm oval that she rubs in circles. She is wearing a green ribbed T-shirt. Through the fabric he can see her belly button, which seems to have turned into an outie. Her nipples too, are huge, bigger than he remembers them, pushing dark through the material. She has no stretch marks yet, she tells him, smiling, maybe she won't get any. She seems younger than she ever seemed before.

All he can think is the word *love*. Love, love, love. Maybe that's what pregnant women emanate: love for a shapeless thing, for a blank. How can you love a blank? Or maybe it's easier to love that way. She rubs it again. He has an impulse to do something violent. It's the smug competence of her hands and her still, placid lips. She knows how to do this without ever doing it before, how to rub a baby in the womb. He doesn't. He can barely understand how it could be real. He wants to ask someone how they breathe in there but he knows it's stupid, that they don't breathe, not really, only he can't understand how that can be.

'Yikes. It's kicking. It kicks my ribs.'

'Can I feel?'

'It's stopped.'

He loves her. The bump is their baby, their love. How can it exist if it wasn't that he'd loved her? How can she be changed like this, her body turned into something else, and still look at him like that, as though nothing ever happened between them? He is getting through life now on the belief that this break-up is a phase, that they will resume things in time. Suddenly this pregnancy has offered an alternative life after another stale summer in Clonmel. He could be a completely different type of man. He could put bread on the table and chop wood for the winter.

Occasionally the recognition that she really doesn't want to be with him again, that she might never kiss him again like that, or eat beans in bed with him, or try to tell him the truth about herself, that they might not spill coffee on the bed sheets in the morning with a baby propped between them, unfolds itself inside him, stretches, opens its yellow eyes like a waking wolf. This is when he becomes an inconvenience, calling her all the time, writing her letters, spitting hurt words onto her answering machine, radiating despair like a noise. Better for both of them if he allows himself the hope that makes him kinder and more pleasant for her to be around.

He wants to be involved, he says. That's the expression, *involved*.

'Of course.'

She smiles again. Pregnancy has put her into a sort of trance. He can't want to shake her, can he? To hit her? To fuck her? Not a pregnant woman? He can't want to, can he? To turn her over, to grip her hips, push her head down …

She rises from the couch easily, holding the bump as though it may topple, and starts to make tea in the neat kitchenette. She has not put on weight anywhere else. She still has a waist. From the back you wouldn't guess she was pregnant.

The flat is very grown up. He gets up and walks to the door of the bedroom, peers in. He wants to own this space by leaving no corner unseen by him, by striding through it as though it were his right. Her CDs are in CD racks and her clothes are all in their drawers. The room has a sense of air, of being able to breathe. He tells her that.

'Yeah,' she says from the kitchenette, clanking the tea things. 'I got an air purifier for when the baby comes. A medical one. It cost a fortune.'

It's blank though, the room. No pictures. Nothing to disclose what kind of life she will live here, what kind of person she will be. No mess of graffiti, nothing that says 'Helen'. Her duvet is cream and there are neat Venetian blinds on the large windows. Her father must be helping her out. Oisín wants to be the one to help her out. He will tell her so when she comes in with the tea. He will leave college and get a better job and save for her and their bump.

'I'm making bread,' she says, 'It will be ready in ten minutes, but we'll have to leave it to cool. I'm addicted to baking. They say that happens. You get broody. I keep making bread.'

He tries to love her in the pure way, in the way that would mean he would be happy that she was happy, but his heart opens into darkness and a thought strikes him over the face like a wet towel: *she will be here with someone else.* It will be beautiful to wake up with her in this room with the sunlight and the cream duvet. Someone else will make her happy and love her and be loved and spill coffee on the clean sheets. He could never afford this flat, not on a barman's wages, not with a 2.2 in English studies. That is his baby. This should not be allowed. He thinks the word 'man' and his pelvis feels like it is collapsing. He wants to punch something.

As he leaves he hears her mutter about the bread. For the first time in months he hears her laugh as he closes the front door noiselessly behind him. Helen's laugh is belly-real and girlish. He had forgotten the way she laughed.

Rather than wait for the lift, he takes the stairs quickly, one at a time, his runners shrieking rhythmically on the lino steps. He can forget again. He will forget again.

thirty-two

OISÍN NEVER made it to the end-of-term drama party the night that Helen left for the holiday, the last time she had let him kiss her, the last time he had said 'I love you'. At the time he planted that last kiss he half knew it, but only half. When he remembers watching her through the window of the bus, the limp wave she had given him, he knows that she had no intention of ever loving him again. He should have understood everything from that wave, that polite smile.

He walked around the walls of Trinity and back home, mouth parched, head whirling. He didn't take off the dress immediately. He lay on the bed and thought about each part of his feminized body, his hair, his mouth, his shaven underarms. He laughed to the ceiling until he felt sick. Then he stripped it all off and took a long shower.

It was a different sort of thrill. Defiant. Sometimes he does it again in his flat and it feels like a wonderful fuck-you parody of womanhood. All that faking, all that pomp, how beautiful and perfect they think they are. It feels like a sort of knowledge, shaving his armpits the way they do, painting his lips. It's almost sexy, it's almost like conquering something.

He's ready for the fancy-dress this time. He has improved the outfit over the months. He bought a better top for underneath, ordered a pair of transvestite shoes off the internet. He was terrified that they would arrive in a bright pink package with 'Tranny' or something written on it, but the package was wrapped discretely in brown paper. He had to pick it up from the post office because his mailbox was too small. The shoes are wonderfully gaudy. They are shiny pink crocodile skin with a big diamante jewel on the front of each one. They really make the outfit.

It is with a sense of failure that he stuffs the bra. Everything else about this feels defiant, except stuffing the bra. In fact, it only makes women's breasts seem even more miraculous, the texture of them, soft and firm at the same time; nipples of varying sizes and colours that feed every nerve in a man's fingertips with pure arousal. Nothing can replicate real breasts. Helen told him she was planning on breastfeeding. He wants her to bottle-feed, seeing as he's *to be involved* and he's the father and shouldn't he make the decisions too and how is he supposed to breastfeed the baby, but she dismissed him by flinching as though his deep voice were hurting her in her delicate state of late pregnancy, rolling her eyes, and rubbing her bump. His bump too. That's her way of controlling the situation, of making sure he knows there are things she can do and he can't. Like carrying a baby. Like making milk come out of her tits.

Bitch.

He does the bra bit first to get it out of the way. The rest of it he enjoys. He hasn't walked out like that since the night of the fancy-dress party. He wants to do it again. Just to walk down Grafton Street. It will be wonderful: pure terror.

WHERE DID all her fear go? How can there be so much water? The floor is flooded with it. The water that was around your baby a few moments ago. The water that knows the shape of it, the colour of its hair. You sit down and wait. When you think the water has finished you walk to the bathroom but there it is again, a big warm gush of it down your legs and into a puddle on the floor. Water. What does it taste like? You want to know that. It looks so pure. It is absolutely colourless.

For a moment you think how lucky it is that you cleaned the flat today, how nice it will be to bring the baby back to a clean home. Then you feel it must be madness to think things like that at a time like this. You are relieved, also, because it's late, the baby, and for the last few days you had started to feel as though this were all a joke, this pregnancy thing, as though it might not be in there at all. It seems so unrealistic that soon, any day now, any hour now, there will be another person, something grown from a spark in your own body.

On the toilet there's more of it. Again you think it's stopped but when you stand up another gush drops out. You had been planning to clean it up but you know suddenly that it won't be possible. The pain is undeniable. You have to squat and swing your hips from side to side to try to relieve it. Then it's gone. Still no fear. You know you can do this now. You think you could do it alone, squatting on the bathroom floor. But that must be madness, it must be some sort of hormonal thing, protecting you from fear. You wouldn't know what to do about the cord. Who knows what happens now, how bad it gets? They say you forget. That's how bad it is. So bad you forget. And they say women used to die all the time in childbirth. Who would look after the baby then? Oisín? Your mother? Another one comes; a shudder in your pelvis, an impossible wrenching – and then it eases.

You breathe out slowly, you rock your hips from side to side, bouncing on your shins until it subsides.

They are not wrong about how much pain there is, but what they didn't tell you is the type of pain, the way it's different to hurting your knee, to being tortured, to having an operation without anaesthetic, because nothing's wrong, because your body welcomes it, because you don't hate the pain. You want to be alone with it, with the pain and the birth. You feel you could do it. Surely there is someone you should tell, one of your sisters or someone. You can't call an ambulance, there's nothing *wrong*. You call a taxi. You are going to the Coombe you say, and the girl on the other end doesn't panic so it must be fine. You waddle out of the lift with a wad of towels between your legs, another stack under your arm, your overnight bag on your back. There is a vest in it for the baby. It's white. You held it up to the bump this morning. It measures from your breasts to your navel.

You put the towels on the back seat. It seems ridiculous to be embarrassed. Not now.

'Where are you going, love?'

The operator mustn't have told him. Surely he should know what a pregnant woman, sitting on a stack of towels in the back of his car, squeezing her eyes and exhaling slowly, means. It's 8 PM. He drives in silence, and between contractions you gaze out the window at the swarm of people on the streets, drunk already in preparation for 2008. They do not know the importance of this night.

The taxi-driver clutches the steering wheel and filters a slow breath out through his teeth. He must be worried about his car. How much would he charge you if you got blood all over the seats? Would he really ask it of you, if you were giving birth, or would he turn up to the hospital the next day with a balloon and the bill? You ask him if he has any kids and he nods and makes a V with his fingers – the 'fuck you' sign that means 'peace' if you're looking from the other side.

He has to help you in, and at the entrance a security guard, who sees women in labour every day and doesn't think it's such a big deal, directs you to the admissions office. You don't make it. You have to squat in the hallway and rock your hips to ease the pain. There might be blood or water on their floor, you don't know. You can't see for the pain. The admissions woman comes out. There must be blood or something because she recoils with her hands up to indicate that she won't touch you, 'I'm not dealing with this. She's in labour. I can't deal with this. Can you get a doctor?'

A nurse passing by tells her to get you a wheelchair.

'I'm not a nurse. I'm not dealing with this.'

'Oh for God's sake, we're half-staffed. Just get the security guard to get her a wheelchair and take her up to the waiting room.'

You want to go home. They couldn't stop you, could they? If you just said you're going home. The taxi-driver is gone though. The security guard gets you into a chair. He has a thick Nigerian accent and the bouncing of it soothes you. He doesn't think it's such an awful thing, giving birth, he doesn't think it is anything to panic about. He is not afraid to touch you.

'You will be okay. My wife has seven. All very easy. You will be fine. You are young. When you are young it is easy.'

He looks at you like a father, and smiles – soft eyes, and love. You believe that now – that it is with love he smiles at you. He smoothes a hand over your hair and says something.

Now the terror. You want to go home. You can't sit in a wheelchair. You need to squat. The nurse says stay in the wheelchair and the security guard says the woman knows what she wants, let her out, the body knows. Then he clutches the receptionist's arm and says, 'Never argue with a pregnant woman!' and chuckles at a girlish pitch, and you don't know if it's mockery or mirth, or if the laugh is even genuine.

They brush him away from you and the nurse wheels you up to a waiting-room full of quiet, excited couples. When you have another contraction, bouncing on your shins with your mouth closed, spilling your waters all over their waiting-room, someone brings you into a small room with a bed and says you should call your fella or your mother or someone and that someone will be in to measure your cervix. There is a giant paper towel on the bed, insufficient to soak up all the stuff that is coming out of you. She puts machines on you, this person, all around your bump and makes you lie down. That is what's excruciating, the lying down. You ask her for water and she says no, in case they have to operate. They won't have to operate, you tell her. She goes out. You get up and squat for the next contraction, rocking from side to side. Hopefully they won't give you an enema. That's what your mum said they do. The way she said it: 'They pump fairy liquid up your hole. Then they shave you.' She loves saying things like that. The monitor comes off when you get up but you can't stay still, not with the pain. The machine starts to beep wildly, alerting them all to the fact that you have disobeyed. No one comes to make you lie down. They're half-staffed. It's New Year's Eve.

IN HELEN'S house they're having a New Year's party. The parents have gone away for a week to a health spa and the kids are running riot. Katie invited me by group text, by accident I think. I turned up at seven, an hour early, but Katie was too nervous to chat. She was texting, and calling her friends, and trying on dresses, so I wandered up to the pink attic room and lay on the bed looking up through the skylight at the purple and black clouds.

I haven't spoken to Helen in months. I don't want to bother her, but I thought she might be here. She's moved to a flat in town, I know that from her sisters, but she hasn't called me.

I've gone off books for the year. I went back to my grandmother for a few months and wore my grandfather's cardigan, and read books, and helped her cook. She didn't say anything about my disappearance until two weeks after I came home. While I was helping her to sprinkle a loaf of dough with poppy seeds she said, 'You think my life was just as I would like, Cassandra? You think there is any woman who is suited to their world, do you?' She put her hand on mine to stop me from sprinkling the seeds on. 'Stop. I need to do the egg.' She looked proudly at the dough, neatly plaited into a great fat braid, and picked up the basting brush.

'Your mother disappeared one day. She arrived seven months later on the doorstep with arms thin like you wouldn't believe, and you in her belly.' She dipped her brush in egg white and painted the dough, her eyes never meeting mine. 'You will not disappear like that again. You go where you like, Cassandra, you do what you like, but you let me know that you are safe. You will not disappear from the world just because it is not how you would like it.' I said nothing while we prepared the loaf. Then my grandmother covered it with a linen napkin, and left it to rise in the hot press.

Twenty minutes later she told me to put it in the oven. She opened the door while I slid the delicately bubbling dough in, keeping it as still as I could so as not to collapse the yeast.

'Good girl,' she said, closing the door, 'You are a good girl, Cassandra.'

'But I don't know –' I said.

'Don't worry so much,' she said. 'You do know. You are a brave girl. You will be fine without me. There are beautiful things you will know. There are such beautiful things you don't know yet. You will know what to do with them. You are brave.'

I have a flight booked for New Year's day. I'm going to go to Paris. I'm going to just live somewhere else for a while, I told her, but I'm going to keep in touch. I promised I would keep in touch. In Paris I will stay in Shakespeare and Co., a bookshop run by an old man who lets people stay in beds that smell like urine, with brown sheets that are never changed, beds erected between the bookshelves. The conditions under which people can stay are that they must write for three hours a day, or read a book a day, or work in his shop, or you can sell him old books in exchange for a bed. It's out and out the falsest of false bohemian. I visited with my grandad five years ago. The other kids there are Cambridge or Harvard, interrailing through Europe for a summer – 'backpacking', the Americans call it – playing at being poor. Like me, I suppose.

Downstairs, the party starts. Katie's classmates have brought friends who have brought friends, who have brought friends, because New Year's is a time for partying and there is nowhere for all the teenagers to go. New Beetles and pink Minis line the drive, I can see them through the front window.

The numbers are rising and they are starting to pull up on the road at the bottom of the house. Beautiful young things, their bodies ripe and bored, teeter and strut up the gravel driveway. They are exciting to watch. Even the chubby, insecure ones in outfits that are less-brave versions of their best friends'. Especially the girls whose breasts are brand new, who still have a ring of puppy fat around their waists, spilling over the tight jeans. Their fresh pink skin, their moist lips, are all blanked with orange foundation and gelatinous lip gloss, but they can't hide their beauty. They don't even have to put their vodka into Coke bottles because there are no bouncers. They traipse up the drive, through the house, hordes of them. High heels and Dubes, badly applied hair gel spiking the boys' heads, some of them gilded with bleached tips, some of them already beefed with steroids, biceps bursting through pre-distressed T-shirts. They're going to pull tonight.

There's fear in the air too, as tangible as taste. No one wants to be standing alone for the New Year countdown. No one wants not to have kissed anyone.

Katie is excited. She was afraid no one would come. She was afraid she'd be the loser who had a party that no one came to, but there are kids everywhere, even upstairs, sorting themselves out in the bathrooms, reapplying their mascara and fluffing their breasts.

Some of the Blackrock boys have brought pills! It's going to be brilliant!

HE COULDN'T GO home to Clonmel for New Year's, not with the baby due so soon. He wants to see his son when he's born. He doesn't want to come back from Clonmel and find that Helen has taken over, telling him how to hold him and what food he likes or whatever. She wanted him to go to parenting classes. As if she knew any more than him about parenting. But he's not going to sit in like a loser on New Year's Eve. That's just what she'd like. He'll go to the drama party. It's fancy-dress again, of course. *Grease* is the theme. Maybe he'll ride Sharon, maybe even ride someone new, who knows. No, not with his shaven armpits and eyeliner on. Or maybe. You never know. Drama girls are weird and there aren't that many guys in Players.

This time he will have to push it even further to get the same thrill. He wears eye shadow and a wig. It's a cheap wig. Just from the joke shop. He can't remember what hairstyle the bird from *Grease* wears but the wig is blonde anyway, and he knows she is blonde. There is a net inside to tuck his hair into.

He has four beers before he leaves the flat. He has never fainted but he feels he might now. He looks like a proper tranny in the wig and high heels. He opens the front door of his flat and has to run back into the toilet urgently. When he has emptied his bowels of everything he puts his head between his knees. Is Sharon even going to shag him if he's dressed like a woman? Of course she will. Drama girls like this sort of thing. He's not gay. He knows that. He knows that so well he can even dress as a woman. He stands up, fixes himself back into the tights, pulls down the skirt. He can do this. He wants to.

YOU HAVE CHANGED into the gown like they told you. When did you do that? The calm between contractions, the bliss of those painless minutes, is incredible. But you need a drink. You need them to switch off that beeping. The baby doesn't like it.

There is no one at all in the hallway. It is lined with doors like yours, and behind each one a woman is starting to give birth. She is in pain, or her pelvis is contracting, or her waters have broken. There are other machines beeping too. Maybe it's normal not to want to lie down. A warm forest would be a better place to give birth; your back against a tree and no beeping, no paper towels scrunched with blood and water.

You peer into the room where some of the couples are still waiting. They look horrified at the sight of you. Then a scraggy-looking man. Not a doctor. Who is he?

'You alright love?'

'Can I have some water? Do you know where there is water?'

'There's a water-cooler by the lockers. I'll get you some. What room?'

Crouched on the floor again, eyes squeezed shut, you point at the room.

'I'll get you some. Go back. I'll get you some.'

After the contraction you make your way back to the room.

You sit with your knees up and your back to the wall, swallowing to moisten your mouth. Your lips are like wounds and your throat tastes of metal. At last he comes and you take the water, surprised that you can only sip it. You ask him for a nurse and he says he will look. After the next contraction you finish the water and hide the cup behind the monitor before she arrives.

She is frowning. 'You need to lie down. What are you doing?' You get up quietly and she straps the monitor back on. She is irritated at being called. 'What's the problem?'

'Could you examine me? Could you make sure everything is okay?'

She tells you to part your legs and shines a light in. She puts something in and it doesn't hurt as much as it should because the other pain has started again, rising and falling like waves. You can't lie down.

'Not even three inches. We'll bring you to the delivery room in a little while. You've a good bit to go yet. The head is engaged. It's all fine. We'll bring you down soon. Stop. Lie down. Don't get up again.'

I SIT at the top of the first flight of stairs, under the grandfather clock, beside the six studio photographs of the O'Brien girls, and watch the teenagers coming in.

Jeffrey is here, who was Katie's best friend in primary school. He's a 'total coke-head' now and she doesn't see him that often. He has some other guys with him she has never met. There's a sound system in the living room but there's music coming from somewhere else. Hip-hop. The arrivals have stopped now and no one knows what to do. The house is packed but people have stopped moving up and down the stairs.

I pace the landing. I am invisible amidst all this excitement. I can see the kitchen and living room through the glass floor of the landing. They are sitting on all the couches and at the big oak table that seats twelve. They are standing in all the doorways. Katie forgot to buy paper cups so people are drinking out of glasses and mugs and bottles. She is standing talking to her school friend, who is hanging out of her new boyfriend, who is slightly shorter than her. He keeps kissing her neck and rubbing his hand over her bum. Katie keeps chewing her lip. She is nervous. She can sense the lull but she doesn't know what to do about it. She switches on the speakers in the living room. It's some rave thing of Laura's. Now there are layers of sound, now there is noise and a proper sense of crowd. Rachel and the new guy start to sway and kiss and feel each other and so do a few other couples. Some of the boys start to whoop and someone is passed over their heads from the hall to the kitchen. The party is taking off again. Conor, who Katie went out with last year for a month, swoops in from behind her and grabs her around the waist and starts chatting, and all around her the party begins. There are shouts and the dog starts to bark and someone turns up the music.

AS SOON AS the nurse is gone you get up. You can't do anything else. The beeping starts again but you press a button with a picture of a bell crossed out and it stops. You shouldn't have come here with the corridors and the metal beds and the cold strips of light. It is not what you want the baby to see first. You should give birth in the dark or the yellow sunlight, labouring together towards your separation, feeling your way. You should not be glared at like this.

OISÍN DOESN'T even feel drunk any more. He makes his way out to the corridor. The Polish woman is in the lift. She had her baby ages ago but she still has that smug look on her face. Her bump never properly went. She still looks loose around the belly. Or maybe she's pregnant again.

Oisín almost steps back and let the doors close. He wants to be alone in the lift. Then he thinks, *fuck what that fat bitch thinks.* He steps in and swings around, facing the door with his back to her so as not to see her. His face is pulsing, his fingertips. Does she recognize him? He forgets to swallow and splutters on his own spit. Can she tell from his back how nervous he is? Is he sweating?

It's a relief to get out onto the cold street. There is a sense of crowd and everywhere packed with people. He hasn't walked out of the flat in the costume since the first time. He was wrong: he didn't need to go further with the outfit to get that thrill. His head is whirling. He hardly knows where he is going. He walks as though deaf and blinkered. He doesn't know whether he is being stared at or not. He knows, suddenly, that he can't go to the party. He can't bear to be recognized like this. He can't shag a woman while he's wearing eyeliner. He wouldn't be able to get it up. He doesn't want to go home yet, though. That would be defeat. He will walk up Grafton Street. He can do that.

AT LAST another nurse comes in. She has a softer face. She says is it a boy or a girl and you say you don't know. She says you'll know soon enough and that makes you sad. You do not want it named and sexed. Will you really hang it, so soon, with the weight of all those words? You will dress it in white.

You have to lie down so she can measure you, but as you lift yourself onto the bed another contraction starts and you push her away and squat. She's talking to you but the force of it is too much. You want to be alone, you and your baby. You can do this alone. You both know how. When the contraction is over she says she'll bring you to the delivery room and they'll measure you there. You don't see the journey because another contraction comes on the way. In the delivery room someone else measures you. Someone holds you down while they do it because you can't lie down with the pain. You scream something at them and the nurse tells you to keep your dignity, for goodness sake.

'Have you not taken anything for the pain?'

'No, I don't want to.'

'There are other things than the epidural. Would you like Pethidine?'

'No it's too late anyway. It will sedate the baby. It won't know how to be born.'

She smiles, 'You've a while to go yet, pet. You're not even four inches. It'll help. Stay steady.'

'No I don't want it. Just let me stand. It's fine.'

They let you squat for the next contraction and you ask the soft-faced nurse for water.

'You can't drink. But I'll get you ice. You can suck on ice. Here. I'll put a damp cloth on your neck. That will help.'

On the next contraction you need to push and someone starts to shout at you, 'Don't push yet, it's not time, don't push yet!' But you can't do anything else.

After the contraction they make you lie down again and the other woman starts to explain it to you. 'You'll feel like pushing, but don't. If you do you'll be too tired by the end.'

'Then why does it feel like I should?'

When the next one comes you scream and the nurse comes up to your face. 'Like this – don't waste energy on screaming. Keep it in, keep your mouth quiet. Squeeze your lips. Don't push.'

She squeezes her lips shut to show you what you should do.

'Bite down on your lip. And don't push.' You bite your lips and there is a release of blood into your mouth, which eases the thirst a little. You try not to make a sound. You will have to do this in secret.

'Are you pushing? Stop pushing! Stop pushing! We need to measure her.'

'It's coming!'

'Believe me pet – you'd know all about it if it was coming! You wouldn't be talking to me if it was coming!'

'It's coming!'

'Get her onto the bed, I need to measure her.'

'Don't make me lie down …'

The soft-faced nurse is not soft at all. She holds you down. Are you strapped? Surely they haven't strapped you?

'I need to measure you. Stop. Don't push.'

She doesn't measure you. She takes one look and starts to shout at you. 'Push! Push! Push!' You try to get up but someone is holding you down.

'We need to see. You need to lie down. Push! Push! Push!'

She turns to a young blonde in white overalls with a notepad, who you hadn't noticed before.

'Now that's very unusual. I had no idea that would happen …'

The blonde looks at you and disregards you at the same time, and writes something on her chart, frowning.

thirty-three

THEY HAVE BEEN following him since Tara Street. He knows it. He recognized them because one of them looks like Kev. He nearly said hi, only when they got closer he saw it wasn't the lads. Just a group of lads very like the lads. One of them even has a bald patch like Denny. It was stupid to walk to such a secluded place when he knew they were following. But he didn't want to be seen. He couldn't stand to be seen suddenly. What was he thinking? Why did he do this in the first place?

AT HELEN'S house, there are people in the hot press. Donna and some boy, fucking in the hot press. I saw them going in. I heard her say 'Get the condom then,' and she sounded older than her sixteen years. If one of Katie's sisters comes home there'll be war, but Katie doesn't know. She's out back with Conor, who I can see through the window of the floral bedroom, who is touching her elbow, imploring. On the windowsill is a little tube of paste called 'Fat Lip'. I go back up to the attic and look out through the bathroom window at the garden.

On the lawn, Jeffrey, off his face, is opening champagne that must be the parents'. He has a collection of expensive bottles that Katie should have locked away, and he is opening them and taking a swig, opening the next and taking a swig, and Conor, who hopes that he might be one of the few to get more than a kiss from an O'Brien girl, shouts 'What the fuck?' and takes a bottle off him, as though to tidy up, put them back, save Katie from the shit she'll get for this.

Inside something smashes.

I peer over the banisters from the top floor and down through the two glass ceilings. In the kitchen one of the French doors has just shattered, miraculously, into a million little cubes of glass. It causes a sudden moment of silence, and whoever smashed it – the guy who was pushed or the girl who threw a glass – is horrified and delighted at the shock of it. Kids start to hurl themselves at the second glass door until that smashes too – not as completely, not as deliciously – and then they stomp the glass, and kick the remaining shards from the door frame, shout and laugh and keep stomping, fuck you fuck you fuck you, to the French doors, crushing it into the antique oak floor.

I go back upstairs before I am compelled to join them. Their energy is magnetic, pulsing throughout the house, *fuckyoufuckyoufuckyou*. Outside something has changed. Someone has dragged the harp from the music room out onto the lawn, and grown bored of it. It's sitting slantwise on the grass with all its taut strings intact, and now Conor is not trying to stop Jeffrey from opening the wine. Conor is pouring one of Pat's seven hundred euro bottles of red wine – the ones they keep locked in the pantry in a special rack on the top shelf – over his hair and face, his lips not even open, and the thrill of that – of the deep red over Conor's forehead, staining the bleached hair – fires them all, and they are smashing bottles into the shed wall, into each other, onto the expensive paving stones of natural granite, over the lawn feature, over the heads of those misproportioned bronze children on their bronze bench, grinning like lovers, that the O'Brien mammy loves and the O'Brien children hate, that sits on the lawn in mockery of it all. They know, these kids, that a seven hundred euro bottle of wine is worth shit, and up in the hot press Donna is fucking a stranger amid dry-cleaned suits, though she was a virgin until twenty minutes ago, because they all know, suddenly, that none of that matters the way they were told it would. The dog bounds down the stairs, covered in shaving foam, followed by a group of boys who are trying to kick and kick it, and the dog is running through the house looking for an ally. This dog has never bitten, never growled at anything but a cat, and it won't bite when they corner it and kick it and keep kicking, flattening the shaving foam into the glossy black coat, kicking the teeth that could take a chunk out of them, the eyes that are squeezed shut, kicking until the dull blood mats its fur, he will whimper, and whimper, and wait for it to end while they kick fuck you fuck you fuck you—

—And the same nurse who wouldn't believe you when you told her you were giving birth, still thinks she knows better, and tries to make you lie when you tell her you need to squat. They hold you down and peer at the head, which doesn't look like a head at all, which looks like a crumpled, wizened, purple passion fruit, like an internal organ, and when you say fuck you she tells you to keep your dignity, show respect for your child, for her, and orders the other nurse to hold you firmly and says to make you take the gas, says she is panicking, give her the gas, says she is panicking, which you are not. You are clear now, very clear, and not panicking.

Angry, very angry, but not panicking, and you have never once in this labour lost your dignity and you kick away the peering face with small bare feet, small and white like the feet of maidens in old songs, and say fuck you—

—Oisín can't try to fight it, not dressed like this. He has given them the right already to throw a punch into his face, kick his flaccid dick, topple him out of the transvestite shoes against the wall where he once fucked Helen from behind, a secluded alley designed for illicit fucking and for kicking guys to a pulp – gays or transvestites or schizophrenic homeless guys – anyone who tells you you're not who you think you are, that you're a little bit the same as them actually. Oisín understands. This is their right, and that's why he finds it impossible, even when he tries, to punch back, or to keep from falling, because that guy is just like Kevin, who might do just the same, and the other one, the one in the T-shirt that has something written on it, has a face like Denny's.

Kevin once sent him a video of a kid being raped in an alley like this one. Someone's cousin being raped in an alley by three sons of three mothers, one after the other. And so he can't do anything but fall against the wall, because there are only two roles for Oisín, and he would as soon be this freak, the kicked, as a kicker, and suddenly his submission seems like honour, and he takes the kicks until he can't feel the impact any more, because the body does that after a while, to protect itself from the pain, it shrinks back into itself and waits.

epilogue

THIS IS WHERE I lose you, Helen, this is where you leap into a place I cannot understand. This is where you go alone, where you have to speak for yourself, or choose to be silent. I know what happens from your emails, from my grandmother's phone call after she visited you, but I don't know the rest, not really. I knew only what you might have felt, what those things might have meant, what your blonde ringlets might have represented—

—YOU DON'T TAKE the gas because you want to feel it when it happens. You've come this far and you want to know it. You want to feel it alone but the lady is screaming push push *push*, and she takes a scissors with long, curving blades, and says she will have to cut if it doesn't happen in the next push, says she will do it in the next contraction and you won't even feel it, the pain is so slight in comparison, and you tell her fuck you and she has given up telling you to keep your dignity and the other one has given up trying to gas you and when you push something happens that no one ever told you happened – no one ever told you that in the final moment what happens is not pain at all, what happens feels like an orgasm of the best, most dignified kind.

acknowledgments

THANKS TO my editor, Lisa Coen, for her dedicated work on this novel, Daniel Caffrey for the sound advice and uncalled-for labour, and my publisher, Antony Farrell, for his patience.

Thanks also to Neil Belton and John Hobbs for encouragement at crucial moments.

Finally, my partner, Seán, for all the stubborn love, steadfast faith, and support in every sense. Also for reading, re-reading and providing invaluable editorial advice on the earliest drafts of this novel.

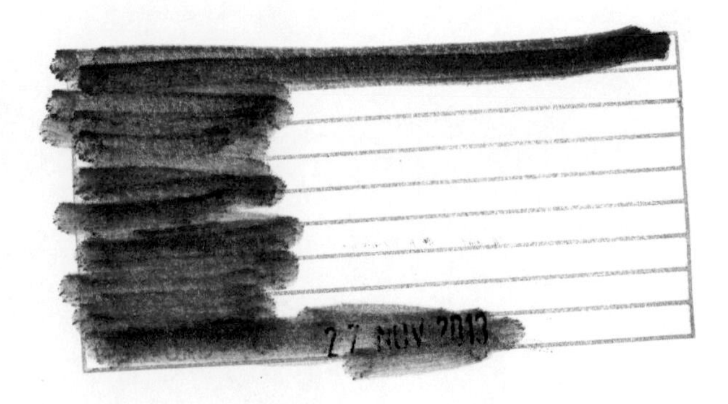